THE EVENTS IN THIS BOOK ARE REAL.

NAMES AND PLACES HAVE BEEN CHANGED
TO PROTECT THE LORIEN,
WHO REMAIN IN HIDING.

OTHER CIVILIZATIONS DO EXIST.

SOME OF THEM SEEK TO DESTROY YOU.

THE LORIEN 🔲 LEGACIES

BY PITTACUS LORE

Novels

I AM NUMBER FOUR

THE POWER OF SIX

THE RISE OF NINE

THE FALL OF FIVE

THE REVENGE OF SEVEN

THE FATE OF TEN

UNITED AS ONE

The Lost Files Novellas

#1: SIX'S LEGACY

#2: NINE'S LEGACY

#3: THE FALLEN LEGACIES

#4: THE SEARCH FOR SAM

#5: THE LAST DAYS OF LORIEN

#6: THE FORGOTTEN ONES

#7: FIVE'S LEGACY

#8: RETURN TO PARADISE

#9: FIVE'S BETRAYAL

#10: THE FUGITIVE

#11: THE NAVIGATOR

#12: THE GUARD

#13: LEGACIES REBORN

#14: LAST DEFENSE

#15: HUNT FOR THE GARDE

The Lost Files Novella Collections

THE LEGACIES *(Contains novellas #1–#3)*

SECRET HISTORIES *(Contains novellas #4–#6)*

HIDDEN ENEMY *(Contains novellas #7–#9)*

REBEL ALLIES *(Contains novellas #10–#12)*

ZERO HOUR *(Contains novellas #13–#15)*

I AM NUMBER FOUR

THE LOST FILES

ZERO HOUR

PITTACUS LORE

HARPER

An Imprint of HarperCollinsPublishers

I Am Number Four: The Lost Files: Zero Hour

I Am Number Four: The Lost Files: Legacies Reborn © 2015 by Pittacus Lore

I Am Number Four: The Lost Files: Last Defense © 2016 by Pittacus Lore

I Am Number Four: The Lost Files: Hunt for the Garde © 2016 by Pittacus Lore

www.epicreads.com

full
fathom
five

ISBN 978-0-06-238771-4

Typography by Ray Shappell

16 17 18 19 20   CG/RRDH   10 9 8 7 6 5 4 3 2 1

❖

First Edition

CONTENTS

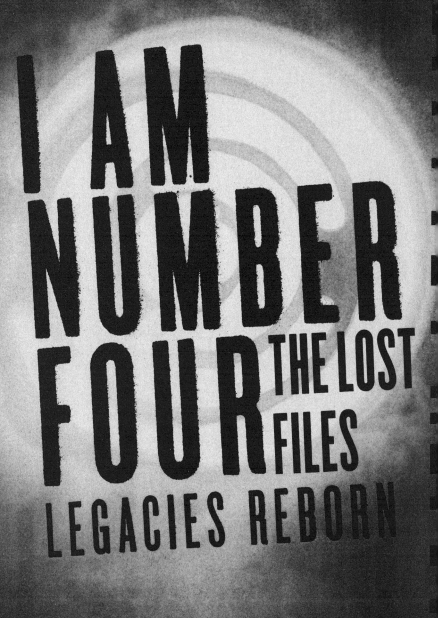

I AM NUMBER FOUR
THE LOST FILES
LEGACIES REBORN

CHAPTER ONE

AS USUAL, BENNY IS AN ASS AND I CAN'T KEEP my mouth shut.

Lunch had been going okay. We'd walked to the diner a few blocks down from our apartment. Everybody in Harlem seemed to be out on the streets, enjoying the first warmish day in weeks. Mom looked radiant in her crisp white button-down. She's always been able to make her work clothes look fashionable instead of like something she was forced to wear while serving fancy customers at a restaurant down on Wall Street that we could never afford to eat at. Benny, my stepdad, was quiet most of the meal, except for a groan here or there—based on his swollen eyes, I'm guessing he had a little too much fun out with his boys last night. All in all, things had been smooth sailing.

Then I had to go and ask if I could get some new headphones. Nice noise-cancelling ones that'd block out the world around me, or at least the noises in our apartment. That seemed worth fifty dollars to me.

The request doesn't go over well.

"Sure, baby," Mom says as she tries to nab the last grape from a side of fruit salad with her fork.

Benny looks like she's just agreed to buy me a Lexus for my sixteenth birthday or something.

"Hold up, now," he says. "What's wrong with the ones you've got?"

"They're busted," I say, pointing to the headphones slung around my neck. "Only one ear works."

"Then deal with one ear," Benny says. He wolfs down the last bite of a burger. "Your mom works six shifts a week. Sometimes more. I support us too. What do you do?"

I almost laugh at the word "support." Benny's been off work for a few months now on paid "disability," even though I haven't seen anything wrong with him. It definitely hasn't stopped him from drinking beer all day while shouting at our TV, driving me crazy.

"I put up with you," I mutter, staring down at the half a waffle floating around a little syrup lake on my plate.

"Dani," Mom says.

"What'd you just say?" Benny asks, his voice a low boom.

I bite my tongue. For Mom's sake, I keep quiet.

"She's having a great semester in school," Mom says. "Lord, *I'll* pay for the headphones. Don't worry."

"Oh really? Where's this money coming from, then?" he asks.

"Benny, don't spoil the meal. You know I set aside a little tip money for things like this."

"At least she *works*," I say. It slips out before I can stop it. Benny snorts and I can tell I've crossed the line.

When he speaks again, his voice is deep and full of anger.

"Listen here, you spoiled little—"

"*Benjamin*." Mom cuts him off.

He looks back and forth between us, jaw flexing as he clenches his teeth. Benny's pretty much always an asshole, but it's when he gets quiet and silently rages that I know I've hit some kind of nerve. I haven't seen him look this angry in a long time, and that's saying something, considering we never see eye to eye on anything.

My body tenses up with anger. I want to hurl my plate at him, or flip this whole table over. I wish I could do *something*.

He stands up abruptly, his knees banging against the table and causing our plates to rattle. On his feet, he's a behemoth, six foot two and thick from years of manual labor and Mom's cooking. A couple of people look over at us, and Mom puts on a smile to show them that everything's all right.

"You got so much spare cash lying around, then you won't mind paying for this shit," Benny says, waving at our table. And then he's off and out the door.

Mom slowly takes her napkin from her lap and dabs her lips.

"You want dessert, baby?" she asks.

I shake my head and suck my teeth, looking across the room at nothing in particular. If I look at Mom I'll apologize for what I said and take responsibility for starting the argument, and I don't *want* to be sorry.

She shrugs and glances at her phone. "I gotta get down to the restaurant. My shift starts soon."

"I'd hate for those rich-ass bankers to have to pour their own drinks."

"Language, Dani," she says. Then she smirks. "Besides, those rich-ass bankers are the ones buying you a black and white."

And before I can protest she's up and across the diner, chatting with our waitress at the bar as the woman makes me a to-go milk shake.

I walk Mom to her train. We cut through Morningside Park, which is kind of crowded because of the nice weather. There are all sorts of families grilling and having picnics. A bunch of kids playing pickup basketball on the courts. We don't really talk—Mom just hums some song I don't recognize and I try to cool off. We've done this a million times. Walking beside her always makes me feel better, no matter what's been going on at home or at school.

But we can't spend all day strolling around. Eventually she has to leave.

We come to the subway entrance.

"Text me which headphones you want, and I'll go pick them up," she says. "It'll be our little secret."

"Until Benny finds out," I say.

"He won't. He's not exactly the most observant guy. He'll forget all about them by tomorrow. Maybe we'll do something fun if the weather stays. Just you and me. I've got the day off."

This is what it should always be like. We don't need anybody else in the world except each other.

"We'd be better off alone."

"Dani . . . ," she says.

"It's true. We were fine before he came along."

"Not always, baby," she says. "You're forgetting he's the reason we can afford to stay in our apartment."

"If that's all it is, then I can get a job," I say. "I'm almost sixteen. We can get along just fine without him."

She smiles, but I don't think it's because I've just come up with some brilliant solution to our problems.

We've had this conversation a hundred times before.

"He's a good man," she says slowly, patiently. "He's just going through a rough patch."

As far as I'm concerned, this "rough patch" has lasted for the last three years, ever since he moved in with us.

"Besides, you need to be focused on school." She smirks a little. "I'm going to find some SAT vocabulary lessons for you to listen to on those fancy new headphones to make sure you're putting them to good use."

I roll my eyes. She kisses me on the forehead, squeezing my shoulder gently.

"I'll see you tonight, Dani," she says. "I love you."

"Yeah." I stare down at the concrete. "Later."

She lingers.

"I love you too," I say finally.

She smiles, and then disappears down into the subway.

Thinking about going back to the apartment makes my blood start to boil again, and with Mom gone there's no one left to keep me calm. I know from past experience that it'll be best if I give Benny a little while to cool down. Besides, I don't want to be stuck in my room avoiding my stepdad when it's so nice outside. So I walk for a while until I finally come to the Cathedral of St. John the Divine. I cut through the groups of people snapping pictures outside and go into the little park beside the church where this weirdo statue of an angel and a bunch of giraffes stands. I think it's really called Peace Fountain, but I've always called it Big Crab because that's what all the animals and the winged man are standing on—a Big Crab. That's also what Mom called it when I was just a kid and she used to take me on walks through the university campus nearby and talk about how if I worked really hard I'd be one of the students there when I grew up.

Now I come here when I want to get away from everything else.

I grab a bench, stretch out my legs and cross my arms, enjoying the feeling of the sun shining down on me. Music blasts from one ear of my headphones. I try to completely zone out.

I don't know how much time passes before my phone starts to vibrate in my pocket, the music in my ear suddenly replaced by a ringtone. I sigh, fearing that it's Benny asking me where the hell I am, or if I'll run by the store and pick something up for him.

But it's Mom.

"Hey," I say when I answer. "I thought your shift star—"

"Where are you?" she cuts me off. Her voice is short and on the verge of a yell. It startles me so that I don't answer at first. She continues. "Did you hear me? Where are you?"

"At the Big Crab."

"Go home."

"Mom, what's—"

"Dani, baby," she says. She sounds like she's about to start crying or something. "You need to go home. Right now. I'll be—"

I don't hear what she says after that, if she says anything at all. There's some yelling and then a loud bang, and suddenly our connection is gone.

I try to call back, but I've got zero bars.

"What the . . . ," I mutter, jumping to my feet. I pause for a few seconds, staring at my phone, my heart pounding against my ribs. I'm not exactly excited about going back to the apartment and spending the rest of the afternoon hearing Benny shout at sports teams. But Mom sounded so worried . . .

The sky becomes overcast, and all of a sudden I feel like something bad's going to happen. I keep hearing the concern in Mom's voice repeating through my head.

I start to run towards home.

As I dart through the park and past the short blocks to our apartment, I can tell something's not right. I hear shouting from inside apartment buildings as I run past open windows. A couple of other people are sprinting through the streets, in a hurry somewhere. I speed up, continuously checking my phone to see if I've gotten a message from Mom or something.

Finally, I'm home. The metal security gate bangs behind me, loud, and I'm guessing every other apartment in our crappy building hears it. Someone yells from inside 1B as I run past the row of mailboxes in the entryway and then up the hard, worn stairs to our place on the fourth floor. I'm shaking as I try to get my key in the door, but I can't tell if it's because I'm completely out of breath and drained from running all the way here, or because I'm so spooked by Mom's call.

I start yelling as soon as I get inside.

"Mom?" I ask. "Benny? What's going on?"

Benny's in his big blue recliner. There are a couple of empty beers on the coffee table, and I'm hoping that means he's forgotten all about the headphones.

"Benny, Mom jus—"

He shushes me, waving a hand in my direction, not taking his eyes off the TV, where a blond boy with glowing fireballs in his hands is fighting a gross-ass giant.

Anger builds up inside me. Benny is watching some crappy sci-fi movie while Mom might be in trouble or something.

I'm about to start shouting at him when I recognize the United Nations on the screen. Then a reporter from one of the news stations Benny loves to yell at comes into frame. That's when I realize that this isn't some movie: it's live.

CHAPTER
TWO

NONE OF THIS SEEMS REAL.

A giant spaceship is hovering above Manhattan. It just rolled in out of nowhere. A freaking *spaceship*. I've tried to catch sight of it myself, but the only windows in our apartment face the building a few yards away from us, and all I can see when I look out are bricks and dirty glass and the little alley below us.

But it's all over the TV. We sit glued to the screen. Benny keeps crossing himself and whispering prayers I didn't think he even knew. He's got a baseball bat in his lap and hasn't moved for hours. I split my time rocking back and forth on the couch and pacing through the living room, constantly checking both my and Benny's phones to see if either of them gets any service. We don't really talk to each other except for when we hear a bunch of people running up to the roof. I start towards the front door, but Benny says "Stay here" in a way that has my butt immediately back down on the couch.

Besides, I keep waiting for the door to swing open and Mom to walk in. I don't want to be up on the roof when she does.

Whatever this is, it's not just happening here in New York, but in cities across the world. Some are calling it an invasion. Others war. None of it makes sense. It's impossible to wrap my head around it. The weird-ass aliens with laser guns they keep showing on TV have just got to be CGI. Or this is just some big viral marketing campaign for a movie or something. I remember learning in school about some old radio broadcast back in the '30s that was about aliens invading. People thought it was real, but it turned out to be a big hoax. This has to be like that, right?

Or at least, that's what I keep trying to believe.

If this *is* a joke, it's the best, most expensive damn joke in history. The news keeps showing footage taken from phones and tablets—I guess some people are managing to get a cell signal. A lot of it is shaky and blurry. Some of it's a little more high quality. A few stations start showing a video pulled from YouTube. It's got a girl doing a voice-over in it like some kind of PSA and talks about the blond boy I saw fighting on TV earlier— apparently his name is John Smith—and how he's a good alien. And that a bunch of bad aliens are here to take over Earth.

This is the craziest shit I've ever seen.

Every time the security gate bangs, I jolt and stare at the door, hoping it's Mom. But it never is. The dozenth or so time I hear it, the clanging metal is followed by the sound of some guy screaming.

"Holy shit, they're here." His cries echo up the stair-well, through the building. "They're on the block! They're on the block!"

I recognize the voice as the old man who sits on our stoop and sometimes talks to birds. I turn to Benny, but he just clicks his tongue and shakes his head a little.

"Dude's losing it," he says, not taking his eyes off the TV. "Those pale freaks ain't gonna bother with Harlem. We're safe here."

He turns the news up louder. The station we're watching is broadcasting live from Midtown, where most of the NYPD has been sent—it seems like the aliens are more concentrated there. Benny leans for-ward in his chair, muttering something I don't hear. Somewhere on our block, a few car alarms start to go off. Even though he may be convinced no aliens are coming to Harlem, I get up and tiptoe over to the front door, moving the little slider out of the way so I can see through the peephole and into the small landing. But there's nothing there—just the two doors of the apartments across the hall and the blinking light that's needed to be fixed for months now.

Behind me, the reporter talks.

"The—the—the Mogadorians," she says, and I roll the word around in my head. "They have taken to the streets en masse and appear to be, ah, rounding up prisoners, although we have seen some further acts of violence at—at—the slightest provocation. . . ."

Prisoners?

"Jesus Christ," Benny says.

I keep my eye up to the peephole, trying to catch anything out of the ordinary.

There's a huge bang downstairs and the sound of wrenching metal, like the security gate's being torn in half or something. I leap back from the door, screaming a little bit, and proceed to freak the eff out.

"It's them!" I say, louder than I mean to. My heart is suddenly pumping a thousand beats a minute as I look around for some kind of weapon.

"Shut up!" Benny says, jumping out of his chair and muting the TV. I'm so scared that I hardly get angry at his words. When he sees my face, his expression softens and he lowers his voice to a whisper. "I mean, keep quiet. Damn."

There's screaming somewhere downstairs. Loud and panicked. Terrified. My breath catches in my throat as I take five steps away from the door all at once and back into Benny. There's another scream, one that's cut off suddenly. I start to shake. My breath comes out in quivery gasps.

Benny grips my shoulder and pulls me back. For a second I think he's just dragging me away from the door. Then I realize he's trying to get me behind him.

"Go hide," he says, letting his arm fall away. I turn to him. There's something in his eyes I've never seen before.

Fear.

"Go on," he says.

I start to think of the few places I could try to hide in our apartment—under my bed, the closet—and suddenly I feel like I'm five years old and playing games. But these alien freaks are definitely *not* playing. Our apartment is so small. If they want to find me, they will.

The screams are getting louder, closer. They're moving up the floors. I can hear the doors being kicked in now, along with electronic noises like the ones we heard on TV—the sounds of their weapons.

What the hell is happening?

There's shouting now, right outside our apartment. Deep, bellowing orders to open the doors. I stand frozen in our living room.

Benny takes his bat and walks slowly to the door, half on his tiptoes. He leans up against the corner in the entryway and raises the bat like he's ready to hit a homer. He glances back at me, and his face contorts into an expression I'm more familiar with coming from him: anger.

"Wake up, stupid," he says. "*Go.*"

He nods to the window on the other side of the living room, where the gauzy white curtains Mom loves are billowing out in the slight breeze.

The fire escape. He wants me to make a run for it.

I listen and bolt, and am halfway down to the next floor when I realize Benny is staying back to fend off the aliens and give me a chance to escape. He should be coming with me. What would Mom say if she found out I just left him behind?

Oh God, I hope she's safe.

So I climb back up and stick my head through our living room window right in time to see our front door fly in.

Any hope that these guys were only actors in really great makeup dies as four of the freaks stomp through the front door, all pale skin and jagged teeth and gross noses. There's no question that these are beings from another planet.

And they're not happy.

One of them sees me through the window, his black eyes narrowing. I duck down, hoping that none of the others notice me.

"Surrender or die," the alien says in a deep, grating voice.

Benny steps out of the corner and swings like a pro, slamming his bat into the alien's skull. The bastard falls hard to the floor, and then disintegrates. Just turns into freakin' *dust* like he's a damn vampire that's been staked or something.

But that's the only swing Benny gets. One of the aliens—*Mogadorians*—fires a laser gun at him, and Benny flies backwards a few yards before crashing through our coffee table. He convulses on the floor.

I clamp my hands over my mouth.

When Benny regains a little control of his body, he looks out the window. We lock eyes for a moment. Mine are wide, scared. His are pleading.

"Run!" he shouts, and it looks like doing so causes him a ton of pain. Blood drips from his ears and nose. "Run, damn it!"

And so I do. As I run down metal steps, I hear more of those electric noises coming from my apartment. Benny screams a few times. Then it gets really quiet. I pause on the ladder at the end of the fire escape. I just want to hear Benny cursing at the aliens or the sound of his metal bat hitting someone else's skull. Instead, I look up and find one of the pale-faced bastards hanging out of *my* living room window. He's got a gun pointed at me.

"Shi—," I exclaim, but I never finish the curse. He fires and I just let go of the ladder. I'd rather take my chances falling to the ground than getting zapped by some alien's gun. The electric blast must come within inches of me, though, because as I fall I can feel some kind of static shoot through my body. But then there's nothing but the rush of wind as I claw at the air, plummeting towards the ground below.

I land in an open Dumpster—saved by trash.

I scramble out and stumble through the little alley between our apartment building and the one beside us, trying to make sense of the chaos around me. I pause at the corner and look out onto the street and my block. Some cars have been turned over. Alarms are going off everywhere. One of the alien spacecrafts I saw on TV is parked smack in the middle of the intersection at the end of the block.

Across the street, half a dozen aliens lead a line of people out of an apartment building. People I recognize from the neighborhood. Men, women, kids. They're forced to drop to their knees with their hands in the air on the sidewalk. The Mogadorians keep poking at them with the barrels of their guns. I want to help them, want to do something to save them, but I can't bring myself to move. I'm hardly even breathing, I'm so scared, and have to keep swallowing down the urge to puke. I feel like my heart is trying to burst out from inside of me.

This must be what complete and utter fear feels like.

Tears fill the corners of my eyes, but I'm not sure if they're for me or Mom or even Benny. It's only then that I realize he's the only reason I escaped. He distracted the aliens, tried to keep them from getting me. He didn't have to do that. Hell, he could have abandoned me altogether.

But he didn't. He told me to run while he stayed behind. My stupid stepfather protected me and it got him killed.

For a second, there's a pang of guilt in my gut for every bad thing I ever said about Benny. But then I hear clanging coming from the alley: one of those pale bastards is starting down the fire escape, maybe chasing after me. So I whisper an apology to Benny and to my neighbors on the sidewalk, and try to save myself. My legs start moving, running. I head away from the ship and the people lined up on the streets and towards the park. If I can get across it, I might be able to reach the subway. Maybe the trains are still running and I can get downtown to Mom.

I stay low and use the cars on my side of the street as cover. I make it past several other apartment buildings and the fire hydrant I used to play at during the summers when I was a kid. Water spews out of the broken hydrant onto a body that's lying on the sidewalk. A body that's not moving. I try not to look at it as I make my way around the corner, where I come across three aliens who have their backs to me. I'm so surprised that I trip over my own feet, twisting my ankle and hitting the ground hard. Hard enough that I can't help but let out a short cry. They turn. The one closest to me has dark tattoos along the top of his skull. He lets out a noise that sounds like sandpaper. It takes me a moment to realize he's laughing at me.

I'm toast.

I try to scramble to my feet, but the three of them are on me too fast. They train their guns at me, and I know that no matter how quick I move, I won't be able to get away from them. They'll shoot me if I run.

"Surrender or die," the Mogadorian says.

I look around, but there's no one nearby to help. I can barely even see the people from my block anymore from where I am. I guess everyone's been rounded up, or is hiding, or . . .

My eyes fall on the unmoving body by the hydrant.

These aliens are going to kill me on my own damn block.

The one closest to me bares his gray, jagged teeth in what might be considered a smile on Mars or wherever the hell he came from. His finger on the trigger twitches.

There's a sharp buzzing in my chest. I can hardly stand it. I feel like someone's blown up a balloon inside me, the pain so bad that I'm sure I'm about to be ripped apart.

My heart thumps.

This is the end.

Mom. I'm sorry.

I throw my hands up in front of my face to shield myself. As if that will do anything to protect me.

And then the impossible happens.

CHAPTER
THREE

THE ALIENS' GUNS FLY OUT OF THEIR HANDS AND through the air, clattering onto the street halfway down the block.

What the . . . ?

Something is different. Something inside me has changed. The *buzzing* has changed. Now I can sense it coursing through my veins. I feel powerful. I feel *electric*, and for a second I wonder if I was actually shot with one of those laser guns. But that can't be true. I feel too alive.

What the hell is going on?

I don't know how to even begin to answer that question. The alien douche bags look just as confused as I am—and really pissed off. The one with the tattoos sneers and lunges for me. I push my hand out in front of me, hoping to stop him.

His body shoots through the air, crashing through

the windshield of an abandoned taxi that's on fire a few buildings away from us.

I look at my hands, and then to the two remaining Mogadorians. They take a few steps back.

They're *afraid* of me.

In spite of everything that's happened, I can't help but smirk at this.

"Who's laughing now?" I ask as I get to my feet.

"Garde," one of the aliens says. I don't know what he means, and I don't really care.

I feel like a puppeteer, like everything has invisible strings I can push and pull. I raise my hand above my head, and the alien on my left is thrust into the air. He lets out a deep growl.

I don't have any damn clue what's happening to me. All I know is that these monsters attacked my city. My neighborhood. My family.

I narrow my eyes and bring my hand down. The floating Mogadorian slams into his friend. And then I take him up in the air and hammer him down again, over and over, until the two of them fall apart, bursting into little clouds of ash.

My hands shake. I stare down at them in disbelief, but I don't have time to try to make sense of this. More Mogadorians spill onto the street a few blocks away, shooting into a crowd of people who run after them. The humans have weapons of their own. They're coming at the invaders with guns, knives, hockey sticks and bats—a few police officers head the charge in riot gear. Someone throws something that's smoking; there's the sound of glass breaking, and then one of the aliens goes up in flames.

People are fighting back.

I wonder if I should stay and try to protect my neighborhood, but the only thing I care about in the world right now is getting downtown to Mom. And so I break into a run, this time slightly less afraid, fueled by this new energy that's flowing through me. My brain feels like it's sparking, and all I can think is that if this is real—if I've got *superpowers* now—then I can still hope that she is okay. That we'll be reunited soon. It's not impossible. Nothing is impossible.

Morningside Park is dark. Normally it's not the kind of place I'd want to hang around at night, but I don't hesitate to sprint into it. All I have to do is climb a few flights of stairs and cross a few streets and I'll be at the same train station where I said good-bye to Mom just a few hours ago. As soon as I get inside the park itself, though, I start to rethink my route. It seems like every bush is shaking, and I can hear whispers in the air around me. I tighten my fingers into fists as I run along.

I'm almost to the stairs when suddenly there's a light in my face and someone pulling on the back of my shirt. My hands go up and I'm ready to try to dust a few more of these pale suckers, when I hear someone say, "Be cool, it's just a kid."

"Who's there?" I ask, not letting my guard down.

The light moves away, and after blinking a few times I realize that it's shining on a small group of people. Maybe fifteen of them. Then the light goes out.

"Sorry," the person with the flashlight says. "We thought you might be one of them."

"Do I *look* like one of them?" I ask.

As my eyes adjust, I begin to see the boy holding the flashlight at his side. He's only a few years older than me, if that, and he can't stay still, his head and eyes darting around the park.

"I have to go," I say, starting towards the stairs again.

The boy grabs my arm.

"It's bad up there," he says. "They're everywhere."

"It's bad down *here*," someone in the group says.

"I'm not afraid," I say, shaking loose from his grip.

"They came into our building," the boy says. "My parents and a few others tried to hold them off in the front while we all made it out through the back. I don't know . . ."

He trails off. I look back at the rest of the crowd. That's when I realize most of them are either pretty young or pretty old. Those who wouldn't have stood a chance against the Mogadorians.

"We'll be safe here," a little girl says. "Until help comes."

I wonder if that now includes me. If *I'm* the help.

Before I can answer that question, another light is on me. On all of us. This time from the air, coming from one of those damn spaceships. Black masses jump from its sides—more aliens.

"Run!" someone shouts. And we do.

We scramble up the stairs. Behind me I can hear the electric sounds of their weapons. An older man is hit and falls. Flashlight Boy grabs him, dragging him along. We keep going. We have enough of a start that we're halfway up the seemingly never-ending steps when they finally start to gain on us.

"Go! Go!" I shout, but there's no way they can move any faster. Not this group.

So I try to buy them some time to escape. I turn my attention to the Mogadorians.

They're a few yards behind me, their boots smacking against the white stone steps.

"What are you doing?" Flashlight Boy shouts at me.

"Saving you!" I yell back.

Or getting myself killed.

"Yo, ass faces." I crack my knuckles. "You never should have messed with Harlem."

They raise their guns, but I'm faster. I push my hands forward. The aliens fly back, tossed through the air. One of them lands in a nearby pond. A couple more tumble down the steep steps. They must have bones, because I can hear them breaking. One of them turns to dust halfway down, the other one disappears at the base of the stairs when he lands on his head.

But I don't get them all. A big one somehow missed my magic Jedi attack and is still coming at me, his blaster raised and ready to fire. I reach out my hand and clench my fist. The alien stops, lifted off the ground by a giant, invisible hand.

"Yeah, sucker," I say. "Whatcha gonna do now?"

He squirms in my grip, saying stuff in a language I've never heard—though it's pretty obvious that he's cursing at me. For some reason I think about Benny's quiet prayers as we watched the news.

And I think of my mom, who has to be all right and waiting for me at her restaurant.

She has *to be.*

"This planet has already fallen," he says in English. I don't know if he's got a weird accent, or if his voice just normally sounds like someone trying to make a gravel smoothie in a blender. "You can't win. Your people will bow before us when—"

I throw my hand to my left. The alien flies, smashing into the rocky side of the embankment beside the stairs. He turns to dust before his body ever hits the ground.

It's only then that I realize it's gotten really quiet behind me.

I turn back, and find a dozen eyes staring at me. Some of them are above gaping mouths, others are wide with fear.

"Uh . . ." I have no idea what to say.

"You," Flashlight Boy says. "You're like the dude in the videos. John Smith."

"Whoa, no," I say. "I'm not with him."

"Are you, like, a good alien?" someone asks.

"What? I live on 120th Street."

Everyone starts to whisper to each other. The murmurs quickly grow louder, until everyone's trying to talk to me, thanking me or asking what else I can do, or telling me to go back to my own planet.

"What now?" a little girl asks. Her eyes are wet and bloodshot.

There's an explosion somewhere close, back from the direction my apartment is in. Or *was* in, maybe. The steps rattle beneath our feet.

I don't know what to tell these people to do, but *my* mission is clear. I've got to get downtown.

And if any of these shark-faced freaks get in my way, I'll destroy them, leaving mountains of dust behind me.

CHAPTER FOUR

I RUN UP THE LAST OF THE STAIRS AND OUT OF the park. The others follow.

"You're like a mutant or something," Flashlight Boy says from behind me. "You been exposed to some radiation or toxic waste or something?"

"Do you have a spaceship?" a girl asks, totally ignoring the fact that I already said I'm not some alien.

"Why is this happening?" another girl asks. She just keeps repeating the question over and over again.

I don't say anything—wouldn't know *how* to even try to answer these questions that don't make any sense to me either. But that doesn't seem to matter to any of them. They just keep on chasing after me, the younger ones sometimes slowing down a little bit to get the old-timers moving faster. I know that if this group stays on my heels I'll never make it down to Wall Street and

Mom, because there's no way I can avoid these alien bastards with fifteen people hobbling after me. I've got to lose them.

So I figure if I can find a good, safe hiding place or something, I can slip away and not feel bad about abandoning them. The only problem is that the safest place right now is probably in, like, Montana or Wisconsin or, I don't know, *Antarctica* or something—just anywhere far enough from New York or other big cities. I know this neighborhood like the back of my hand, and my mind races trying to think of some kind of place they can hole up and wait for actual help from the army or whoever. I make for Columbia since the university is only a block away and has big metal gates at its entrances that at least *look* like they might be strong. But I don't even have to get close to the campus before I can see a small spaceship in the air over it and hear the shouts and sounds of those electric weapons firing. Some of the buildings are on fire. It sounds like the entire school's under siege. I guess some of the nerds didn't like the idea of being invaded and decided to put up enough of a fight that the aliens are taking notice. Or maybe they were having one of those protests they're always doing, and the pale freaks thought it was a threat. Whatever happened, shit's definitely going down on campus.

Normally I'd cut across the university at 116th Street

to get to the train, but that's obviously not happening. Taking out a few pale-faced dudes in the park is one thing, but I'm not gonna test my luck by trying to face off against a *spaceship*. I doubt I'm that strong. Besides, I don't even know how I got these powers, much less how long they'll last, and I don't want to use them all up when I've still got to get across the whole damn city. So I take a quick left and head down Amsterdam. There are people everywhere, mostly running, some who look injured. No one seems to know where to go or what to do. My legs keep moving, and it's a few more blocks before I realize where I'm leading us.

The Big Crab.

Or, more specifically, the Cathedral of St. John the Divine.

I stop at the bottom of the steps leading up to the church and turn to the group behind me, the kids, old people and a couple of wide-eyed teenagers around my age. There's a little pang in my side from running, but I'm in great shape compared to the others, who are wheezing.

"Inside," I say, nodding to the church. "You'll be a lot safer in there than on the street. Just wait until the army or marines or coast guard or *whoever* shows up and takes out all these pricks. They're probably marching across the bridges right now."

"What are we supposed to do inside?" Flashlight Boy asks.

"I don't know. This place is gigantic and, like, a hundred years old. There should be plenty of places to hide. Plus, it's a church, so . . . you know. It's probably extra protected or something."

A couple of the elderly people who are hunched over and trying to catch their breath look so relieved that we've stopped that I think they might cry. Or maybe they're on the verge of tears because of everything that's going on around us. I don't know. Whatever the case, they start up the steps, glancing around and looking for any more aliens on the block. Three of the teenagers stand their ground, though. Flashlight Boy puffs out his chest.

"Where are you going?" he asks.

"Downtown. That's where my mom's at."

"You're gonna need help," Flashlight Boy says. "I'm fast. And I can fight."

I catch him flexing his wiry arms a little, and in other circumstances I'd probably laugh at the fool. The others nod in agreement. One girl starts saying how much safer they'd be with me to protect them, while Flashlight Boy goes on about not wanting to sit around with nothing to do just waiting for the demons from another planet to show up, and all I can think about is how with every second I waste here, Mom might be in more and more danger.

"You wanna see a demon?" I ask, shaking my head at them. "Spend five more seconds standing here talking instead of getting inside."

Flashlight Boy looks taken aback. He cocks his head to one side.

"You can't stop us from coming."

My nostrils flare as I push my hand out to one side. At the top of the stairs, a big set of doors fly open with a bang, almost tearing off their hinges.

I've got to be more careful with this whole mind-power thing.

My point gets made, though. They look back and forth between me and the doors for a few seconds, faces all twisted up in a mixture of confusion, fear and something like awe.

"Go," I say. It sounds more like I'm begging them than commanding them. I've got to go. I've wasted too much time as it is.

Thankfully, they trudge up the stairs. At the top, Flashlight Boy takes one look back.

"Well, you better fuck all those aliens up," he says. "Any of 'em come busting in here and they'll be sorry."

I nod and turn away, cutting across the road. A few cars and a taxi whizz by me, but in the distance, farther down Amsterdam, I can see another alien ship landing. The cars are headed right for it, right into the arms of the aliens. My blood pumps faster. How many obstacles stand between my mom and me? I shake the thought from my head and focus on continuing to move. It's only then that I realize how truly messed up this must be for Flashlight Boy and the others. If their families made some kind of stand or distraction back at the apartments, there's a good chance they met the same fate as Benny. Or they were captured, which, hell, might even be worse for all I know. I'm just glad I have Mom to run to. Otherwise, what the hell would I even be doing right now?

I turn off Amsterdam before I get to a bigger intersection. There are only a dozen people on the street, but I see lots of faces in windows looking out with wide eyes. I try to think about what this means. If the Mogadicks are at the university and hit my block in Harlem, maybe they're working their way down from the Bronx. They were in Midtown on the news, and I know they were at the UN. Maybe they haven't gotten down to the Financial District.

Halfway down the block, I hear a huge explosion from somewhere behind me. I look over my shoulder to see smoke rising from the area the church is in. I stop. My stomach cramps up. For a second I think about running back, but I bury that idea in my head and start towards the train again, telling myself that it must have been a car getting bombed or one of those alien ships going down. The church is probably fine. I have to keep focused. I can't stop and help every person I see.

Still, my heart's in my throat.

But it doesn't stay there. Instead, it drops to my guts when I come to a corner and see dozens of Mogadorians four or five blocks up the street. There are tons of police cars too, their flashing lights reflected in the hulls of two spaceships hovering over the street. I can't tell if there was some kind of police resistance that retreated into campus or if some kind of student revolt spilled out onto Broadway. Whatever's happening, the Mogs are fighting back with everything they've got. The ships fire into the crowds. There are exploding bottles being thrown by the students and a steady pop of gunshots. It's chaos. It's hard to even take my eyes off the crumbling buildings and the faces of the people fighting back. But I do. A hundred feet in the other direction is a subway entrance at 110th. My goal. The trains still have to be operating, helping get people out of the city.

Right?

I practically slide down the stairs when I finally get to the entrance. For a second I actually wonder if I have my MetroCard on me, as if with everything that's going on someone would try to stop me from hopping the turnstile.

Only, that's not a problem, because the subway station is packed full of people. It's madness. If I were claustrophobic at all, it would be my worst nightmare. There have to be a hundred men, women and children between me and the turnstiles. A steady stream of panicked people leap over them, one by one, and jump down onto the tracks. They hold their cell phones out, using them as flashlights. Someone's opened up the emergency gate, and a high-pitched alarm squeals as people shove through it.

"What the hell?" I wonder out loud. "They're going to get run over down there."

"Oh, honey," a woman beside me says. She's got a handful of photos and a small, rat-looking dog pulled close to her chest. "This train hasn't been running for hours."

"What are you talking about?" I ask. The trains have to be running. *Shit.*

"The aboveground tracks are out at 125th," she says. The dog yaps. "Bastards destroyed them. Not that I'm guessing any of the other trains are running now either. Lord, I hope not if there are other people in the tunnels."

My pulse is pounding so hard that nothing's computing in my brain. Before I can even formulate another question, someone runs into me, knocking me into the woman and causing her photos to fall to the ground.

"They're coming!" It's a college-aged dude with blood running down his face. "They're all moving this way. Go! Faster! Run!"

CHAPTER FIVE

THE ALREADY MESSY SITUATION QUICKLY TURNS into pandemonium as everyone tries to jump the turnstiles at once. Screams bounce off the tile subway walls, blending in with the screeching alarm. People fall and don't get back up, trampled. Others are wedged against walls or turnstiles. I realize that I'm probably not going to make it onto the tracks unless I unleash my power on these folks and carve a path by pushing everyone out of my way, and I'd probably end up crushing half of them if I did that. I don't know how I can help. But if some aliens with heavy firepower start down the stairs, I'm screwed. We're *all* screwed, because while I might be able to take out a couple of bastards in a park or on the street, fighting down here in close quarters with a ton of people around is a whole different thing. So I climb back up to the street level, figuring I'll just keep running down to the next stop. The bleeding guy wasn't lying—a few blocks up, about ten aliens have broken off from the rest of the fighting and are marching down Broadway, blasters out in front of them. I turn and start for a side street, when out of the corner of my eye I see a bunch of people all rushing through the open doors of an MTA bus. One of the giant ones that looks like two buses shoved together.

"Come on," I hear someone yell as she pulls a kid half my height onto the bus. "We're getting out of here."

I'm over a hundred blocks away from where I need to be. The trains are down. I can't run all the way down-town. Not with evil aliens lurking around every corner waiting to take me prisoner or shoot me full of lasers or whatever. Despite the voice screaming in my head that this might be a bad idea, I sprint towards the bus. I get on just as the doors close behind me. There are maybe two dozen people huddled together in the seats in various states of shock. A woman a few seats from me cranks the handle on a little emergency radio while trying to find a broadcast, to no avail. At the front of the bus, two guys are crouched in front of the steering wheel.

I hear the firing of weapons on the street. Some-where way too close to us.

"Go!" I shout. "Go, go, go. Downtown! Just drive!"

One of the guys at the front glances back at me and sneers but doesn't say anything.

"We don't have keys," one of the people in the seats says. "They're trying to hot-wire it. . . ."

"You've gotta be shitting me," I mutter, wishing I'd kept on running. Now I'm trapped on a bus, bad guys about to show up at any second.

My fists clench at my sides. These people have no idea how lucky they are that I got on board.

I shove my face up against the back doors, trying to get a look at the approaching aliens, but the way the bus is angled makes it hard for me to see up the street. I glance at the front of the bus over my shoulder. The men are talking excitedly, but I can't hear what they're saying. Suddenly, there's a rumble that shakes the floor. At first I think it's from an explosion, but then I feel cold air being pumped in through the AC: they've got the engine started.

That's when I turn back to the doors and see the gnarly gray teeth of one of the aliens. He's got his blaster pointed right at me.

I shout in surprise, and my hands go up. Before I realize what I'm doing, I can feel the power pouring out of my body. The door to the bus rips off, slamming into the Mogadorian and sending him sailing through a coffee shop window across the street. I fall on my ass. Some of the other people inside the bus start screaming too, and rushing away towards the front. And then we're moving, slowly at first but quickly accelerating.

A few electric shots bounce off the side of the bus, but we get away.

"They've got ships!" I shout as I try to get to my feet. "We gotta get off Broadway."

"I'm working on it," the man behind the wheel shouts back at me.

Right on cue we take a sharp turn. It feels like the bus is going to tip over for a few terrifying seconds. I slide across the floor, knocking my head against one of the handrails. I'm pretty sure the wheels on the left side actually come off the ground, but we level out, taking half a dozen side mirrors off cars parked on the street as we race by. I grip onto one of the poles, trying to pull myself upright.

"Where are we going?" someone asks.

"Riverside to Hudson," the driver yells. "It's the fastest way down."

Down. It's the only word I need to hear.

Air rushes by the hole where the doors used to be, filling the bus with a low roar. When we get to the road that runs along the Hudson River, there are burning cars all along the sides of the park. It looks as though something blew them up. I wonder if the aliens took one of their spaceships and just flew down the highway, blasting everyone who tried to escape when they first appeared. For a moment I'm thankful for whatever cleared the road for us, and then I shudder at the thought.

Taking prisoners. Destroying buildings and cars. Killing who knows how many people. What the hell do these douche bags want?

My body is sore all over, and I let myself sink into one of the seats lining the side of the bus to catch my breath. A few of the other passengers are staring at me. Maybe they're wondering if I was the reason the doors flew off. The last thing I want to do is try to explain what's going on with me, since I have no damn clue myself. And I definitely don't need another group wanting me to keep them safe. So I pull out my phone and try to ignore them.

Still no signal. Still no messages.

And my battery's starting to get low.

There's a pulsing pain in my head, and I rub my temples to try to make it stop. If anything, I think I actually make it worse, so instead I lean my head back against the window and try to take a few deep breaths and figure out what the hell is going on.

That's when I see it for the first time with my own eyes. The giant spaceship that's hovering over the middle of Manhattan, the one that was all over the news. I knew it was big, but seeing it in person is totally different from watching it on our crappy TV. It blots out part of the sky. It's hard to even imagine how something that size was built. I can make out things that look like weapons sticking out from its hull.

"Holy shit," I murmur, and there's such a sinking feeling in my stomach that I have to clamp a hand over my mouth, scared that I'm going to hurl.

Mom. She's so small compared to that thing. We all are. What if . . .

But I don't have much time to worry about what kind of damage the ship has already done to the city: our driver starts yelling.

"Shit! It looks like something went down at the Lincoln Tunnel. Oh Jesus, it looks like it got blown up! We'll have to try the Holland."

The driver keeps cursing, and people start to shake their heads and mutter about how we're all going to die. It takes me a little while to realize what this means. The Lincoln Tunnel—they're headed down but not *downtown*, just to a way off the island.

I get to my feet and walk to the front of the bus so I can try to talk them into going towards the Financial District, or at least letting me off before I end up stranded in Jersey. Through the front windshield I can see a pileup of cars all sprawled out in front of the Lincoln Tunnel ahead of us. Several of them are burning. A couple look like they've been completely mangled. It looks like two of the tunnels have collapsed, brick and dust spilling out of them. My stomach twists as I wonder how many cars might have been inside it when they were destroyed. There are plenty of people around.

They climb over the piled-up cars, disappearing into the darkness of the remaining tunnel. Desperate to get out of the city I'm working so hard to get deeper into.

The driver doesn't slow down even though cars jam the street. Instead, he just slams on the horn, causing people to scatter as we race towards them. We take the bumper off a taxi and then clip the front of a little red sports car. The bus shakes and I have to hold on to the rails above me to keep from tumbling back.

"Dude, we can't get through there," the other guy who helped with the hot-wiring says. "Take a side street or something."

"Everybody hold on," the driver shouts as he shakes his head.

"This isn't your *taxi*. Are you sure you know how to handle this thing?"

"I see a path but it's gonna be tight. Besides, you really wanna risk going through *Midtown*? You saw the news right? Midtown's a war zone."

"Yeah, but . . ." The other guy notices me coming to the front. "What do you want?"

"Just seeing if I can help," I murmur.

"Are you crazy, girl? Sit back down and hold on. We're gonna . . ."

I stop listening and try to focus on the cars we're rushing up on. Maybe I'm powerful enough that I can push them out of the way. Maybe I can help get us through this—*then* I'll worry about where we're going.

I don't know if it's because we're moving so fast, or that the cars are too heavy, or that I'm too far from them—whatever it is, they don't budge. I concentrate harder, ignoring the pounding in my head.

Focus, Dani. If you can help clear the path, you're that much closer to Mom.

The right side of the windshield suddenly breaks, fracturing like a spiderweb. The left windshield is separated by a piece of metal and is fine, but the driver still swerves a little, startled. He hits the side of a stalled-out car, sending me falling back into the laps of some of the passengers.

So much for helping.

"Here we go!" he shouts.

He leans on the horn again as we blow through more parked cars. The passengers cry out. The woman whose lap I've fallen into holds me close, but I don't know if it's because she's trying to keep me from being thrown to the ground or because she's just scared out of her mind. I don't see what we hit but I feel every impact. Everything around us lurches and shakes, but hardly slows down. Sparks fly into the back of the bus through the opening where the door was.

Somehow, we make it through.

The driver lets out a whoop as we hit clear-ish road again.

"All right," he says. "Everyone pray that the Holland Tunnel is clear. We're getting the fuck out of the city."

"Hold up," I say, getting to my feet again. "I'm *not* going to Jersey."

"Don't be stupid. We can't stay here."

"I have to get downtown! My mom—"

"Kid . . ." He cuts me off, but he doesn't finish his sentence. Instead, he just points to the massive spaceship over Midtown.

The bus has done a fine job of getting me farther downtown, so I really hesitate to cause a scene or yell at the driver. On the other hand, the only person I have left in the world is somewhere down by Wall Street, and I've got a badass superpower. I don't have to take no for an answer.

"Stop the bus before you get to the tunnel," I say firmly, calmly. "I'm getting off."

The driver laughs a little.

"Like hell you are." He glances at me. "There are aliens attacking the goddamn city. I'm not slowing down until that ship is a speck in the rearview mirror."

The other guy standing beside him looks at me with shifty eyes. I can see him wondering if he's going to have to push me back to the rear of the bus. If I'm going to be a problem. Over his shoulder, through the cracked windshield, I see a sign for the Holland Tunnel whiz by.

"I don't wanna have to make this a thing," I say.

"Then *don't*," the driver responds.

"Damn it," I mutter.

I could try to brake the bus myself, but I'm afraid I'd slam on the pedal too hard and send us careening off into the Hudson. So instead, I lock eyes with his friend so that he knows exactly what I'm doing. Then I push one hand out. If I concentrate hard enough, I bet I can break the cracked window and control the glass or plastic or *whatever* it is that the windshield is made of. Show off my power. The people might think I'm a crazy alien, but at least they'll listen to me. They'll have to go—

"Hold on!" a voice shouts from the back of the bus. At first I think she's talking to me—that she's somehow figured out what I'm about to do—but then I realize it's the woman with the emergency radio. She rushes towards the front, warnings pouring out of her mouth.

"The Holland Tunnel is out too." I can hear a man's voice crackling through the radio in her hands the closer she gets. "It sounds like all the tunnels in the city are either blocked or collapsed. The bridges are the only way out. There's a big evacuation site at the Brooklyn Bridge they're telling people to go to if their homes have been destroyed."

"Are you sure that's right?" someone asks, voice shaking. "Maybe the tunnel's been cleared up since then or—"

The bus suddenly jerks, brakes squealing as we slow down rapidly. I turn my attention back to the front and see that a few blocks ahead of us the highway is littered with abandoned cars. Some of them are smoking. Others have been overturned. Flames reflect off the water of the Hudson River.

Something bad happened here.

"Damn it," the driver says. "Damn it, damn it, *damn it*."

It gets quiet in the bus except for the sound of the man on the radio. Static keeps interrupting him as he talks about how none of the other boroughs have been hit yet, only Manhattan. Then suddenly everyone's talking, trying to figure out what to do.

The woman with the radio stares at the driver. "What do we do now?"

He shakes his head a little as he goes over his options in his head. Finally, he puts his foot on the gas again, and we all jerk back as the engine revs.

"We're heading for the Williamsburg Bridge," he says.

"But the Brooklyn Bridge is where—," the woman starts.

"Yeah, which means the streets down there are probably a shit show. We've got to get out of the city and that's our best bet. Once we're across we can cut down through Staten Island to Jersey and get as far away as we can. I doubt Staten Island's on their hit list."

He doesn't wait for a response, just takes a sharp left turn and barrels down a side street, threatening to tip the bus over again.

I try to go over geography in my head as we cut through narrow streets with names instead of numbers. I don't know this part of the city well at all, and it's not like I can use the map on my phone since there's no signal. I try to make sense of things. Tunnels are out. An evacuation spot off the Brooklyn Bridge. Mom's work wasn't *too* far away from that. It's possible she might have headed that way.

But she wouldn't have just gone off to Brooklyn and left me with Benny, right?

My head starts to pound again, jumbling my thoughts and making it hard to concentrate. I start back down the aisle, looking for a bus map or something hanging on the walls, asking no one in particular if they know where we are—but there's so much shell shock in the damn bus that no one answers me. We take a few more sharp turns, slowing down a little each time. The driver seems to know these streets well and keeps us moving. Eventually, we're shooting down Houston. And I keep my eyes on the signs at every block we pass until I finally see a cross street I recognize.

Bowery. It's almost a straight shot to where Mom works if I follow it downtown. Once I met her at the restaurant and we walked all the way up to Central Park just because it was a nice day, and I remember taking Bowery for a part of the trip.

I'm about to yell for the bus driver to stop when he slams on the brakes anyway. A few people scream, and it's only then that I see it: one of the alien ships sits in the intersection a block ahead of us. I don't see any pale monsters around, but still, they've got to be close. The driver looks around nervously as the passengers grow louder, people yelling at him to go, or turn, or reverse, or that this is the end and we're all going to die. Abandoned cars and debris cut off the side streets on our right, so the driver makes a quick decision and guns it, turning left onto First Avenue, shouting something back to the rest of us about going another way around the ship. His hands are gripped on the steering wheel and sweat is pouring down his face. I think the dude's about to lose it. But more importantly, we're heading uptown now, farther away from Wall Street, farther away from Mom. If I can just get back to Bowery, I know how to get down to her.

And so when he slows the bus to turn right on Fourth Street, I take a deep breath and step to the empty space where I blew the doors off the bus earlier.

"Good luck in Brooklyn," I murmur.

I jump onto the road, stumbling a few steps before slamming into the side of a parked car and catching myself. The bus doesn't stop. It just drives off without me.

I make sure that I'm not hurt or anything, and then I start to sprint, back towards Bowery, hoping that the aliens from the ship we just saw are busy somewhere off in another direction. I'm getting closer and closer to Mom. Step by step. Inch by inch. But it gets harder and harder. As I turn the corner, my lungs are full of fire. My heart pounds, and my legs scream out for me to stop. On top of that, the throbbing in my head is starting to get to me. It's a weird kind of pain I've never felt before. I'm not even sure it's pain, more like a building pressure behind my eyes.

What's happening?

The streets are pretty empty, and suddenly I feel so alone. Where is everyone? Maybe this area has been evacuated. Or maybe . . .

What if the aliens from that ship have been through here already and rounded everyone up?

Doubt starts to creep into my head. I'm finally getting closer, but what am I supposed to do if she's not there? What do I do if she's gone?

Tears sting the corners of my eyes, threatening to spill as I approach a big intersection. That's when I see a dozen Mogadorians marching into the street, and my whole pity party comes to an abrupt end. I stop, almost falling down. I put my arms out, trying to balance, and end up letting off some kind of force wave that knocks a trash can into the street.

Crap.

I dart inside the nearest building—a bank—hoping the aliens didn't notice. I back away from the door slowly, keeping my eyes on it, my hands stretched out in front of me, ready to use my powers. It's pretty dark inside and my eyes slowly start to adjust. I wonder if the lights are off, or if the electricity's been knocked out. I should have been paying more attention to stuff like that on the street. I should have—

"Uhh . . . ," a voice comes from behind me.

I turn around, keeping my hands raised, ready to dust some aliens. Instead, there are three figures wearing ski masks. Humans. Two of them are in the back, stuffing cash into a duffel bag. The other's just a yard away from me, his eyes wide, mouth hanging open in confusion.

He's pointing a gun at my face.

CHAPTER
SIX

I GET READY TO KNOCK THIS GUY BACKWARDS AS tears start to stream down my cheeks, brought on by a mixture of exhaustion and the thought that in the middle of an alien invasion, I might get killed by some punk human.

"Uh, don't cry?" the man murmurs.

Despite the tears, I manage to laugh a little at the guy who's telling me to get ahold of myself *while holding a gun to my face.*

Luckily, I don't have to go all Jedi on him. His buddies interrupt.

"What the *fuck*, Jay," one of the guys from the back says. "She's just a kid."

Jay lowers the gun, his hands shaking. "Sorry," he says quietly. He doesn't sound *too* much older than me, maybe in his twenties.

The reality of the situation dawns on me.

"The city is being invaded by aliens and you ass-holes are *robbing a bank*?" I say loud enough for all three of them to hear me.

"Hey," Jay says, defensive. "We're just trying to make the most of a bad situation."

All the sadness that had taken me over morphs into rage. I spit venom out of my mouth before I even realize that I'm shouting.

"Do you have any idea what it's like out there? My stepdad just got murdered trying to protect me. I have no idea what's happened to my mom. I'm pretty sure I saw a bunch of people get *trampled* in the subway by dudes just trying to escape. Not killed by aliens, but by other people. Who knows how many have been killed by these alien bastards? And you want to tell me that making the best of this situation is you and your boys robbing a bank while all this is going down? How can you be so selfish? Jesus. You could be helping people get out of the city or something." My thoughts imme-diately go back to everyone I've left behind—everyone I haven't protected or fought for because I've been try-ing to get downtown. The neighbors on my block. The group I left at the church. Hell, even the people on the bus, who for a second I was going to force to take me downtown. My head starts shaking and the tears well up again because even though I know I should be going to find Mom, there's a voice in my head telling me I should be taking my own advice. That of course she wants to see me and be reunited, but that helping other people is just as important. Maybe *more.* I should be trying to do some good where I can.

Jay looks at me with wide eyes, like this is all stuff that might have been in the back of his mind already, and he's furious with himself *and* with me for bringing it up. His two friends don't seem to care, though, because once their duffel bag is full, they slap him on the back and nod towards the door.

"We're done," the guy with the bag says.

I wipe my eyes, feeling stupid for crying in front of them. "Maybe you forgot, but there's a bunch of aliens out there," I mutter. "Go outside and you're toast."

"I'm not sitting on top of all this money and waiting to get caught."

"We run across 'em, we'll take 'em out," the other dude says, holding up another gun.

"No, like, they're *right outside.*" I try to talk some sense into them. "That's why I ducked in here in the first place. There's a dozen of those pale freaks."

"Maybe we should hole up in here for a little while until the coast is clear," Jay says. He peeks out the window, but from here he can't see far down the block.

"Dude, our car is just around the corner," the third guy says. "We get in, we punch it and we're out of the city in ten minutes with an assload of cash. Don't be stupid." He points to me. "The next person who comes in might not be some dumb girl. It might be cops or the National Guard or some shit. You wanna be standing around like this when they get here?"

I somehow manage to keep my cool and not slam him against the wall.

"I'm betting the cops have more important things on their minds than you right now." I turn to Jay. "Don't say I didn't warn you."

My mom's voice might be telling me to slow down and help people, but I'm guessing she'd take exception to these fools. If they want to get wasted stealing a bunch of cash that's their problem, not mine.

The guy who's not holding the duffel bag lets out a big exaggerated groan and pushes past Jay. In seconds he's out on the sidewalk, looking around. He calls back to the others inside.

"Street's empty." He waves his gun around. "Come on, you bitches."

Jay gives me one last look, and then makes for the exit. They're a few steps away from the door when the guy outside yells and fires off a few rounds farther up the street. Some kind of blast rips through the guy outside. He drops like a rock. Suddenly, the street gets bright. A light drops down from above and shines into the bank, blinding me. I raise my arm to cover my eyes and back away out of instinct. It takes me a second to realize that it's not just a spotlight hovering in the air, pouring light inside.

It's a ship.

"Holy shit, get do—"

I don't get to finish the sentence. An electronic sizzling fills the air as the small ship fires on us. The windows shatter. I hit the ground hard, army crawling to cover behind a kiosk in the middle of the bank. Jay and the other guy stay standing, guns drawn, firing at the light. Idiots. I shout at them again, but it's no use. Jay doesn't last long. Some kind of light bursts through his chest, different from the electric shots I saw earlier. I wince. The guy with the duffel bag turns to run, but he doesn't get far before he's taken out too, the bag sliding across the floor towards the back.

Three people dead, just like that.

I lie motionless, hoping there's not some kind of heat-seeking missile or something on the ship that can find me. Maybe if I don't move, don't even *breathe*, I'll be okay.

Then I hear the footsteps. A group of aliens—probably the ones I saw earlier—are congregating outside.

Shit, shit, shit.

They bark at each other in their weird language. Then one of them steps forward, creeping through the shattered window. He's dressed in black tactical gear like the others and has spiraling tattoos that run from the top of his shaved head to down behind his ears. His boot kicks Jay, who doesn't respond.

He does the same thing with the other guy, who's also toast. I pray that he's just going to turn around and leave. Instead, he keeps wandering farther back into the bank, his weapon drawn, looking for other people. I make myself as small as possible, curling into a ball against the kiosk. But I'm not small enough. He's coming from the back of the bank when he glances over and locks eyes with me.

I'm screwed.

My hands shoot forward and the alien flies, slamming into the back wall of the bank hard enough that he turns into a cloud of alien dust. I can hear voices from the front again, and I peek around the kiosk to see two other freaks stepping forward, blasters out. My mind races. I don't know if the kiosk can handle much more damage. There may be a way out the back or something, but if the ship starts blasting again, I'm probably dead.

I try to prioritize and deal with the closest danger. With a wave of my hand, the guns the two Mogadorians in front are carrying fly away, thrown back into the street. There's a moment of stunned silence from the rest of them before the others start firing into the bank without any real target. I wave my hands again, and the two unarmed aliens float in front of the rest of their troop, shielding me from gunfire long enough that I can bolt to a spot behind a leather sofa farther back inside and at least put some distance between me and the monsters. But the alien shields don't hold up for long before they turn to dust too, so I send a desk flying out towards the blaster fire. I think I even hit a couple of the bastards.

Maybe I stand a chance against these dudes after all.

That's when I realize the ship is repositioning to shoot into the bank again. I can hear some sort of whirring that sounds like an engine warming up.

And I'm hiding behind a dinky couch.

I swallow hard. My head pounds.

"Mom . . . ," I whisper as I raise my hands in front of my face.

A fireball flies through the air from somewhere down the block. There's an explosion, and suddenly the street goes dark.

CHAPTER
SEVEN

WITH THE SPOTLIGHT OUT, I'M SUDDENLY BLIND
as my eyes try to readjust to the darkness. Blaster fire
sizzles against the leather sofa, and I duck down, pressing myself as flat onto the floor as I can in case the
ship's guns go off. The world slowly comes back into
focus in the inch of space between the floor and the
couch that I can see through. Weapons fire constantly,
though there seem to be fewer and fewer of them. I
peek around the couch just in time to see what looks
like some dude—I think it's a dude, he's just a shadow
to me—hanging on the edge of the alien ship. He must
have a flamethrower or something, because fire is filling the cockpit. Then he leaps off it, landing on the
street again while the ship spins and crashes into a
building across from the bank. It's some real Spider-
Man shit. There's a big explosion, and I duck down
again, covering my head.

I think this guy just saved my life.

I wonder if it's the army that's finally come to anni-hilate these pale motherfuckers. Whoever it is must have won, because I don't hear any more of the alien weapons going off, and I can make out voices from the street that sound human.

Okay. So I'm not dead. That's good. I'm also not that far away from Mom's restaurant. Or at least I'm a lot closer than I was an hour ago.

Slowly, I stand, keeping my eyes on the street outside. After a few small steps, I almost trip over the duffel bag full of money that the robber had been carrying. I stare at it for a second, and suddenly my head is flashing back to the last time I saw my mom, arguing with her about Benny and keeping our apartment. Even though I don't think any of that matters now—if our apartment is still there at all—I pick up the bag. I know I gave Jay and the others shit about being *felons* when the city's going to hell, but this totally isn't the same thing. It's a lucky break. I'm not going to just leave, like, hundreds of Gs on the floor here. Mom and I might need it to survive. And isn't that what all of this has been for? Us living through this and starting over? If—*when* I find Mom, this cash means we could go anywhere, do anything we wanted. Go somewhere far away from all these ships, even if the world does go to hell.

Only now I look like a robber. If it's the army that

saved me, they may not even know I'm in here. They were probably just killing any aliens they came across. If that's the case, maybe I can sneak out the back.

I sling the duffel bag over my shoulder right as two figures come into view, silhouetted in the broken window. I duck back down behind the sofa.

"Just keep walking," I whisper.

"Hey, it's all clear out here," one of them says.

Crap. They must have seen me. Stupid.

Then, a light comes on. I think it's a flashlight or really powerful phone at first, but when I peek around the sofa it looks like it's actually coming from this guy's *hands*. I can see just a glimpse of his face and blond hair. Something about him looks familiar, but I'm not sure why.

"Nine?" he asks. Then his voice lowers a bit, getting kind of an edge to it. "Five?"

That's when it dawns on me why I know this guy— he's the dude who was fighting the big ugly alien on TV. He's like a legit superhero. The good alien from that cheesy-as-hell YouTube video they kept playing on the news.

John Smith.

Maybe he knows what's going on. Maybe he knows why I can suddenly move stuff by waving my hands around.

I take a step forward, into the light coming out of his

palms. It feels warm. Which had better not mean it's got radiation or some weird alien stuff in it that's going to make me sick one day. My eyes have to readjust again. When they do, I can make out the other figure coming up to John's side. He's kind of a scrawny, indie-band-looking sorta dude. Not John, though. He's tall and buff, even though he looks younger now that he's in front of me and not on the news.

He's probably the most famous person in the world right now. Other than the aliens. It's kind of weird that he's standing there looking at me like *I'm* a surprise.

"You're him," I say, taking a few more small steps forward. "You're the guy from TV."

He turns off his flashlight hands and gets a weird look on his face. I can't tell if he's relieved or disappointed to see me.

"I'm John," he says.

They ask me some questions about other people being in here with me, but I'm pretty sure they aren't talking about any of the robbers. Both the guys look at me like I'm about to pull a knife on them or something. Then I show them that I've got powers too, by floating the gun from the alien I smashed against the wall over to me.

That definitely changes their expressions.

They seem surprised. Not about the powers themselves, but that I have them. I've seen John do some crazy stuff on TV, and he and his buddy just took down a whole squad of monsters from space *plus* their ship. I wonder if they know why I suddenly have telekinesis— their word for what I can do.

I try to make sense of everything as we talk. I'm a human, but I've got the same powers John and his friend have. Benny didn't have them. None of the other scared people I met tonight have them. But I do. Which means that either I'm just the luckiest—or maybe unluckiest, I don't really know yet—girl in the city, or there's a reason I've been turned into a superhero. It seems like someone or something *chose* me specifically. I just can't figure out why.

It's time I got some answers.

"So, um, can I ask why you picked me?" I raise my eyebrows and look back and forth between them. The scrawny guy's mouth just hangs open like I've asked him to fly me to the moon. John's eyebrows are scrunched together.

"Picked you?" he asks.

Yeah, fool, as in why do I have alien powers?

A bunch of questions fly out of my mouth, but neither of them seems to have any idea why I'm a mutant now. So what gives? If they don't know, then who would?

John's got other things on his mind.

"It's not safe here," he says. He looks so earnest, eyes all big as he nods. "You should come with us."

It's not like I can just follow these guys. I still have

to find Mom. Besides, if they're out fighting aliens—
Mogs, as they call them—that means joining up with
them would probably put me on the front lines of this
attack. I'm not exactly thrilled by this idea.

"Is it gonna be safe wherever you're going?" I ask.

"No. Obviously not."

"What John means is that this particular block is
going to be crawling with Mogs any minute now," the
lanky one says as he starts walking away from the
bank, looking really skittish. Watching him makes *me*
start to worry, like maybe he knows something I don't.

"Your sidekick's nervous," I say to John.

"My name's Sam," the other guy says.

"You're a nervous guy, Sam."

I bite the insides of my cheeks, trying to make heads
or tails of what I should do. They're right; we probably shouldn't be hanging out where a whole squad of
bad aliens just got blown away. Even though they don't
have any answers for me, they're the closest thing I've
got to any sort of explanation of what's going on. And
they're obviously powerful—they took down a *ship*.
Maybe they could actually *help* me get to Mom.

And there's something about John. It's hard to
explain, but I feel drawn to him. It's got nothing to
do with his piercing eyes or cheekbones—the dude's
totally *not* my type. It's something else, on a deeper
level. I feel connected to him somehow. When he talks

about doing good and fighting, I hear my earlier words to Jay in my head.

But when he starts talking about me helping him win some war and finding some buddy of his, I realize how far away they would take me from Mom. I don't even know these guys. It's not like I can trust them to help me out if I say I'll join them.

Besides, I know it hasn't been all that long since these Mogs appeared out of nowhere and ruined everyone's lives, but the military is probably gearing up to take back the city right now. They'll be flying in on jets and parachuting down into Central Park by the thousands, guns blazing.

"Seriously?" I ask. "I'm not fighting any war, John Smith from Mars. I'm trying to survive out here. This is America, yo. The army will take care of these weak-ass dust aliens. They got the drop on us, that's all."

John looks confused about this—I'm getting the feeling he's not exactly someone that others say no to a lot. I'm betting some people really fall for his whole Superman routine. But before he can argue with me, there's an explosion somewhere a few blocks away. I'm almost knocked down by it. Car alarms start going off on the street. Over the rooftops, I can see a bunch of smoke rising into the air.

My grip tightens around the Mog weapon I've still got in my hand. John starts in on his pitch again, trying to tell me how it's my duty to help them and that I should go with them to Brooklyn or something. Everybody is trying to force me out of the city, but I'll worry about a safe zone when I know I've done everything to find Mom. Outside, explosions keep going off. I point a finger at John. A little bit of my telekinetic energy pushes him back, which seems to shut him up.

"My stepdad got roasted by those pale scumbags and now I'm out here looking for my mom, alien guy. She worked down here. You saying I should drop all that and join your army of two, running around my city that you played a part in getting blown up? You saying the friend you're looking for is more important than my mom?"

Another explosion outside. Sam says something, but I've got my eyes locked on John's and don't really pay attention to his friend. Then there's movement in the sky that I catch out of my peripheral, and I turn to see the big-ass ship floating into view. Some kind of energy starts to charge up on a cannon-looking thing sticking out of the bottom of its hull.

We're totally in its target zone.

"Hell with this," I say and start running away from the ship. Famous alien superhero or not, I'm not going to stand around with John Smith and get blown up.

CHAPTER
EIGHT

"DO YOU KNOW WHERE YOU'RE GOING?" SAM YELLS.

I glance over my shoulder. The two of them are trailing me by a few yards but catching up. What is it about me today that makes people think *I'm* the one in charge?

"What?" I turn my attention forward again. "You guys are following *me* now?"

"You know the city, don't you?"

Goddamn alien tourists.

An explosion rocks the street somewhere behind us. I glance back to see that Sam and John are okay, but half the block is nothing but smoke, dust and debris now. The bank is gone. Just, not there anymore. This is some next-level shit. The city's getting demolished.

I gulp down my worry and focus on moving.

"We need to get off the street!" John shouts.

Sure. No problem. I'll just pry up a manhole cover or something.

I spot a green subway lamp a block over.

"This way!" I yell back, taking a left and cutting across the street.

The smoke and debris roll past us, and I cough through it, until we're off the main avenue and onto a side street where the buildings block most of it. Eventually, we make it underground at one of the Bleecker Street subway entrances. We're inside for only a few seconds before the whole station starts to shake. At least this stop is empty—though that's not exactly comforting. The vibrations intensify, and I don't waste any time hopping the turnstiles. I head for the 6 since that tunnel will take me in the right direction. I think. It's hard to map out routes in my head while I'm afraid that the subway is going to explode around me at any second.

Tiles fall off the walls. Pieces of ceiling rain down. John and Sam follow behind me, yelling for me to go faster, deeper into the station, as if I'm not running as fast as I can already, taking an entire flight of subway stairs in just a few steps. When we finally get to the tracks, I hesitate for a second, thinking of my mom's warnings about getting hit by a train and of electrified rails. The kind of things she's drilled into me since I was a kid. Only I'm guessing she never imagined I'd be in a situation where a subway station was literally falling down around me because of some damn alien warship. I jump down. There's a splash when I land. The tracks are full of liquid that rises over my shoes, and I hope to God that it's just water. At least I guess the third rail is out because I'm not electrocuted. The boys follow behind me, and John's flashlight hands come back on to light our way and scare a fuck-ton of rats.

"Oh, gross, gross, gross," I repeat to myself as I keep running into the tunnel. Everything around me is shaking. It feels like the earth is going to swallow us.

And it kind of does.

There's a crack above me. I look up just in time to see a giant piece of cement falling down on top of me. I scream, covering my head.

But I don't die. When I look up again, my nose is a few inches away from a slab of tunnel ceiling that's just hanging in the air. I think for a second that maybe I'm the one doing this somehow, but then I look back and see John. He's on his knees in the gross water and it looks like he's being crushed, muscles all straining like the weight of the world is on top of him.

"We have to hold up the ceiling!" Sam shouts. "We have to help him!"

His hands go up in the air and I see a hint of relief flash on John's face.

I look down the tunnel. I can't see the other end, but I know if I just keep going I'll eventually be close to the Brooklyn Bridge. Then it's just a little more running until I'm on Wall Street. Till I'm with Mom.

I could just go. Could leave these guys behind. Maybe they'd be okay without my help.

But a thought I've been trying to silence rings in my head.

You don't know that she's alive.

It's true. I know it is. I just don't want to consider it. But it's getting harder to ignore, when there are aliens obliterating entire buildings in front of me. When I've seen everything that I've witnessed in the last few hours. And as I look back and lock eyes with Sam—his expression frantic, veins bulging in his face and neck— I know I can't abandon these two. It's not what Mom would want me to do.

Besides, I owe them one.

I raise my hands above my head, pushing up with my telekinesis. I can feel a little bit of give in the cement as my strength is added to theirs. The pounding in my head comes back, and I bite my lip, trying to ignore it.

John takes a few rasping breaths as he moves forward,

until all three of us are standing close together. Behind him, some of the tunnel—or, more likely, the whole *street* above—falls with a splash.

"Walk . . . walk backwards." Dude sounds like he's about to pass out. "Let it go . . . slowly."

We go one step at a time, trying to keep the tunnel reinforced with our telekinesis. It's heavy at first, but with every move it gets worse. Almost unbearable. My arms get all wobbly. My brain feels like it's going to explode.

"Shit, shit, shit," I keep repeating.

John whispers some kind of encouragement, but I'm concentrating so hard on not getting crushed that I hardly hear him. I glance over at Sam, who looks like he's having just as bad a time as me. We keep walking, little by little, letting bits of the tunnel fall when we're a safe distance away. At some point, it actually starts to feel easier. I think my mind muscles must have suddenly bulked up before I realize that we're just finally getting far enough into the tunnels that we've managed to outrun the collapse.

Finally, we can stop holding up the ceiling. When I let go, I feel sick. I've totally overexerted myself. I take a few shaky steps to the side of the tunnel and lean against it. The last bit of lunch in my stomach comes up, splashing in the filthy water at my feet.

John takes a few steps towards me. As shitty as I feel,

he looks even worse. Sam's by his side in a flash, struggling to hold the guy up.

"Oh man, is he dying?" I ask.

"However much ceiling we were holding, he was probably carrying four times as much," Sam replies. "Help me with him."

I hesitate for a moment, trying to make sure that *I'm* not going to collapse, before I pull John's arm over my shoulder, the duffel bag butting up against his side. He's sweaty and gross and I try not to grimace—or think about how gross I probably am by now too.

"He just saved my life," I murmur.

"Yeah," Sam says. "He does that kinda thing a lot."

We only get a few steps farther into the tunnel before John's flashlight hands turn off. Then he goes slack.

"Oh fuck, he's dead," I say.

"No," Sam corrects me. "He's just passed out. Why would you *say* that?"

"I don't know! This morning I didn't even know there were aliens, jeez."

We trudge on. The tunnel is dark, but I manage to take out my phone and turn the flashlight on, which lets us see a little ways in front of us. At least the collapse must have scared off all the rats. It's a small miracle.

John weighs a ton, and if it weren't for our combined strength, I doubt Sam or I would be able to drag him far. But we do, somehow. We pass what I think is the

Spring Street station. It's hard to tell because the station platform is completely caved in as well. Destroyed. I don't say anything when we pass by it, just shake my head and focus on keeping my legs moving.

"Do you have any idea where we are?" Sam asks a few minutes later.

"Uhhh . . ." I try to envision subway maps in my head. "Maybe under Little Italy? Or Chinatown? I think the Canal Street station is next."

"Crap."

"What?"

"Nothing. I think we were over here earlier. We were heading the other way. To Union Square."

"Long ways from there, now."

Sam just grunts in reply.

Eventually we come to a spot where a bunch of tunnels run side by side. There's a train that looks like it must have stalled out or jumped off a track. Whatever happened, it's abandoned. And dry.

"Let's rest in there," Sam suggests, and I don't know that I've ever been so happy to get on a train before.

We lay John out on one of the benches and then just stand there catching our breath. My whole body is tense. My arms and legs shake from overuse. The drumming in my head is getting worse.

"Well," Sam says finally. "We should probably let him rest for a little while."

I move my phone's flashlight to Sam's face like I'm in some kind of cop show. He winces, raising a hand to block the light.

"I guess it's just us," I say, dropping my duffel bag to the floor of the train. "And I've got lots of questions for you, Sam the Martian."

CHAPTER
NINE

IT TURNS OUT SAM'S NOT AN ALIEN.

John Smith, though . . . he's a different story.

"So . . . ," I say, trying to wrap my head around everything Sam has said. "He really *is* a good alien."

"I just told you everything I know about him," Sam says. "If you're not convinced that he hasn't been tainted by the dark side yet, I don't think you ever will be."

"Why didn't you guys tell everyone about all this sooner? Recorded some better commercials maybe. Put on, like, a protest or something."

Sam turns to me, squinting his eyes.

"Do you really think a protest would have stopped them?"

"No, but at least we woulda been prepared for this shit. We could have nuked them in space or something."

He shakes his head. "You *were* listening when I said

some of the government is in on this, right?"

"Damn," I mutter. "Guess you got a point."

We're a few subway cars away from where we left John sleeping like a rock. Benny used to pass out that hard sometimes—though it was always from too many beers—and would be completely immovable until morning. I'm guessing John's not waking up anytime soon either. As weak as my body feels, I can't say I blame him.

I carry a knockoff Prada purse slung over my shoulder. Sam's got a tote that says "Music Is My Bag" on the side. Scavenging was Sam's idea. He said it was in case we had to make a speedy exit and didn't have another time to loot the train, but I think he was just hungry—which, after having hurled earlier and spending most of my night running, I totally understand. Luckily for us, whatever happened to this train caused a lot of people to leave their shit behind. I've already found some meal bars, little hundred-calorie packs of cookies and even a few bottles of water. Not to mention a couple of phones—which is great, because my battery is dead. No luck on finding a mobile charger or something yet. Not that I'd get any signal all the way down here, even if the network was up.

"You're heading down to Wall Street, right?" Sam asks. He's on his hands and knees fishing a plastic bag out from under one of the seats.

"Yeah," I say. "That's where my mom works. She

waits tables. Sometimes bartends. The restaurant's nice as hell. Lots of rich bankers."

"That's cool."

"I guess."

He stands back up and looks at me all serious-like.

"Do you have any idea . . . ?"

He trails off, but I know what he's getting at.

"She called me when it all started," I say. "Told me to go home. Then there was some kind of . . ." I struggle with the word. "Loud noise. An explosion maybe. I'm not sure. I had no idea what was going on. Didn't realize what was happening until I got home and saw your boy John on the news beating up on that big alien guy. Citrus Ramen or whatever."

"Setrákus Ra."

"Or *whatever*," I repeat. "Anyway, I haven't had a signal or anything since then. I'm sure she's fine. She's tough. Well, not really. She's the nicest, most loving person ever. But she's a survivor."

Sam looks like he wants to say something, but I'm so physically and mentally and emotionally tired that I just hold a hand up and walk away. If we keep talking about this, I'm going to break down.

"Daniela—," Sam starts.

"Here, nerd," I say, holding a granola bar I've just found on the ground out to him, cutting him off.

He looks at it for a second.

"Wait. Why am I a nerd? Why does everyone assume that?"

I shrug. "Just a guess. You've got that vibe coming off of you."

He looks like he's about to protest, but he doesn't. Instead, he takes the snack. "You don't like these?"

"No," I lie.

I stretch and yawn. Sam does too like it's contagious. I'm so exhausted that I'm wondering if I could use my newfound powers to float myself back to the car where John is.

"We should head back," Sam says. "Get some sleep. We're no good if our energy's zapped."

"I can't believe I'm about to sleep in a subway car." I wonder what Mom would say.

"There's a whole other half of the train we haven't gone through. We can hit it in the morning. Then we should get aboveground and see . . ."

He doesn't finish. I don't ask what he's wondering. I've got too many questions of my own going through my head. Too many grisly images of what might be happening on the surface.

I shake my head. We start back the way we came.

"You were at the UN earlier?" I ask.

"Yeah. It was crazy."

"How come I didn't see you fighting?"

"Hey, I was doing my best," he says. "Besides, I didn't

have these Legacies yet. And I haven't exactly trained with guns that much."

"Legacies?" I ask. "John used that word when we were on the street. Is that what you call the telekinesis and his light-up hands?"

"Yeah."

I twist my lips a bit. "It's kind of a dumb name. Wait— oh shit—did someone *die* for me to get these? Did I inherit, like, alien ghost powers? That's messed up."

"Uh, I don't think so," Sam says. "I mean, I think they're passed down from those Elders I mentioned earlier for John and the Loric, but as far as we're concerned . . ." He shrugs.

"So you don't have any idea why we were chosen?" I ask as we step across the gap between two cars. "What's so special about us?"

He shakes his head, and I can tell that this has been on his mind.

"Man," he says, "I've been asking myself that all day. Honestly, until we met you I thought I was the only one." His voice gets a little quieter. "I thought maybe I was being rewarded for helping the Loric."

"Well, I sure as hell wasn't being rewarded for anything, unless this is some kind of weirdo prize for finally getting my grades up in school." I think about this for a second. "Guess that really doesn't matter anymore." Harlem and the diner and my apartment seem so far away. Was I really sulking over headphones earlier today?

"Whatever the reason, I'm going to use them." Sam nods as he talks, like he's telling me the most important thing in the world. "Now I can finally help everyone else. I won't be stuck on the sidelines. I can protect my friends. I can protect the *planet*."

"Right," I say. John's whole pitch from earlier comes back to me. About how I should use these powers to help him win a war. Sam's obviously on board. "Maybe it'll be you on TV fighting aliens next time."

He smiles a little bit.

"Maybe. I don't know that I'll ever look like John when I fight, though. He's a hero." He sounds so genuine when he says it. There's such awe and respect in his voice.

It makes me wonder.

"Are you two, like . . . a thing?"

Sam looks confused for a second. Suddenly he understands what I'm asking.

"We're . . ." He hesitates. "Best friends I guess? We both have . . ." He pauses again. "Girls," he finally says, a little awkwardly.

I stare at him for a few seconds. Then I shrug. "Because it's totally cool if you are."

"We're *not* a thing."

"I know. You both have . . ." I pause dramatically. "Girls?"

Sam rolls his eyes and jumps across into the car we left John in. He's still out, snoring a little.

"It's just a complicated situation. His girlfriend is with her ex-boyfriend right now trying to expose the Mogs. They're the ones who made that video you saw. They've got some mysterious hacker friend on their side who's helping them uncover classified government info. And my . . . the girl I've been . . . Oh man, I'm not sure what Six is doing right now. She's in Mexico looking for a Loric sanctuary."

"Your girlfriend's name is 'Six'?" I ask. "Weird."

Sam looks up at me. "*That's* what's weird to you out of all of this?"

I shrug, and then let out a massive yawn.

"I know," Sam says with a smirk. "Intergalactic space wars and the fate of the world are so boring."

"Shut up," I say, trying not to yawn again.

"With so many tunnels caved in, I doubt anyone's going to be down here looking for us, but we should probably sleep in shifts just in case," he says. "I'll take first watch and wake you when I start to fall asleep."

"I guess. You sure you won't just immediately pass out on me?"

"Are you kidding? I've got granola bars and . . ." He pulls a crumpled plastic bag out of the tote. "Someone left their entire comic shop haul down here."

"Yep. Nerd."

He kinda grins, then gets a sad look on his face.

"Hey," he says quietly. "I hope your mom's all right. My dad . . . He was missing for a long time. There were days I thought I'd never see him again. *Logically* it made sense to move on, but I never really gave up hope. Eventually we were reunited. I'm not saying it's the same thing, obviously. But you just have to keep fighting and believing. You have to honor the person who's not there with your actions." He shakes his head. "Sorry, I'm really tired. I think I'm rambling now."

"Thanks," I murmur. "For real."

I ball up the fake Prada bag and use it as a pillow on one of the benches, turning away from Sam and John, my face almost touching the back of the subway seat. I'm too tired to even care about how gross it is to be lying here. Instead, now that it's finally quiet and I'm not running or foraging for snacks and left-behind electronics, all I can think about is her. The uncertainty. Sam's words repeat in my head. Tears start to come, silent and pooling on the seat in front of me. They take away my last drop of energy, and before I know it I'm asleep.

CHAPTER
TEN

I WAKE UP WITH A START. TURNS OUT FIGHTING aliens all night and then sleeping on a gross subway bench doesn't make for the best sleep. Half-realized nightmares about Mom linger in my head as I get over the initial shock of waking up in a strange place. My eyes burn from lack of sleep, and the pounding in my head is back. For some reason I think of school when we had to read *The Iliad* and learned about Greek gods and stuff. I remember that one of the goddesses broke out of her dad's skull. Aphrodite, maybe? Or Athena? Whoever it was, that's how my head feels: like someone's taking a bat to the inside of it, trying to get out.

It's weird the thoughts that cross your mind when you wake up on a stalled train with an alien and his super-powered human sidekick.

The subway car is pitch-black except for the faint glow of a cell phone in Sam's hands. He's sitting straight up in one of the seats, passed the eff out. A handful of comic books have slid onto the floor in front of him. So much for keeping watch or waking me up.

I get up and stretch and walk over to him. There's drool coming out of one corner of his mouth. I wonder how he can sleep so soundly with everything that's going on, but I guess he's had more time to process the idea of aliens being real than I have. I slip the phone out of his hand, which doesn't get any kind of reaction from him at all. I probably couldn't wake him up if I tried.

The cell phone tells me it's just after 5 a.m. I don't know if the sun would be up aboveground yet. Don't even know if there is a sun still, actually. I turn the phone's flashlight on and wave it around our car. John hasn't moved. I keep the light on him long enough to make sure his chest is still moving up and down before turning my attention to the big duffel bag of cash sitting under the bench I slept on. I haven't actually looked through the bag, so I unzip it, in case there are weapons or something inside we can use. I find myself looking down at more money than I'd ever know what to do with. I pick up a wad of hundreds and think about what this money would have meant just twenty-four hours ago. Everything. And now . . . who knows? The future seems so uncertain.

The money's the only thing in the bag.

I stand, spreading a fat stack of cash out into a half circle and then fanning myself with it as I try to figure out how far away I am from Canal Street or whatever the next subway station is. But I don't know where I'm at. Not for certain. My light falls on the closed train doors. I could just leave now. Take my bag and go. These guys would be fine without me. It's not like when the tunnel was falling in around us. They'd wake up and move on. Keep fighting.

Keep fighting.

Sam's words. Maybe it's because I only got a few hours of sleep, or maybe it's because *evil aliens attacked our city*—whatever it is, I suddenly feel so lost and alone. So much so that I almost shake Sam to try to wake him. I could just pretend to be ragging on him because he fell asleep.

But he needs his rest. They both do.

Regardless of whether I go out on my own or stay with them, I'm going to need some supplies. Even if I have a dozen phones on me, if I get lost in the tunnels I don't want to risk being stuck with a bunch of dead batteries. So I pocket the cash and start down the other half of the train that Sam and I didn't get to. It's pretty much the same scene as the cars we explored last night. A lot of trash on the floors. A couple of purses and grocery sacks every now and then with usable supplies. I find a few more phones and two giant Whole Foods bags full of groceries—probably a hundred bucks' worth. My stomach growls. I dig out a jar of almonds and eat them by the handful as I continue.

Three cars into my search, I find a small blue book bag on one of the seats. There's a baggie of baby carrots and an applesauce pouch in the front pocket. The big zipper compartment holds a stuffed animal and some picture books. This is some elementary school kid's bag. Maybe even a preschooler. Left behind when the train stopped for whatever reason.

Suddenly I don't feel so hungry anymore.

I take a seat with the bag in my lap, feeling a little woozy.

I try to shine the light of the phone out the window, but it just reflects off the glass. There's nothing but darkness waiting for me outside, and the idea of going through the dark tunnels by myself seems crazy.

But then, *everything* seems crazy now. I concentrate on the book bag. It floats away from me and bobs in the air. I look down at my hands. This power. What am I supposed to do with it? I realize now that I've been running—mostly *literally*—ever since I first took out the Mogs with my telekinesis. I haven't had time to just sit and think about what all of this means. What my next steps are. I've had such tunnel vision about getting down to Mom's restaurant that I haven't let myself consider what happens if she's not there. That hasn't really even been a possibility.

What would I give to go back to the diner eating waffles? To walk with Mom right now? I'd even be nice to Benny—would see him in a whole new light. How does life get so messed up so fast? Yesterday morning I was just a normal girl. My biggest concern was getting some new headphones. And now . . . now everything's different. *I'm* different. I'm powerful. And the world is falling apart.

But maybe I can help stop that. I'm just not sure what I'm supposed to do.

Honor the person who's not there with your actions.

My hands start to shake and I make the kid's bag return to my lap, where I hug it tightly. I wonder what its owner is doing now. I hope to God that he's safe. Maybe the kid and his parents made it to the Brooklyn safe zone John and the guy on the radio talked about.

Brooklyn. I try to put things into perspective. This whole time I've been counting on Mom being down at her restaurant. Hiding. Safe. But realistically, that's not what she'd be doing, right? Not if she survived. She'd come looking for me. She'd try to make her way up to Harlem. She could be anywhere.

Or maybe she was taken to Brooklyn against her will. If she was hurt, they might have sent her there. Or if the army finally showed up they might have forced everyone to evacuate. She was pretty close to the Brooklyn

Bridge at work. Maybe she's there now, waiting for me.

Maybe Brooklyn is actually my best shot at finding my mom.

And John and Sam can help me get there.

I realize that I've started rocking in the seat, and at that moment the last place I want to be is all by myself in an abandoned subway car, alone with my thoughts. I've got to get moving again. If the sun's not up yet—if it's still there—it will be soon. A new day's starting; my mom will be wondering where I am.

I stand up, putting the little blue book bag on the bench carefully. Then I take a deep breath, gather up the rest of the stuff I've found and return to the car where my new weirdo friends are sleeping.

When I get back I try to sit still and wait for the boys to wake up on their own. I check the battery power on some of the cell phones I've collected, leaving a few fully charged ones on to try to make the inside of the train car feel less depressing. After a minute or two, though, I start to worry that they're both going to sleep all morning, and I'm too fired up to get going again to wait for that. So I cough a few times and chuck the fake Prada purse onto the seat over by John's head.

He bolts straight up.

"You're alive," I say. I don't have to fake my smile.

John seems groggy, but that doesn't keep him from going pretty much straight into another recruitment speech after giving me some shit for having a duffel bag full of money, *as if I'm some kind of common thug.* Like he even knows me. I don't know where he gets off with this "I know everything you should be doing with your life" tone. He gets all serious and tells me about how he was too young to fight back when the Mogs came for his planet, but that I'm not and can make a difference on Earth. The words make sense. Maybe if I wasn't so scared about Mom and the aliens and everything I'd jump at this chance. I don't know. It's hard to process right now.

John's not as smart as he thinks he is. He doesn't even know about the YouTube video of him they've been showing on the news, and he gets the dopiest look on his face when I tell him about it.

Eventually he wakes Sam up and tells us we should get moving. Before I agree to come along or even ask where they're going, I want to know everything he does about what's happening in Brooklyn.

"You mentioned getting some people out of New York. . . ."

"Yeah," John says. "The army and the police have secured the Brooklyn Bridge. They're evacuating people from there. At least, they were last night."

I nod. In my head, I try to figure the odds of where Mom could be. But it's all just guesswork. I could try to make it down to her restaurant alone, or I could go to Brooklyn with two dudes who can move stuff with their minds and shoot fireballs and see if she's there first.

It would be nice not to be alone in this search. Especially if there are still Mog squads roaming the streets.

"I'd like to go there," I say, getting to my feet. "Maybe see if my mom made it."

"All right." He gets a smile on his face like he *knew* I was going to ask something like that. I roll my eyes and start for the door. What a punk.

"We should head that way too," he says.

"Whatever," I murmur, even though a wave of relief crashes over me when he says this. I don't know that either of them heard me. That doesn't really matter. I'm glad they're coming along, that I don't have to go alone.

Sam yells at me not to forget my duffel bag. I lock eyes with John, ready for him to give me some spiel about how this money should go towards Earth's war fund or something. I know I said similar stuff to Jay about this earlier, but I do *not* need a lecture from John Smith about—

"Use your telekinesis," he says, pointing at the bag. "It's good practice."

Okay, maybe he's not such a Boy Scout after all. I shoot him a grin and head out the doors, the bag floating after me. Today is going to be different. Today I'm going to find Mom and we're going to pick up the pieces.

I'm one step out of the train car when I see guns pointed at me. My hands go up, and I'm ready to scream and use my telekinesis. Then I realize the guns aren't like the Mog blasters. These are human guns, held by human soldiers.

Oh shit, I'm under arrest. Earth's going to shit and I'm going to prison for taking money I technically didn't even steal.

"Whoa, whoa," I say as I step back into the train, using my powers to try to hide the bag under one of the seats.

I see John move out of the corner of my eye. His hands are on fire.

"Wait," Sam says. "They aren't Mogs."

One of them recognizes John as they shine flashlights in our faces. I notice that they don't immediately put their guns away.

"Friends of yours?" I ask.

"Not sure," John says.

"Sometimes the government likes us, other times not so much," Sam says.

"Great," I murmur. I've done a hell of a job picking my friends. "For a second there, I thought they were here to arrest *me*."

Some woman's voice comes out of one of the military dude's walkie-talkies. I see John stiffen a little when he hears it. The guy steps forward.

"Please come with us," he says. "Agent Walker would like a word."

I glance at John, who nods at me. I guess Walker *is* a friend.

"Hey, where are we going?" I ask.

"The Brooklyn evacuation zone," the soldier says before turning around and heading back into the tunnel.

I guess things are finally looking up.

I don't know how to explain my duffel bag to these dudes, so as much as it pains me to do so, I leave it.

Somewhere between Spring and Canal, I repeat in my head. *I'll be back for you. Mom and I both will.*

CHAPTER ELEVEN

IN FRONT OF THE BROOKLYN BRIDGE I SEE TANKS in person for the first time. They're bigger in real life, with their guns pointed into the city, like they're going to fire on Manhattan.

"Whoa," I whisper as we walk by.

I follow John and Sam, who follow some soldiers. They treat John like he's hot shit, calling him "sir" and stuff. I can't help but smirk every time they do. Don't these fools realize John Smith is only sixteen? I get that he's, like, the guy everyone knows about thanks to him fighting at the UN, but he should be going to prom or something, not getting treated like he's the president.

I guess it could mean I'm not the only one who feels a connection to John. Maybe these soldiers feel it too, and that's why they treat him with so much respect. Or it could be that getting people to follow you comes with having Legacies. I'm still trying to catch on to how all this works.

Heading away from the city, it's almost like nothing bad ever happened. Brooklyn looks untouched in front of us. If it weren't for all the people in uniform and the lack of tourists hanging out on the bridge, I could imagine that I was just out on a nice walk with Mom, clearing my head. Once we got to the Brooklyn side we'd have a slice of pizza and sit in the park and just look out at the water for a while. Quiet but together.

It's a nice image, but when I turn to look back at Manhattan, the whole dream falls apart. Plumes of smoke rise from all over the city, including downtown. The skyline looks different than it was the last time I was on the bridge months ago.

I swallow down the lump that's suddenly formed in my throat, hurrying to catch up with the others.

On the other side of the bridge, the park's been turned into some kind of combo hospital and military base for the National Guard and whoever else has shown up from the Pentagon or wherever all the military higher-ups hang out. There are people everywhere, in various states of injury and unrest. A few Red Cross stations have been set up, handing out supplies and bottles of water. Most everyone's got dust and blood on them. Looking down, I realize I'm no different. Buses seem to be carting people off to somewhere else. Somewhere safer, I'd guess, farther away from the city.

There are a few tables set up where people look like they're signing in. My heart flutters.

I turn to one of the soldiers.

"They have a list or something I could check? I'm . . . looking for someone."

"Sure," he says. "You could ask."

He's not very helpful. I'm about to point that out when I realize John's staring at me.

"I'm gonna—," I start.

"Go," John says. "I hope you find her."

I force a smile. I realize I don't know when I'll see him or Sam again. "Um, about that whole saving the world thing . . ."

"When you're ready, come find me."

"You're assuming I'll ever be ready," I snort.

"Yeah," he says, eyes looking all serious. "I am."

I nod, raise my chin up at Sam and then run towards one of the sign-in stations. There's a line dozens of people long, and it takes everything in me not to bat them all out of the way with my thoughts and jump straight to the front.

"This where people are checking in?" I ask an older Asian guy in front of me.

All he does is nod a little. His eyes are wide and he looks like he's in shock, like he might pass out at any moment. He turns away from me. Others in the line are louder. Some cry. A few just keep talking about how they're going to kill every alien they see as soon as they find a gun. I keep quiet, wishing I'd brought one of the phones with me or that I had my headphones. Even the broken ones, which are back in an apartment I might never get to return to. Without music or some kind of distraction, I'm left alone with my thoughts. I worry.

After what feels like hours, I'm finally at the front of the line.

"Can I get your name?" a woman asks. Her hair's tied back in a black bandanna and there are dark bags under her eyes. I wonder how long she's been at this.

"Daniela Morales," I say. "Look, I'm trying to find my mom."

"We're just taking information here," she says, looking up from her electronic tablet. "There are systems being put into place at our secondary evac site to connect missing persons. The bus will take you there once I have your info."

"But I need to know if she's there," I say. "If she's not . . ." I'm not sure what to say next. I'll go back to Manhattan? Would they even let me back across the bridge? Doubtful, but I could find a way.

The woman's eyebrows draw together and she purses her lips. She looks like she's tired of hearing this. I'm guessing I'm not the first person trying to find someone I love.

"If you'll spell your full name—," she starts.

"You're checking everyone in? My mom's name is Roxanne Morales. She's a waitress downtown. Please, can you just look?"

She looks at me for a few seconds. I can feel my eyes stinging. Finally, she taps on the electronic screen a few times. After scrolling through some lists, she lets out a small sigh. She doesn't say anything, just looks up at me and shakes her head.

The stinging gets worse.

"Morales," I say again. "M-O-R-A-L-E-S."

"I'm sorry, Daniela, but there's no Roxanne Morales in my database. Now, we're only getting updates from the other sites every hour or so. Maybe she went to one of the other evacuation points farther uptown."

I shake my head. My fingers grip the edge of the table in front of me. I don't want to leave. I can't walk away.

"No, she worked in the Financial District."

The woman's eye twitches a little.

"Where, exactly?" she asks. "Where does she work?"

I tell her the location, just off Wall Street, not taking my eyes off hers. I'm so focused that I don't even notice she's moving her hand until it's on top of mine.

"That area was hit really hard in the initial attack, Daniela," she says quietly but firmly. "We haven't seen many survivors from that location. There's always hope, but our rescue teams are still having trouble navigating much of downtown. The best thing for you to do is to give me the rest of your info and go to the secondary site. That way if your mom comes through here, she'll—"

I run. I don't know where I'm going, I just go. The woman shouts my name but doesn't follow. I pass a makeshift emergency room, doctors, injured bystanders, firemen, policemen who look like they haven't slept in days. National Guardsmen and -women eye me as I pass by, but no one stops me. I keep going, until I finally find myself down by the water, staring at the smoke rising from lower Manhattan.

We haven't seen many survivors from that location.

She told me to go home. There was an explosion—of course it was an explosion, no matter how much I try to tell myself that it wasn't—and then silence. We were disconnected. She was gone.

Mom's not here. She could be dead. She's *probably* dead.

My eyes start to water. I can feel them getting red as I clench my fists and think of all the things I've done to get to her, to get here, only to find that I'm no closer to reuniting with her. The people in the park, the bus, the bank, almost dying in a tunnel with Sam and John. Maybe I should have gone to the restaurant after all. Hell, maybe I should have stayed hidden in our apartment or somewhere in our neighborhood and waited for her to come back. I could have fought the Mogs off probably.

Maybe.

What would she have wanted me to do?

And then, new words start to float through my head. Sam talking about his dad and how he didn't give up hope.

She could still be out there. She could be fighting her way uptown to find me. Or hiding out somewhere safe, waiting for the right moment to run. Or she's at another evacuation zone for all I know. I still have to have hope. I mean, shit, I've got *telekinesis*. Anything is possible.

You have to honor the person who's not there with your actions.

What would Mom want me to do *now*?

There's screaming behind me, and I turn expecting to see a bunch of Mogs. Instead, I watch a stretcher rush by. There are two people in scrubs—young, nurses maybe—pushing it towards one of the medical tents. The woman lying on it is covered in blood. Another woman chases after them, holding her hand out in front of her, tears streaming down her face. I don't know which of them screamed. It could have been the nurses, or someone else in the safe zone for all I know. There are plenty of reasons to be screaming or crying or shouting here.

We've all lost something. Who knows how many people are just like me right now, trying to find someone who means the world to them in the middle of all this shit?

I turn back to the city and wipe the hot tears from the sides of my eyes. My gaze lands on the giant spaceship hovering above the city, just waiting to attack us again. John and Sam called it the *Anubis*, I think. I have other words for it, most of which Mom would be pissed at me for saying out loud.

My fists curl into balls at my sides.

I know one thing for sure: if my mom is still alive, she's not safe while those bastard aliens are here. None of us are.

"I'm not giving up on you," I say quietly, hoping that wherever my mom is she can hear me. "I'm going to see you again. But until then, I think I'm going to kick some alien ass. Help some people. Make you proud."

I turn and start running again. This time I know where I'm going. I have to find John Smith. I can't just sit around here with the rest of the evacuees or I'll lose my damn mind. I'm going to do some good. I'm going to fight.

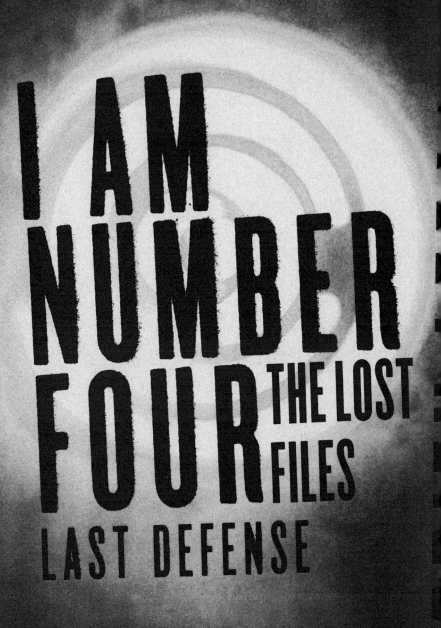

CHAPTER ONE

THE MOG SKIMMER RISES ABOVE ASHWOOD ESTATES and shoots off towards the horizon. Six, Marina and Adam are on board. A handful of kids—teenagers, technically, but still children to me—ready to cross the continent in search of a place called the Sanctuary. Somewhere they only know about because years ago, during one of the many gaps in my memory, I told the Mogs it existed and that it was important to the future of the Loric.

I hope for our sakes that this is true. Earth is facing invasion, and we need all the help we can get.

I've been racking my brain trying to remember anything else about this place that's apparently so important to the Loric. Any details at all. But I come up with nothing, and there's not really time to dwell on recovering these memories. I have so much else to worry about. The most important thing is my son, Sam.

He's putting himself in danger. Again. He's about to head to New York with John and Nine and a few of the FBI agents who've joined our side in order to stop a corrupt politician and expose the Mogadorian threat.

As I watch the skimmer disappear against the morning sun, I wonder what kind of father lets his only child get wrapped up in so much violence and death. I lose myself in this question, unable to find a suitable answer, until John Smith's voice breaks my daze.

"Damn, this place looks like a war zone. I thought we'd gotten most the fires out last night."

I turn and find him stomping on a blackened spot on the grass, a wisp of smoke drifting up around his shoe. Behind him stands Adam's childhood home, the front windows knocked out from yesterday's fighting. Now it's our makeshift base of operations.

"I think the remodeling you guys did is actually an improvement," I say, and then motion to a house towards the end of the block that's been completely demolished. "I always hated these kinds of cookie-cutter houses."

I'm attempting to keep things light to hide my worry about everything that's to come. To put on a brave face.

"If I were you I wouldn't mind seeing this place go up in flames either."

He locks eyes with me and smiles, but I can tell he's sizing me up. As the unofficial leader of the Loric, John must think it's his job to worry about everybody. And it makes some sense that he'd have his sights on me. It wasn't long ago that I was in captivity in the facilities located far below our feet—the tunnels, research labs and operating tables found underneath Ashwood, where the Mogs' brutality was allowed to incubate and flourish. If not for Adam I would have died here. Or worse. I can't fathom what "worse" might have been in my case, but I have no doubt that the Mogs are capable of something more terrifying than death. If anyone here is going to freak out, I'm the likely candidate.

Still, it makes me feel terrible somewhere deep in my gut, like I need to prove my worth to the cause. Maybe I wouldn't feel that way if it hadn't been me who spilled so many Loric secrets to the Mogs, even if it was against my will. That's one of the worst parts about not remembering so much of the last decade: all I have to show for those missing years is betrayal, pain and the knowledge that my family was out there without any idea of what happened to me the whole time.

I shake my head, trying to refocus my thoughts. One of the side effects of having my mind tampered with by the Mogs is that I'm easily distracted, prone to chasing long-forgotten memories like rabbits through Wonderland.

"I guess you're right," I say.

"You should try to get some rest," John says, a slight

crease forming between his eyebrows. "Try not to over-work yourself. When was the last time you slept?"

"Who needs sleep when I've got coffee and Mogador-ian home movies to watch?" I ask with a limp smile. I've been going over videos found in the archives below Ashwood since we took the suburb yesterday.

"Thanks for helping out with that. Who knows what we could learn from those files? You're the only one here we can completely trust with important stuff like that. Even if Walker's men are on our side now."

He means this as a compliment, I'm sure, but there's a subtext to his words. He may not even realize it, but he's reminding me that there's no room for me on this upcoming mission. Someone needs to stay behind and sift through the data, and I'm just an old man who's pretty good with a rifle, not a fighter like they are. My place is here. He's a remarkably charismatic leader for his age. I have to keep reminding myself that he's really just a teenager, at the point in his life where he should be learning precalculus or chemistry. All these kids act like they're ten years older than they actually are (except, perhaps, for Nine, whose personality seems to have stalled at the age of thirteen).

John nods to a large hawk perched on a tree limb above us.

"The Chimærae are patrolling the area in case the Mogs realize that no one's checking in with them from

Ashwood and decide to investigate."

"If the Mogs really are gearing up for an invasion, they'll likely have more important things to worry about than Ashwood," I say.

"Still, they've got your back. Plus . . ." He takes a look around, making sure there's no one in earshot. "Walker and her crew are helping us out for now, but I feel better knowing the Chimærae will protect you just in case anything happens. They'll look after you until we get back. Do you know how to whistle?"

"Sure."

"Good. Gamera up there is your new personal bodyguard. You whistle and he'll come running. Or flying, or whatever." He shrugs a little. "That was Sam's idea. He thinks you've got a soft spot for Gamera since you named him. Anyway, I told all of them to stay out of sight for the most part. Walker's agents know what they are, but if anyone else shows up they've got instructions not to morph in front of them. The fewer people who know about the Chimærae, the better."

The front door springs open, and Sam starts down the porch holding a plate piled high with yellow disks. One of them hangs out of his mouth, flapping as he jumps down onto the lawn.

"Dude, they've got frozen waffles in there," he says to John as he chews. "I don't know if they were Adam's dad's or if the Feds brought them or what, but there are like ten boxes in the freezer." He shakes his head. "All these waffles and no syrup. The monsters."

"Sweet," John says, reaching for one.

Sam shirks away, twisting around so the plate's out of reach.

"These are mine. Go get your own. I'd hurry too. Nine keeps challenging the FBI dudes to arm-wrestling matches, and I'm pretty sure Walker is about to sedate him or something."

John shakes his head and looks at me again.

"Remember: just whistle." Then he heads inside.

"Did you like that?" Sam asks, his face lighting up. "The whistling, I mean. It was totally my idea."

"That's what John said. Brilliant."

He grins and holds out the plate.

I raise my eyebrows. "I thought those were for you."

"Just eat some waffles, Dad. I doubt you were raiding the fridge during your all-night cram session in the archives."

As if on cue, my stomach grumbles.

"See?" He pushes the plate into my hands, taking two more waffles for himself. "They're making coffee inside, but these agents are just as addicted to it as you. I tried to get a cup, and one of them actually growled at me."

"Sam," I say. I don't want to spoil his mood, but our time together is getting short. "I know this isn't news to you, but this trip to New York might get pretty dangerous. If Setrákus Ra is planning on making a public appearance and it goes wrong—"

"I know," he cuts me off. "I'll be careful. If we get into a fight, I'll leave the heroics to the actual alien superheroes as much as I can. Don't worry about me. Just see if you can find something here that'll help us take down these Mog shit heads."

I give him an exaggerated sigh.

"What would your mother say if she heard you talking like that?" As if cursing even registers as a problem at this point in our lives. I'm honestly not sure where this reaction comes from. I guess part of me is still trying to mask my concern, as if letting these kids know how scared I am about them—about *Sam*—going to the front lines might somehow destroy their seemingly limitless capacities for bravery.

"I'm kind of more afraid that when I get home after all this is over, Mom's going to chain me up in my room and never let me see the outside world again. Oh, speaking of, maybe I should call her on the drive and let her know I'm still alive."

I think of my wife. The last time I saw her—when I showed up after years of being gone only to discover that Sam was missing too—she wasn't exactly thrilled to hear that I blamed my disappearance on aliens. Since then she hasn't been too keen on talking to me.

"Do that," I say. "Just remember that her phone is probably tapped, so no details. I'll . . . I'll wait until I have something good to tell her. Then I'll call."

"That reminds me—here," he says, holding a black satellite phone out to me. I pat my pockets, realizing I haven't been carrying mine around. Sam continues, "*Yes*, this is yours. Adam was messing with it. Apparently Earth's understanding of communications systems is really basic. This is supposed to get a signal, like, anywhere. Or so he says."

"Excellent," I say. "We should all start carrying these."

Sam shrugs. "I guess. But you know how much fighting we get into. Electronics don't really last that long around us. That's why I'm giving it to you. I'll talk him into making me one whenever he gets back."

The door opens behind him and John comes out, followed by Nine, Agent Walker, and a few other Feds I haven't been introduced to yet.

"All right," Nine says with a smirk. "Let's go knock some evil politician heads in the Big Apple."

Sam rolls his eyes. "Keep that phone with you, Dad. I'll call you when I have news."

He tries to give me a quick side hug, but I pull him in closer.

"Good-bye, son. Be careful."

"I will. I'll see you soon."

And just like that, he's gone.

These kids all think they're invincible, but they're not. Even some of the Garde, with all their abilities, have been killed. For a second I wonder if I can talk Sam out of going. Call him and tell him to get dropped off at a gas station or something where I can pick him up. He could help me sift through the years of Mogadorian data stored in the underground facilities. But I know he'd never agree to that, and I'm pretty sure I don't have the authority to flat-out forbid him from going. He's already made so many tough choices on his own without me. Why would he listen to me now?

CHAPTER
TWO

GOD KNOWS I'D PROBABLY BE MORE ALERT IF I
had a few hours of sleep, but I can't imagine closing my
eyes and drifting off while Sam is en route to New York.
Not when there's work to be done. So instead I manage to snag a cup of coffee from the pot in the kitchen
and head back into the bowels of Ashwood. With any
luck, I'll find some kind of secret weapon that'll take
down the Mogs. Or at least some information we can
use against them.

Anything to make me feel like I'm actually contrib-
uting.

A long stairwell leads into the tunnels from a back
room in Adam's home, plaster and brick giving way
to concrete and eventually smooth metal walls as I
descend. Everything is hard, gray and clinical. The
hairs on the back of my neck start to prickle the farther
down the steps I go, though I'm not sure if it's because

the air is getting cooler or because terrible things happened to me here, even if I barely remember any of them. Gamera follows close behind me in the form of a dragonfly hovering over my shoulder. I nod to the Chimæra. It's good to know my son is watching out for me, of course, but at the same time it makes me feel like a failure. I should be the one protecting *him*.

The underground portion of Ashwood Estates is a labyrinth. A sublevel snaking through the entire community with tunnels that stretch on in twists and turns for what seem like miles. As if that weren't confusing enough, several of the passageways and rooms are completely caved in—something we have Adam to thank for, that eternity ago when he freed me from captivity here and let loose his newfound earthquake Legacy. Who knows what hides behind the collapsed hallways, what knowledge we lost when equipment was smashed? If we weren't on the brink of losing the Earth, maybe we'd have time to find out.

There are plenty of rooms still standing, though. Laboratories and detainment cells, for example. I pass them, eyeing strange devices and surgical tools that send shivers down my spine. This place is still dangerous to me. Not just because of the questionable structural integrity, but because of the feeling I get when I walk through its hallways: the faintest wave of recognition followed by a stabbing pain in my head.

There is something in the smell of the place—musty, charged with electrical equipment—that is familiar, like all the memories I've forgotten are just out of reach, waiting to be reclaimed. These tunnels fill every cell of my body with dread.

Fortunately, most of that subsides when I reach the facility's archives. I don't think I ever entered it during my imprisonment, because I can breathe a sigh of relief when I step through the doorway. That's not to say the room is exactly cozy, nothing like the dusty libraries full of books and overstuffed chairs from my days at the university. This archive is just as uninviting as the rest of the underground level. Monitors and computer terminals line steel tables, their keyboards an unfamiliar shape and covered in markings I don't understand. Cabinets full of servers and hard drive storage banks line the walls, humming in tune with the fluorescent lights overhead. There's even a shelf holding a row of blasters on the far side of the room—the Mogs can apparently never be too far away from their weapons.

I stretch, my back cracking, and take a seat at one of the metal chairs in front of a computer terminal. This is the little space I've made my own over the last day: a computer, a handheld electronic tablet, a notebook, a small duffel bag full of tools and documents that might prove useful and a graveyard of dirty mugs. I put on a pair of headphones and flit through the list of Mog recordings on the screen until I find where I left off. Then I start watching.

Apart from being ruthless warriors, the Mogadorians also seem to be absurdly thorough when it comes to recording themselves, though I'm not sure whether this is strictly for some kind of historical record or is the by-product of a fascist regime wanting to keep track of its many moving parts. I fast-forward through dozens of videos, almost all of which are in the Mogadorian language and useless to me now that Adam is gone. Occasionally I find one in English, but those are mostly communiqués between human MogPro associates that contain either nothing useful or information we already know. I log anything of the slightest interest in my notebook. The whole process is mind-numbing, and at some point my eyes must start to glaze over, because I don't realize someone else is in the room with me until there's a hand on my shoulder.

I spin around, almost falling out of my chair as I try to get to my feet.

The man behind me is an FBI agent wearing a black suit. He's younger than me, maybe thirty, with olive skin, short dark hair, and several days' worth of stubble. On the stool beside me, Gamera has taken the form of a cat, eyes locked on the agent, ready to pounce and morph. The animal must have realized his usual turtle form might draw unwanted attention from the agents.

The man holds out a hand.

"Agent Noto. Walker"—he hesitates slightly—"*insisted* that I might be a valuable resource to you."

I wave my hand towards the feline at my side.

"I've already got a bodyguard." He doesn't find this funny. I continue. "I'm sure your Bureau skills will be more useful up there instead of watching me sift through alien data files."

He smirks a little, but it's hard to tell if it's out of annoyance or amusement.

"I assure you I'm more than just a gun, Dr. Goode."

It's been so long since someone called me "doctor" that the word sounds strange attached to my name. I almost can't believe there was a time when students and colleagues called me that on a daily basis.

Noto continues.

"In the past I served as a liaison to the Mogadorians. Before we realized what their true intentions were."

"Ah. So you have a good idea of who we're dealing with."

"I can even understand some of their language. Though I admit that I'm probably on the equivalent of a kindergarten level when it comes to reading it."

Finally, a windfall.

"Please," I say, shaking his hand. "Call me Malcolm."

He takes a seat on the other side of the desk and I get him caught up, pointing him towards a set of files to examine. I try to explain that we're looking for any-thing useful, even if that's a vague description. He seems to understand. We work in relative silence for hours, talking only about our findings, comparing notes. It's fruitless work. I don't uncover anything par-ticularly helpful, and Noto's progress is slow. He often spends fifteen minutes on a file before realizing it's an order for more food supplies or inconsequential reports on traffic around Ashwood.

Eventually I open up a file that causes me to freeze, my heart pounding in my chest. I *recognize* the face of the human on camera. I can even give him a name, though it takes me a moment to pin it down in my head.

Ethan.

The problem is, I don't know *why* I know his face and name.

The file appears to be a video conference between Ethan and a Mogadorian. Based on the tattoos, I'm guessing it's a high-ranking official. Ethan is recit-ing a list of names, giving facts about them and their locations. The words trigger something in my memory, illuminating one of the dark places I'd thought long lost. Faces flash through my head of men and women who helped the Loric refugees when they first arrived on Earth. People *I* recruited.

Greeters.

That's when I realize who Ethan is. He had been one

of them. A Greeter. No, that's not right. He was *going* to be one, but I cut him loose before he fulfilled his duty for some reason. He wasn't there when the Loric landed. There's something else, just out of reach. I didn't trust him—but why not?

As I continue watching, I start to understand a little more. He worked with the Mogs. A traitor detailing everything he knew about the Greeters and the Loric, which wasn't much. Still, it was probably enough to give the Mogs a few leads.

In fact, it sounds like the Mogs already had at least one of the Greeters captured at the time this video was taken thanks to Ethan's information. I wonder, was it me?

New images shoot through my mind. Some of the same faces as before, only this time they're pale, broken, bloodied. They're *here*, at Ashwood, being shown to me as a threat or a warning that if I don't tell Dr. Anu—the head scientist at Ashwood—everything he wants to know, I will end up like them.

Dead. Murdered.

I swallow down the waffles and coffee that are rising in my throat as Ethan continues to talk. Based on what he says, it sounds like the message is old—from before everything happened in Paradise. Even so, Ethan lets a bombshell slip: he's been put in charge of training and *recruiting* Garde Number Five. He's already had contact with the boy.

The video ends, and everything comes crashing down on me. Despite all the confusion and gaps in my memories, I know some things to be true. I was in charge of recruiting the Greeters. I must have brought Ethan on board at some point, even if I did kick him out of the group before the Loric arrived. Ethan turned on us and likely molded Five into the traitor he is now.

And because of that, Eight is dead.

It's an easy line to follow, the dots almost connecting themselves and creating a direct link from me to Eight's corpse. I take my glasses off and squeeze the bridge of my nose, trying to shake the pounding that suddenly fills my head as these memories and realizations flood in. Not only did I give the Mogs knowledge of the Sanctuary, I helped them turn one of the Loric into a Mog sympathizer. Who knows what other terrible things I did while under their control—or that I accidentally set into motion just trying to help the Garde. Will I wake up tomorrow and suddenly discover that I helped plan this invasion too? How do I begin to atone for all this?

I realize Noto is staring at me. His face is steely, but there's a hint of concern behind his eyes. Or maybe suspicion.

"I'm fine," I say. "Just a headache."

"Maybe you should take a break," he suggests. "Get some air."

I nod, but make no effort to move.

"I'm sure none of this can be easy, coming back here," Noto says. "Walker gave me a quick overview of what happened to you. It's kind of funny, actually. I investigated your disappearance from Paradise." He pauses. "Well, I guess 'funny' isn't really the right word."

This is something I didn't expect. He looks far too young to have been involved in the case.

"You did?" I ask.

"Not originally, but after the Mog incident at the high school—you know about that, right?"

"I do."

"That's when our team went to Ohio. I spent some time looking into your old missing person's case. It was a hell of a puzzle. Like you just vanished off the face of the earth." He squints a little, staring at me. "You still don't remember what happened?"

"Nothing about my abduction," I say with a sigh. "I'm not sure I'll ever know what happened. I've tried putting everything back together. Strange things will trigger a memory. Mostly just flashes of images and feelings. But even those are difficult to hold on to or understand. There are even missing spots from years before I was taken. Whatever they did broke me. They took so much of my life away."

"I can't imagine."

I think of the Greeters again, and of the video I discovered earlier where I'm drugged or brainwashed, being controlled in some way.

"That's probably a good thing," I say. "The Mogadorians did terrible things here—to me *and* to others. Still, I'd gladly remember every excruciating detail if it meant having all my good memories back as well."

"When you put it that way"—he flounders for the right words—"it's a lot of lost time."

I cock my head to one side a bit. Something he said earlier isn't adding up.

"Why were you looking into my disappearance? That was so long ago, and with everything that must have been happening after the attack on the school, surely you had more important things to worry about."

"Your son was a prime suspect and was missing. We couldn't rule out the idea that you were working off the grid somewhere with John Smith or the Mogadorians even. If they had only told us they had you. . . ."

He stops, realizing that he's digging himself into a hole, reminding me that while I was in a coma a few rooms down, he and the rest of Walker's agents were working with my captors.

"We didn't know." His eyes meet mine. He sounds earnest, though I can't tell if he's trying to convince himself or me. "All the civilian casualties and detainments, the plans for invasion . . . Jesus, we just thought we were getting high-tech weapons and medical enhancements out of helping them find some alien fugitives."

Anger bubbles in my stomach as he speaks, not at him but at all of it: the FBI, the Mogs, my imprisonment. I try to push it down and focus on what's important.

"Well, we'd better make up for both of our sins. Taking down the Mogs might not absolve us of the things we've done under their influence, but it sounds like a pretty good start to me."

Noto nods a little. We sit in silence for a few moments before a new question comes to my mind.

"You were investigating Sam. What did you find?"

He takes a deep breath, looking a little relieved. "Solid grades. Exceptional aptitude in sciences. An understandable obsession with conspiracy theories and space. I wouldn't want to poke around the internet history of most teenagers, but Sam spent the majority of his free time researching faraway planets and talking about potential extraterrestrial sightings on message boards. I mean, he also pirated a lot of movies and music, but all in all he seems like a pretty good kid."

"I can't take credit for any of that," I say, a pang of guilt in my gut.

Noto shakes his head. "You're telling me it's just a *coincidence* that your son grew up to become an ally to the Loric? Something you did must have rubbed off on him."

"Now, if only I can remember what that was," I say, trying to make a joke of it but failing. "I swear, if Anu and Zakos weren't dead already, I'd kill them myself."

Noto's face suddenly twists, his brow furrowing. "Who?"

"Dr. Anu. He was the first Mogadorian doctor who—"

"No, the other one," Noto says. He's not looking at me now but tapping on the keyboard.

"Zakos," I mutter. "He . . . After Dr. Anu died he was the one who oversaw my captivity. He was evil. I mean, they both were, but Zakos seemed to take pleasure in his experimentation. A Mogadorian Mengele. He almost killed Adam, from what I understand. But Adam got to him first, when we escaped."

Noto shakes his head.

"That was in the fall, right? When you escaped?"

"Yes." Once I'd carried Adam out of the destroyed tunnels, sneaking away in the chaos and confusion, we crisscrossed the country trying to avoid being recaptured. Weeks flew by in a haze. We spent a lot of time sleeping in fields and living off scraps we found. "By the time I figured enough time had passed and I dared go back to Paradise to reunite with my family, Sam was gone."

"Right . . ." Noto's voice is quiet, distant, like he's not really listening anymore. His eyes are locked on his screen.

"What is it?"

"I've got a recording here of Dr. Zakos." He raises his head and meets my eyes. "It's from earlier this year. Whatever happened to him here, he survived."

"No," I mutter, coming around to his screen. "That's not possible. Adam knocked him out, and then the ceiling came down around him when—"

But he's there on the screen. In the background his lab is in shambles, the walls cracked and floor covered in rubble. It's obviously after Adam partially destroyed the sublevel. He looks pleased with himself, black eyes shining in the paused image.

It takes me a few seconds to comprehend what I'm seeing, but then it hits me in my chest. Dr. Zakos—the butcher, the mad scientist, the *monster*—is still alive. He's still fighting against us.

Somewhere in the darkest parts of my mind, there's a strange flash. Not joy, exactly, but something like it as I realize I might have the chance to face one of my former captors.

"It sounds like he's been called in for some top secret

project that Setrákus Ra is overseeing. Something they think will ensure Mogadorian victory."

Before I can say anything, though, Noto's walkie-talkie crackles.

"Noto, get up here! Something's happening in New York."

CHAPTER THREE

THE WARSHIPS HAVE COME. THEY'RE REPORTED first over New York and then cities across the world.

"This is it," I murmur to myself. Everything I've tried to prevent is happening. The Mogs are here, in full force.

It's an invasion.

Is Sam safe?

Noto and I gather around several televisions in the house's media room with at least a dozen Feds to watch shocked newscasters and talking heads try to make sense of what's happening. Pretty soon the only thing playing is a live feed of the UN press conference. Ella is there. So is Setrákus Ra, in the form of a middle-aged man. He's saying something about wanting peace. I grind my teeth together.

Then there's some sort of commotion, and the camera pans to John, his face a portrait of rage. That's when everything goes straight to hell.

Where is Sam?

I search for a glimpse of my son. But he's not in the crowds fleeing when John's hands start to glow with fire, and by the time Ra transforms into a horrifying monster, the camera is pointed only at the people on the stage. When the live feeds cut out, the news stations keep playing the footage, over and over again. Still, I don't see Sam.

I try Sam's phone, but there's no answer. Of course not. He's probably there, in the thick of it all, just off camera. My hands start to shake as a feeling of helplessness falls over me. I'm so far away from him. I should have stopped him, demanded that he not go. But it's too late. What can I do now? Suddenly the idea of going back down into the archives seems foolish, like trying to use a water bottle to put out a forest fire. And so I keep watching the footage on loop.

At first it's just the videos on repeat with no commentary, as if the news anchors themselves can't figure out how to respond. Then it's a bombardment of theories, warnings and assurances that either the government will handle this or that it's directly responsible for it.

Gamera, still in the form of a small black cat, winds between my legs, brushing up against me. His green eyes dart about, ears perked. I wonder briefly how much he understands about what's going on. Can he feel that our enemy has invaded? That everything is changing?

Around me, the FBI agents try to deal with what's happening in their own ways. Most are either dumbfounded, standing slack jawed beside me, or they're manic, yelling at every busy signal or call that won't go through on their phones, or shouting into crackling radios, trying to get a handle on the situation. No one's heard from Walker, and I can tell that several of these agents want to be out in the field.

I don't know how many times I watch the footage repeat. Reports start to come in from across the world. Humanity doesn't know how to react. Chinese forces attack the warship over Beijing, sending planes to drop bombs on it from above. At the same time, trucks shoot missiles from below, the sky erupting in flames. But the warship remains unharmed, protected, apparently, by some sort of invisible shielding. The missiles explode against the force field and then fire and debris rain down on the city. A few of the missiles appear to bounce off the ship completely, obliterating towering buildings, destroying the skyline.

When the smoke clears, the warship looks untouched, but Beijing is on fire.

There's riots and looting in cities across the world. It seems to be happening in places where there aren't even any warships. I guess when there's a giant alien craft hovering over your city, you're less likely to rampage through the streets. People are scared, frightened, some ready to fight, others claiming it's the end of days. There's even footage of a group holding welcome banners and signs that say "Beam me up!"

I try to remember how I reacted when I found irrefutable proof that there was life outside of Earth. When I first met Pittacus Lore. Bursts of images and feelings flash through my mind. Awe. Fear. Validation. Pittacus holds out a white tablet. His eyes burning like fire as he asks for my help.

A new video starts to play on one of the monitors, taking me out of my thoughts. I recognize Sarah Hart's voice immediately as she explains who the Garde and Mogadorians are—after spending so much of my life trying to keep the Garde a secret, it's astounding to hear them spoken of on national television. At first it's just on one news station, but then all of them are playing it, talking about how it was found on YouTube. They actually interrupt their coverage of the warships to show it, until Sarah's voice is echoing all around me, coming from every speaker and telling the world about John Smith and the Loric.

The talking heads try to dissect the footage, bringing up screen caps and stories from They Walk Among Us.

I feel like I can't catch my breath as I look on.

Everything is happening, all the dominoes falling. I can barely keep up.

Eventually Agent Noto stands beside me. He doesn't take his eyes off the screens as he speaks.

"We can stream the news footage on a laptop downstairs if you want to get back to work."

"I'm aware of that," I say quietly. "But what's the point? What are we going to find that can fight this?"

Outside, the sun is beginning to set. My eyes feel like sandpaper. They're no doubt bloodshot, and the combination of caffeine and the events unfolding on the screen has me practically shaking.

"Just a suggestion. I can't seem to look away either." He lets out a single, breathy laugh. "The world is shitting its pants right now."

"And we're playing house in a goddamned alien suburb," another agent says, pushing himself between the two of us. "What the hell are we doing here, Noto?"

"Following Walker's orders." Noto's voice is calm and measured. Only a hint of annoyance shines through.

"Walker went to New York. She could be dead for all we know."

I see Noto glance at me before turning his attention to the other man.

"This is a highly valuable enemy base. We can't just—"

"For fuck's sake, this isn't capture the flag."

The man is attempting to whisper now but failing. "I can't get anyone on the line. The Mog loyalists must have shut down communications at the branch offices. Either that or every agent we have is trying to figure out what the hell to do. We're not far from DC. There are half a dozen assets within a twenty-mile radius more important than protecting a bunch of half-trashed Mogadorian shit. Weapons. Civilians. People who know *launch codes*. And that's just off the top of my head. We can't let all that fall into enemy hands."

Despite everything that's happening—or, maybe, *because* of the rush of adrenaline and heightened awareness surging through my body—a memory pings in one of the dark spots of my mind.

The last thing we need is for that to fall into the enemy's hands.

I hear the words again and again. I know it's important, but I can't remember why. Slowly a scene starts to come to light. I'm on the porch of my home. Sam is with me, but so young and fragile. A woman I don't know is there, warning me about something. What is it?

I close my eyes, trying to grab hold of the memory before it's gone. Maybe this is something that can help us.

Then I remember. She's telling me that if she found me then the Mogs will too. That my family isn't safe.

And I'm scared because I know I can't leave, because the Loric are planning to come back to Paradise one day.

And so I stayed.

I swallow down another wave of nausea. For the last few months I'd assumed that the Mogs had taken me by surprise. But they didn't, not entirely. I *knew* they could find me. I was warned. But I didn't listen. What if they'd taken my family? What if they'd taken Sam too? How could I have been so stupid?

But then, who is the woman I was talking to? She wasn't a Greeter or one of the Cêpan . . . but I have the feeling she *was* Loric. Someone I was equally impressed by and afraid of.

Where is *she* now?

"What do you think, Malcolm?" Noto asks, and it takes me a moment to realize he's talking to me.

"I'm sorry," I say. My voice is a coarse whisper. "What?"

That's when the Chimærae outside start to go nuts.

Birdlike screeches sound from all around, breaking through the cacophony of news reports and arguments inside. Gamera hisses, jumping into my arms. Noto and I look at each other, and then he follows me as I dart for the front door, shouting something about being careful. A few more agents are already on the lawn, one holding a pair of binoculars up to her eyes. In the distance, some kind of aircraft is approaching.

"What've we got?" Noto asks.

"Looks like a transport chopper." The agent hands her binoculars to Noto. "Army markings."

"Do we know who they are?" I ask. Despite the agents helping us out in Ashwood, the government isn't exactly to be trusted right now. I try to remember what I've read on They Walk Among Us and everything else we've uncovered, hoping to recall exactly who in the army we can trust, if anyone.

"We're on walkie-talkies here, and most of the cell networks are down," Noto mutters. "Unless you saw some kind of broadcasting equipment underground, we can't exactly call them up. Stay in the house until we've identified them." He unholsters his sidearm. "And tell the other in there to prep the big guns."

Gamera lets out a growl. Overhead, the remaining Chimærae continue to dart around in avian forms, squawking.

"I'll be right inside," I say. "If anything goes wrong . . ."

But I'm not sure how to finish that sentence. Noto just jerks his head towards the door, and without knowing what else to do, I go. When I get inside, I pull open two slats of wooden blinds and watch as the chopper lands on the street in front of the house.

Two men dressed in black body armor hop off the

helicopter when it lands. The one in front keeps his sidearm holstered, but the FBI agents have their weapons on him, their posture rigid. The other man's got some kind of assault rifle slung across his back and a crew cut. He looks like he's made of nothing but muscle, like a pro wrestler.

I can see mouths moving but can't hear anything over the noise of the helicopter's blades beating. Noto steps forward, holding out what I assume is his badge. He talks to the two men for a bit and then raises a hand to the agents behind him. They relax slightly.

Then Noto turns his face to the window I'm looking out of. The others follow suit, until they're all staring in my direction.

"Oh, no . . . ," I murmur.

The men in body armor follow Noto across the lawn. Gamera hisses, jumping to the ground in front of me.

"Easy there," I say softly, watching the men approach. "I think we're okay."

Once inside the house, Noto introduces the man who seems to be in charge as Colonel Lujan. His handshake is firm, and his eyes dark and piercing beneath bushy black eyebrows. The other man goes unnamed, but "Briggs" is written on a patch over the chest pocket of his uniform.

"I'm Malcolm Goode," I say. Lujan and his other man just nod, as if I'm giving them information they already had. Neither of them moves to sit or enter past the foyer.

"Dr. Goode," Lujan says. "I'll cut to the chase: our country is under siege and facing an alien invasion. The president and several other key members of the administration have been transported to a bunker, where they're formulating America's response to this crisis. Your assistance has been requested."

"My *assistance*?" I ask.

"It seems that Walker's been in touch with the brass," Noto says. "They want answers as to what's going on, and she gave them your name. Said you could provide a clear picture of the conflict. Apparently she's tied up in New York with . . . well, you saw what's going on there."

"My son. Did she mention Sam?"

"I haven't spoken to Agent Walker directly," Lujan says. "I'm just here to make sure your collection goes smoothly. As you can imagine, time is a factor here, Dr. Goode."

My mind races, wondering if I even have the option of saying no to these men. And there's still the possibility that something from the archives *could* help—however unlikely that might seem considering the news.

On the other hand, I can almost certainly do more good if I have the president's ear and can lay out exactly what's happening. Doing that will help Sam and the others.

"If you'll give me a few minutes, I'd like to pack up some of my things from underground. My rifle is down there, along with a lot of intel I'd—"

"We can arm you," Lujan says.

"I can keep things going here," Noto says. "If your son or any of the others return . . ." He pauses. "Well, it seems like Walker knows how to get in contact with the bunker."

"But—"

"With all due respect, sir," the colonel says, "we need to move."

I look back and forth between them before nodding. Gamera shifts on the ground between my feet.

"My bag and jacket are in the dining room," I say, darting into the adjoining room before anyone can protest.

Gamera follows. I look over my shoulder to make sure the military men aren't watching before unzipping my duffel bag and motioning for him to climb inside.

"It's not ideal," I whisper as he shrinks down into a beetle and hops in. "But it's the best I can do right now."

I pull out an old satellite phone—I keep the new one in my pocket at all times in case Sam calls—before putting on my jacket and slinging the bag over my shoulder, trying to be careful about not knocking Gamera around too much inside. Back in the foyer, I toss the older phone to Noto.

"It's secure," I say. "I'll contact you when I can. Keep looking for anything that might help us."

He's interrupted by more screeching outside, followed by shouting. Lujan's walkie-talkie crackles.

"Five unknown aircraft, coming in fast!"

"Hold your position!" Lujan shouts into a handset. He turns to me. "We need to get out of here, now. If the chopper gets hit, it's a long way back to DC, and we're sure as hell not getting there on the highway. It's jammed for miles."

"Go!" Noto says. "Good luck."

I nod. And then I'm running.

We're only a few feet out the doorway before I spot the Mogadorian skimmers headed straight for Ashwood.

CHAPTER
FOUR

WE'RE HALFWAY ACROSS THE LAWN WHEN A HUM-
vee crashes through the iron gates leading into the
estates. It speeds towards us, eventually turning on a
dime and screeching to a halt on the opposite side of
a short brick fence separating two lots. Doors open. I
see the pale faces of Mogadorians. And then suddenly
Briggs is pulling me to the ground, shoving me behind
one of the FBI vehicles parked on the grass between the
house and the helicopter. My breath is knocked out.
Glass rains down around me as the car's windows shatter.

"Stay down!" Briggs shouts. He joins the Feds at the
back of the SUV and starts shooting in the direction of
the Mogs.

Behind me, agents break out the second-floor windows of Adam's old house and start firing. From my
position, I can't tell where Lujan's at.

Five birds land on the ground around me. Their claws tremble, hinting at transformation. I look back at the porch and see Noto. Blood's dripping from a burn mark on the shoulder of his suit. I point to him.

"Protect the others!" I whisper loud enough for them to hear me.

They cock their heads and stare back blankly.

"Go!" I shout.

They scatter. Briggs looks back at me, reloading his rifle. He barks something into his walkie-talkie and then turns to me, shouting.

"When I start shooting, you move. Get to the chopper."

I nod while gasping, trying to catch my breath. My bag is undulating on the ground beside me. I pat it, trying to tell Gamera that I'm all right. He could break out if he wanted to, I'm sure, but if we're about to take to the sky, I don't want to risk losing him.

Above us the skimmers have circled and are coming in for a pass. There's a loud banging sound from across the lawn as one of the craft goes up in flames. I follow the trail of smoke from the explosion down to the helicopter. That's when I realize it's a gunship, likely full of all sorts of weaponry.

"Go!" Briggs shouts, opening fire again.

I sprint, focusing in on the chopper and ignoring everything else around me. For someone who's spent the majority of the last decade in an induced coma, muscles atrophying and disintegrating, I make a hell of a good run for it. Ashwood is a blur, but I'm aware of gunfire all around me and can hear the sizzle and electric pulse of the Mogadorian blasters firing. There's another bang from the chopper. In my peripheral vision, I see the Mog Humvee go up in flames.

It turns out Lujan is already in the helicopter, firing from what I think is a grenade launcher. He pulls me inside when I get there, half pushing me towards a seat in the back. I buckle in, wedging my bag between my feet, trying to weigh the pros and cons of unleashing Gamera now. The problem is that I don't know these men, or where I'm even going. With all the pain and suffering that's happened because of my actions in the past, I couldn't stand the thought of Gamera or any of the Chimærae ending up dissected on a lab table in some government research facility in the name of science.

Lujan yells into a walkie-talkie.

"Asset on board. We're taking off in five seconds whether you're here or not."

It's a command not only for Briggs, but for the pilot, who nods.

There's a second soldier in the cockpit in addition to the pilot. I assume he's the one targeting with the gunship's main weapons. Another soldier is adjusting the mount on a huge machine gun pointing out the side of the chopper opposite where I entered. His eyes are on the sky, focused on the incoming skimmers, firing away.

Briggs practically throws himself into the chopper a few seconds later. He shouts when he lands, then scrambles to his knees. One of his boots is covered in blood, and his left arm dangles limply at his side.

"Get us the hell out of here!" Lujan barks at the pilot. He turns to the man on the gun. "Mark your targets."

As the chopper shudders and begins to shoot up, I attempt to help Briggs into the seat beside me, asking if he's okay. But he shakes me off, gritting his teeth as he buckles in. I lean forward, trying to get a glimpse of the incoming ships.

Three skimmers open fire at once. Our chopper veers to one side, throwing us all about as we narrowly evade being hit. Carnage rains down on Ashwood, and we're caught in the cross fire. I brace myself and resist the urge to vomit. This is the first time I've been in a helicopter. At least that I'm aware of.

"Knock those bastards out of the sky!" Lujan shouts.

Machine gun fire fills the air, followed by the acrid, metallic smell of discharged rounds. A bigger weapon fires from somewhere near the front of the craft. I clench my jaw and grip the straps holding me in so hard I think I might be drawing blood.

Shock waves from an explosion somewhere outside rock the helicopter. A skimmer goes down in flames.

"Damn," Briggs says. "One of those Bureau bastards must have been packing a Stinger."

We fly forward. One skimmer circles Ashwood, but the other is in fast pursuit of us, darting and flying zig-zag loops to avoid the shots still being fired from our helicopter.

"Whatever you found in that base," Lujan says, shouting over the noise, "they must not want it to get out."

What did we miss? Or what are we overlooking?

"I haven't found *anything*," I say.

"Yeah, but they probably don't know that."

"Could be they're just pissed-off aliens," Briggs mutters.

As he speaks, he awkwardly tries to pull up his blood-soaked left pant leg with his right arm.

"Let me help," I offer.

He takes a few deep breaths, sweat beading on his forehead, before leaning back into his seat. I take that as an okay and manage to get his pant leg pulled out of his boot and up over a hole that's been shot clean through his calf. He points to a med kit attached to the inner hull and then talks me through cleaning and covering the wound with a compression bandage.

"Caught me midsprint," he says between instructions and long strings of profanity. "Came down hard on my shoulder. Think I knocked it out of the socket."

"I can try to put it back in if you want."

"Are you a doctor?"

"Technically . . . ," I say, "I'm an astronomer."

Briggs just stares back at me, wheels turning in his head as he thinks about how to respond. But he doesn't get a chance to. One of the skimmer shots hits us, and we take a sudden dip, dropping what must be hundreds of feet in the air in the course of seconds. I'm sure we're going to crash, but the pilot levels us out.

"Dammit," I hear Lujan shout as he picks the gunner up off the floor and helps him get back to his post.

"We can't outrun this thing!" the pilot shouts.

As Lujan confers with the other soldiers, I strain to look out the window. That's when I see it: the Mogadorian warship hovering over Washington DC.

"Impossible," I murmur, knowing full well it's not, that it's real. But seeing the giant ship in person is something I'm not prepared for, even after all the TV coverage. It's awe inspiring in the worst possible way.

Below us the city seems eerily quiet, at least from what I can tell. No smoke rising from the buildings. No jets flanking the alien monstrosity blocking the twilight sky from our nation's capital.

"Where's the rest of the army?" I ask. "The National Guard? Where are our *defenses*?"

"Emphasis was put on the evacuation of high-value

assets," Briggs says. "Most of our targets were in the city. You're one of the few we had to secure by air. Otherwise, we're under orders to stay grounded. The chopper's going to drop us near our destination. It'll serve as a distraction if we need cover while we make the rest of the way on foot."

"I don't think we're getting dropped anywhere if we can't shake this skimmer."

Briggs looks at me, confused.

"That's what we've been calling those smaller Mog ships," I say.

He considers this. "Beats UFOs, I guess."

The chopper shakes again. Lujan's yelling at the two men in the cockpit. Something about avoiding collateral damage. Briggs starts shaking his head.

"All right," he says, leaning his hurt shoulder towards me and looking in the opposite direction. "Do it. Fix my arm."

"You're sure?" I ask.

"If we land in a hot zone I don't want to be limping *and* unable to aim. Just get it over with."

While I'm aware of how this should work physically, I've never actually put someone's shoulder back into its socket. Briggs closes his eyes as I take my seat belt off, angling my body as best I can to get some leverage.

"I'm going to count to three," I say, grabbing his arm. "One . . ."

"Hold on," Lujan shouts back to us. "We're going to try something, and this is gonna get bumpy."

The helicopter veers, throwing me into Briggs. There's a *POP* when I hit him.

"Shit!" he shouts.

I think I've accidentally reset his shoulder.

It takes a few seconds to understand what the pilot's doing. Pulling back and slowing down has put the skimmer right beside us: in the perfect line of fire for our machine gun. Bullets rip through its hull, shredding the alien ship.

"Wahoo!" the gunner shouts.

The alien ship's cockpit goes up in flames, smoke trailing out of it.

Briggs lets out a long breath. "That's one way to lose a tail."

"Well, I'll be damned," Lujan says. "You got the piece of shit. Looks like—"

He stops as we watch the skimmer veer to the side, heading right for us. Its pilot is making one final attempt to destroy his target. Our chopper shoots forward, but not in time. The skimmer hits the back of our craft, our tail rotor snapping. And then we're spiraling down towards the grass below, a plummeting wreckage of glass and metal and screams.

CHAPTER FIVE

I'M AWOKEN BY A SLAP TO THE FACE. MY EYES shoot open, but the world is fuzzy and full of smoke, nothing but blurry shapes and disorienting darkness. For a few seconds I'm afraid I'm back inside the Mog containment pod and that everything that's happened in the last few months—my escape, reuniting with Sam—was nothing more than one long dream in an induced coma.

Someone is shouting, but I can't figure out what he's saying, the sound distorted in my head. I feel myself falling forward and then before I can make sense of what's happening, someone's pulling me, *dragging* me.

Another slap to the face. This definitely isn't Anu or Zakos: they both preferred needles and blades over getting their hands dirty with human subjects.

Slowly everything comes into focus, and I start to remember what's going on. I prop myself up on my hands and knees in a soft patch of grass, coughing, trying to catch my breath. My lungs feel like they're full of smoke and fire. The first things I see are the helicopter and skimmer, scorched mangles of twisted metal a hundred yards away. Lujan and Briggs stand over me, the latter leaning against a tree, taking as much weight off his injured leg as he can. Both their faces are smudged with something dark. The edge of the warship is overhead, blotting out the sky.

As I continue to gasp for air, my head spins. Getting to my feet is a wobbly process, Lujan stepping in to keep me from falling over. Finally, though, I feel grounded enough to assess our surroundings. That's when I see it, lit up in front of us and blazing against what is now almost full-on night.

"That's . . . ," I start, but I can't finish the thought. I'm too overwhelmed by the realization of where we are, of what's happened.

"The Washington Monument," Lujan says. "We're lucky we went down here, otherwise we might have had civilian casualties. We're not far from our destination."

The fact that crash-landing in the middle of half a dozen national landmarks is considered a good thing is probably more telling about the current state of the world than it should be.

"The others?" I ask, remembering the men on board.

"They didn't make it," Briggs says.

There's something else nagging in the back of my mind, but my thoughts are a jumble. Blood drips down my face from my left temple. I must have hit my head in the crash. As if I didn't have enough brain damage already.

"We need to move," Lujan says. "Now. There are hostiles patrolling the city, and there's no way they missed our crash."

That's when it hits me.

"My bag!" I shout as I rush towards the wreckage. Gamera's inside. What happened to him?

"You can't—" Briggs starts, but I ignore him. As far as we know, there are only a handful of Chimærae in existence now, and I won't let one of them—my bodyguard—be burned alive.

Lujan intercepts me, grabbing the back of my shirt with a firm grip and spinning me around before I can charge headfirst into the clearing.

"Listen, Goode," he snarls. "Briggs risked his life pulling you out of there, and I'll be damned if I let you die of smoke inhalation or an explosion or *get captured* while trying to rescue your luggage. Our mission is to get you to the bunker, and that's what we're going to do come hell or high water."

"You don't understand . . . ," I begin, but then I hear a familiar screech in the air—the sound of a bird crying out. A big hawk is perched on a tree limb overhead, staring at me. It stretches its wings out as if to signal me.

I shake my head a little, relieved. Obviously I've underestimated how resilient these animals are. Lujan stares at me like I'm an idiot and then pulls me back towards Briggs.

"With any luck we can make it the rest of the way without raising any alarms," Lujan says.

"I wouldn't exactly say luck has been on our side tonight," Briggs mutters.

"Where are we going?" I ask.

"Union Station." Lujan takes his sidearm out and checks to make sure that it's loaded. "There's transport there that'll take us to a secure location."

"The trains are still running?"

"No train the public knows about."

My mouth falls open a little. I remember reading conspiracy theories about secret tunnels that led to and from places like the White House and the Capitol, all connecting through DC's Union Station. I didn't realize they actually existed.

I guess I shouldn't really be surprised.

Briggs steps forward with wide eyes.

"Sir," he whispers while taking the assault rifle from across his back. I turn and find another skimmer approaching the wreckage, a few miles off.

"Move," Lujan says, pointing in the opposite direction. "If they're smart they'll be looking for survivors."

He leads us through the National Mall, keeping to the trees lining the side instead of the open middle area. They offer a little overhead coverage but aren't dense enough to hide us completely if the Mogs bring in a skimmer with a spotlight on it. At least the foliage makes a great pathway for Gamera, who jumps from limb to limb as a bushy-tailed squirrel. It's a small miracle that we have at least some cover of darkness, but there's enough ambient light around that we're not exactly invisible. The US Capitol stands less than a mile ahead of us, its white facade gleaming in the darkness. It's eerily quiet, especially for where we are. I'd feared the cities would be overrun with frantic people and military—or worse, squadrons of Mogadorians.

"Where is everyone?" I whisper as we pass a series of museums. "Isn't this place usually filled with tourists? What happened to all of them? Why wasn't there immediately some kind of response team when we *almost crashed into the Washington Monument*?"

"This area was a priority evacuation zone," Lujan explains. "Blocks surrounding the White House and the Capitol have been cleared. After the resistance in New York turned into widespread destruction, the official military stance became to neither engage the Mogadorians nor interfere with the patrols they sent down from their warships. People are being dragged from their homes in Manhattan. We're trying to keep that from happening here too."

I swallow hard at the mention of New York and tap my pocket to make sure my satellite phone is still there.

Is Sam safe?

"And what's the *un*official stance?" I ask.

"What does it look like? We're covertly pooling our assets and readying countermeasures. Why do you think you're here?"

We're almost to the Capitol when Briggs starts to fall behind. There's blood leaking from the bandage around his leg.

"Shit," Lujan says when he notices. "How bad is it?"

"Go on without me." Briggs leans against a tree. He's sweating profusely now, his adrenaline probably beginning to wear off. "I'll be fine here. Any of 'em come across me, I won't engage."

Lujan stares him down for a few seconds and then nods.

"We can't just *leave* him here," I protest.

"Our mission is to get you to the bunker safely," Lujan says for what feels like the tenth time since I met him. He's already starting to jog away.

"Well, I'm not going without him."

The colonel turns to me, sneering a bit.

"At this point that's not your decision."

I look back and forth between the two of them, but neither seems like he's going to budge on this. So I keep talking.

"You don't know the enemy like I do. That's the whole reason the president wants me, right? If we leave Briggs here and the Mogs find him, what do you think will happen? A wounded, lone soldier near the wreckage of one of their ships? Best-case scenario they kill him immediately. More likely they'll take him prisoner. I'm guessing he knows where we're going. You'd be leading them straight to the president."

"I won't talk," Briggs says.

"You think that matters?" I ask, raising two fingers to the side of my head where the Mogs used to attach electrodes. "They'll rip everything you know out of your mind. They have technology you've never dreamed of. You'll tell them every secret you know and only then will they start to really hurt you."

Lujan grits his teeth. For a second I worry that I've actually doomed Briggs to an early death, and I mentally start readying arguments against putting the man down. Eventually, Lujan points a thick finger in my face.

"Don't move. I'm going to scout ahead." He glances at Briggs. "When I get back, be prepared to run."

Then he's gone. Briggs stares at the ground, seething. He looks angry, but I'm not sure if it's at the Mogs, me or himself. Likely a combination of all three.

"You should just leave me behind," he finally mutters.

"You pulled me out of the wreckage, right?" I ask.

"I was doing my job."

"Well, now we're even."

He gets quiet and keeps his eyes on the grass. I take my satellite phone out and make sure I haven't missed a call from Sam and that it's still intact after the crash. Then I pat my pockets to see if I have anything else useful that I've forgotten about.

"Lose something?" Briggs asks.

"The Mogadorian blaster, in the crash. I'd stashed one in my bag."

He shrugs and pulls a pistol from a holster on his back.

"Know how to use one of these?" he asks.

"I'm better with a sniper rifle, but I think I can manage."

He lets out a single laugh and hands over the weapon. It's got "Beretta" engraved across the side.

"It's not an alien gun," he says, "but it'll get the job done."

Briggs has some extra gauze in his pocket, and I talk him into letting me re-bandage his leg. He needs some kind of real medical attention, but right now I'm all he's got.

I'm just finishing up when Lujan returns.

"We're pretty clear up ahead," he says. "I saw one Mog patrol booking it towards the crash site. They must have been called in to search for survivors. Hopefully the bastards aren't very good at tracking."

He notes the pistol in my hand.

"Don't fire that thing unless you have to. Stealth is our greatest advantage right now."

There's a noise above. Gamera's bouncing on one of the branches, chittering in strange rodent squeaks and looking back and forth between me and the rows of trees we've already walked through.

"Let's get—," Lujan starts.

But whatever he says after that is drowned out by the bellowing roar coming from the trees behind us.

CHAPTER
SIX

SOME KIND OF ANIMAL MOVES OUT OF THE SHAD-
ows. No, more like a demon. Even in the relative
darkness I can make out its grotesque face. There's
something bat-like about its features. Black eyes sit
above what looks like a row of four or five quivering
nostrils—perhaps the creature found us by scent? Its
jaws open so wide that they look unhinged, showing
off rows of jagged teeth that drip thick saliva onto the
grass below. Its arms and legs are too long and muscular to be mistaken for an animal of Earth, each elbow
or joint capped with a jagged horn. In the dim light I
can't tell if its slick-looking body is gray or a dark blue.

"What the fuck is that?" Lujan asks.

A Mogadorian monster, I think, remembering Sam
and Adam and the others talking about such creatures.
But I don't have time to explain. The beast roars again
and then charges on all fours, propelled by its oversize

limbs. I raise my gun and pull the trigger. There's only a click, no bullet.

"Take the goddamn safety off!" Briggs shouts as he opens fire. Lujan joins him, shooting a giant revolver that looks like it could take down an elephant.

The creature seems unfazed, or possibly just isn't hit by any of the shots. Whatever the case, it bats me out of the way with one massive arm as it flies by, sending me rolling into the trunk of a nearby tree. Briggs manages to outmaneuver it, dodging its next swipe and hustling backwards. A barrage of bullets from his assault rifle shreds one of the creature's legs. It hits the ground hard.

I hear someone barking a command behind me in a language that causes every muscle in my body to tense. There are a dozen Mogs—maybe more—darting towards us through the trees, trying to catch up to the beast. Several in front are already aiming our way.

"Mogs! Take cover!" I shout, scrambling to my feet.

Briggs ducks behind another tree near me as blaster fire sends smoking bits of bark falling all around us. I get the safety off my pistol, and we fire into the approaching squad. A few of the Mogs disintegrate. Behind me and several yards to my left, Lujan fires in a steady rhythm, Mogs turning to dust after every shot. His gun thunders like a cannon each time he pulls the trigger.

At some point the monster must have disappeared.

I don't see it anywhere. Or maybe it's turned to dust, destroyed by Lujan.

"I'm out," I say as my weapon starts clicking with an empty chamber. Briggs tosses me a clip, and I fumble to reload.

That's when a roar sounds over my shoulder and I turn just in time to see the creature leap out of the trees, using its remaining muscular leg to send itself flying straight for me. I'm too slow and can't get my handgun loaded and turned in time. The monster holds one of its elbows in the air, ready to plunge the spiked joint into me.

I whistle.

It's a reflex—in my panic I'd forgotten all about my bodyguard, but some primal part of my consciousness must realize that whistling is the only thing that will save me now. Gamera descends in a split second, obviously having been waiting in the trees for his moment to strike, moving so fast that I wonder if he was already in the air when I whistled. He takes the form of a panther, intercepting the Mog beast in midair, gnashing sharp teeth around its one good leg.

"What the hell is going on?" Lujan shouts, aiming his gun at the animals fighting tooth and nail in front of him.

"Don't! The cat's with me!"

He looks at me in confusion. That's when a blaster

shot hits him in the stomach. He groans, clutching his gut as his knees hit the ground.

"Shit!" Briggs shouts. He starts forward, but there's a tangle of beasts between us and Lujan, not to mention half a dozen Mogs still firing at anything that moves.

"Gamera!"

I don't know how much the Chimærae understand anyone who's not a Garde, but the panther looks my way, ripping off the monster's good leg as he does so. I point towards where the blaster fire is coming from in the trees.

"Attack."

He must understand some of that, because suddenly he's a bird shooting overhead. Moments later I hear a roar, followed by the sound of a Mogadorian scream. It only lasts for a few seconds before going silent.

I take a few steps forward, sticking to the trees for cover. When I'm close to the Mog beast, it roars at me, struggling to get up using only its arms.

I raise my pistol and fire over and over again. Each bullet finds a home in the bastard's head. Dark, viscous mucus spurts onto the trees and grass behind it. After a few seconds my pistol starts to click again.

The monster falls to the grass. Lifeless. Then it slowly starts to dissolve, until it's nothing but a pile of ash.

Despite being in a shootout with invaders who've come to take my planet, I can't help but feel exhilaration every time one of them turns to dust.

Maybe I'm not so useless after all.

"Dammit, I'm almost out of ammo," Briggs says.

That's when I realize all the blaster fire has stopped.

Gamera darts out of the trees, back in the form of a black panther, his gleaming coat covered in ash.

"Holy Jesus," Briggs keeps repeating. "What's happening?"

I don't get to answer. Lujan's groaning in front of me, clutching his stomach. There's smoke rising from holes in his chest. He must have been hit a few times when we weren't looking. There's blood everywhere.

I kneel beside him, but it's too late. He points in the direction of Union Station and then his breathing stops. All I can do is close his eyes and mutter an apology that he got dragged into this, telling myself that he'll be the last casualty of this war, even though of course I know that's not true.

"He's . . . ," Briggs says.

I nod my head.

"This thing . . . ," He aims his rifle at Gamera, who stalks the trees around me, sniffing the air. "This . . . this animal . . . it's an alien too?"

"That *animal* is on our side. He just saved our lives."

Briggs steps across from me, not taking his eyes off Gamera until he's standing over Lujan. There's a flash of remorse on his face.

"We need to get to the station," he says quietly. "That gunfire probably alerted every hostile within half a mile. They'll be here in no time."

"What do we do with his body?" I ask.

Briggs just shakes his head.

"He'd want to make sure the mission was completed."

I understand where he's coming from, but the colonel lost his life trying to get me to the president. I can't just leave him here, out in the open. So I drag Lujan to a dense thicket of bushes nearby and try to hide him as best I can. It's all I can think of. I tell myself that when we get to wherever we're going I might be able to send someone to get his body, but in the back of my mind I know that there are much more important things to worry about.

I don't realize how shaky my hands are until I put him down. Despite all the fighting I've been a part of, I am still not used to death. But then, no one should be.

Briggs crouches beside me, collecting Lujan's gun and ammo. When he's done, he nods to me and then we're moving again. Briggs has to be in excruciating pain with every other step, but he doesn't say a word or even slow his pace. I follow behind him, wondering how the hell things got this bad. And about my son.

Is Sam safe?

And I can't help but think of the others as well.

Adam, the rest of the Garde, Sarah—even Noto and the agents who we left behind at Ashwood.

What's become of them? What's going to become of all of us?

CHAPTER
SEVEN

WE KEEP MOVING WITHOUT MUCH INCIDENT, though the journey is a bit of a blur to me. The shock of everything that's going on coupled with my lack of sleep has me running on nothing but adrenaline. A squadron of Mogs races by us in Humvees at one point, but Briggs and I stick to the parks and trees and somehow manage to avoid detection. Questions fill my mind. *Who's supplying the Mogs with transportation? What are they doing now that they have seemingly free rein to move about the city?*

I call Sam along the way but get no answer.

I try my best not to think about what that means, but worry for his safety continues to beat through my mind.

Eventually Briggs and I arrive at Union Station, a giant structure full of shops, restaurants and rail lines. We avoid the main entrance. Briggs ushers me through a side door and pulls an earpiece out of his pocket as we stand in an empty, narrow hallway.

"Major Briggs reporting in." His voice is a whisper. "I've got the asset. Do you have a visual?"

He points to a camera mounted on the wall. Someone must respond.

"Negative," he says. "It's just the two of us." He turns to me. "All rails and buses are suspended. The place should be evacuated, but I'm guessing there might still be hostiles patrolling inside. Our route won't take us anywhere near the main lobbies, though."

"Who are you—," I start, but Briggs puts a finger to his lips and shakes his head twice. Somewhere down the corridor I can hear the faint echo of Mogadorian voices. They're inside.

Briggs limps through a connecting hallway and eventually to a series of twisting staircases, hesitating only a few times to figure out where to go next, holding a finger to his earpiece and, I assume, listening to directions. I'm not sure if our path is chosen to avoid Mogadorians or if it's just necessarily convoluted. He communicates only in hand signals, eyes constantly searching for signs of movement as we dart through the maze of behind-the-scenes hallways and rooms most people never see. Gamera follows, buzzing along as an insect, ready to shift at a moment's notice.

Finally we come to a room that looks like some

kind of suite—though based on the furniture and the avocado-colored carpet, it looks like it hasn't been redecorated since I was a kid. Briggs finds a touch screen keypad on the wall behind a small painting of the White House. It's the only thing that looks new in the room. He enters some code and lowers his head to stare into the pad, which must have some sort of retina sensor. The wall beside him shifts, and a series of thick steel slabs slide away, revealing a small room with a grated metal floor.

He waves me through, finally letting out a long breath as the wall slides back into place behind us. Then he flips a switch and the floor starts to move.

We're on an elevator.

"Thank God," he says, leaning against the wall, finally grimacing and acting like a man who's been injured.

"This is insane," I whisper. I can't figure out how many flights of stairs we've gone down, but it seems like we're definitely farther underground than any normal train station would be.

"There've been hidden tunnels and safe rooms in this building since the Truman administration. When the Cold War really started to escalate, all sorts of secret entrances and exits were added. And . . . well, let's just say the architects got creative."

We finally come to a stop at a small landing. There's one door that has a sign that says "Employees Only" on it.

"That should be an unused janitor's closet," he says, pointing at the door. "Which means . . ."

He heads to a blank wall and starts pressing on bricks at random, muttering to himself. Finally, one of them pushes in, and a portion of the wall slides away.

He turns to me and grins.

"What'd I say? You'd be surprised what kinds of gonzo shit the government designed in the '60s and '70s. It's like they were taking their cues from James Bond movies."

The panel closes behind us as we step into what looks like a museum of old train cars—ten or so of them parked side by side in a tight row in front of us.

"What is this place?" I whisper to myself as I look around. There seems to be no other entrance or exit.

"Union Station's top secret transport hub." He waves at one of the cameras on the wall and then limps forward. "Good. Looks like they sent back our car. We won't have to wait for it."

"How do you know all this?" I ask. Even if he is a major, this seems like it should be far above his pay grade.

"There's a small team of soldiers stationed out of a

secret base here in the city. Our primary concern is the safe evacuation of assets and high-profile targets in the event of an emergency."

He keys in a code on the side of one of the trains and a door opens. The inside is roughly as big as a single subway car but furnished like a private jet: all plush and leather.

"Incredible," I murmur as Gamera lands on a bench and takes the form of a snapping turtle.

"You haven't seen anything. Watch this."

Briggs walks to the front of the car and flips a series of switches. The train shakes, and suddenly we're sinking into the cement, until the entire car is several yards below the floor. A set of lights goes on, and I can see a track disappearing into a dark tunnel ahead of us.

"We'll be there in an hour. Why don't you get some sleep if you can."

The train car starts to shoot forward, taking me off balance a little. I catch myself on the side of a seat before sinking into it.

It's as if just by sitting down, my body gives up, ready to pass out.

While Briggs busies himself at the front of the car, I pull out my satellite phone. Whatever Adam did to it must have worked, because I get a signal.

But Sam doesn't answer.

Please be safe, wherever you are.

Before I can start worrying or hypothesizing what my son might be doing, a dark, dreamless sleep settles on me, and the rest of the world fades away to nothing.

CHAPTER EIGHT

"MALCOLM!"

I shoot up in my seat as I wake to the sound of my name, gasping back into consciousness.

"Finally," Briggs says. "I've been yelling at you for a full minute. I thought I was going to have to slap you again."

He's on the bench across from me, injured leg outstretched. The bandage is starting to ooze blood around the edges. My eyes scan the train car until I find Gamera, still in turtle form, snoring on the floor by my feet.

"Where are we?" I ask.

"Almost to the bunker. I figured you'd want a few minutes to wake up."

I nod, rubbing my eyes. They sting, and I realize I'm probably on the way to being dehydrated if I'm not already. I look at my phone. Still nothing. I've slept less than an hour.

"We're still underground?"

"This whole system is underground," Briggs says. "It's a secret, remember?"

"Fascinating," I say, still trying to wrap my head around things. Since being freed from the Mogs, waking up has been a process of slowly remembering where I am and what I'm doing—especially if I find myself in a strange place. "I have so many questions I don't know where to begin."

"*You've* got questions?" He points to Gamera. "That's a shape-shifting alien pet. This is the craziest shit I've ever seen. Well . . . maybe it would have been a week ago. Before everything else."

Gamera stares at his finger curiously.

"Looks like he's hungry," Briggs says.

"He won't bite," I say. "At least, I don't think he will. His name's Gamera. That was my idea. He . . . always seemed fond of my son."

Briggs mutters something I can't make out.

"When we get to wherever we're going, I'd appreciate you not mentioning him to the others. It's not that I don't trust whoever's there . . . it's just that I'm afraid—"

"Don't worry," he says. "You're right to be cautious. Everyone's on edge. We're all still trying to figure out who's in bed with the Mogadorians and who's not. It's a select group being collected at the bunker, though. Still . . . I mean, aliens are real, so I don't know what to expect anymore."

I have to focus. Names float through my mind—the men and women we know of who are MogPro agents.

"Will the vice president be at the bunker?" I ask. He's the highest official I can think of who's sold his soul to the Mogadorians.

"No. From what I understand he's AWOL. Disappeared along with his entire security detail right after everything happened at the UN. They may have tracked him down by now, but it's standard procedure to keep the president and VP in different locations in a situation like this. You know, so they don't get taken out at the same time if something goes wrong."

"Ah," I say. "That's good."

"You don't think . . ." He doesn't finish the question. Just lets it linger in the air. It's obvious what's on his mind, though.

"The Feds think he's working with the Mogs." This was one of the first things Walker told us when she showed up at Ashwood. Was that really just yesterday?

"Jesus." Briggs shifts his focus and looks me straight in the eyes. His gaze is piercing. "Just . . . *Jesus.* Do we even stand a chance?" he asks.

"I have to believe we do," I say.

Briggs seems comforted by this. The muscles in his face relax a little.

"I won't mention Gamera," he says.

"You know, you never told me your name."

"Major Briggs."

"I meant your first name."

"Oh." He shrugs. "Yeah. You get used to everyone using your last name, I guess. It's Samuel."

Sam.

Of course it is. I smile, even as my worry for Sam pounds against the inside of my chest.

"That's my son's name."

"He wasn't back at Ashwood, was he?"

"No. He'd left already. Headed to New York to try and stop the Mogadorians. He's been fighting against them for months now, trying to keep all this from happening. Working alongside the Garde. The *good* aliens."

Briggs nods but doesn't say anything for a minute or two. When he does talk, his voice has a softer tone to it than I've heard since he showed up to whisk me off to a secret bunker.

"My mom's the only one I have left. She lives in the Bronx, but she . . . she works in the city. I haven't been able to reach her." There's a spark of something painful on his face and then it's gone. He's back to the stony expression that seems to be his natural state.

I hold out my phone. "Here," I say.

"No signal underground."

"I've got one."

He looks at me curiously and then takes the phone. "How is that possible?" he asks.

"It's a long story."

I watch him dial, carefully, his fingers hesitating over each button. He holds the phone up to his ear for a long time before finally handing it back to me, shaking his head.

"I'm sure she's all right," I say, knowing full well what a useless assurance this is.

The train starts to slow. Briggs gets to his feet. "She's a tough old broad. I'm sure she's fine. Say, can I get my gun back? They're kind of particular about who has weapons down here."

I hand the pistol over. He limps a bit as he positions himself in front of the car's sliding door. The brakes screech, and we come to a final stop. He stretches, gritting his teeth as he puts weight on his injured leg.

"I hope they've got a solid med staff here. And hot water."

Gamera shrinks down to an insect again and hops on my shoulder as I stand beside Briggs.

"And coffee," I say. "Wait, is this your first time here?"

"In person, yeah. But I know the schematics like

the back of my hand, so I pretty much know what to expect."

The door slides open, and the first thing I see are five guys in dark suits all pointing machine guns at my face.

Briggs doesn't flinch at the sight of the weapons. I, on the other hand, jump and raise my hands in the air.

"Major Samuel Briggs," a man in black says as he steps forward. Briggs nods. The man holds some kind of small electronic device up to Briggs's eyes and then has him place his fingers on an electronic tablet. He must pass whatever this test is, because the man motions for Briggs to come out of the train car.

"This is the asset, Malcolm Goode," Briggs says as he steps between the men. None of them turns his gun off me. "He's cleared. I've disarmed him."

Despite this, one of the suited men steps forward and pats me down. He holds my satellite phone out to the guy who seems to be in charge, but he just shakes his head.

"Won't do him any good so far underground and with all our shielding," he says, and my heart sinks. He continues. "Hand."

I reach out, obliged to follow any orders at this point, and he guides my palm to the tablet. An old picture of me pops up on the screen—one I know they used in "missing" posters when I disappeared—along with some sort of record full of my information. The man pulls the tablet away before I can actually read anything.

"Welcome to Liberty Base," he says. "I'm Deputy Chief Richards with the Secret Service. Follow me."

"Wait. How do you have my fingerprints?" I ask, pocketing the phone the other man gives back to me and silently thanking the entire universe that the guy didn't check for a signal on it. "What information just got pulled up?"

The man lets out a short laugh and doesn't bother to answer the questions. Instead he turns away and starts walking towards a door on the other end of the room, which is nothing but a big concrete box. It's only then that I notice a man in a lab coat hovering over a control panel in one corner.

"Keep the train here," Richards says to him as we pass by. "This is the last of our guests from Union Station."

He leads us into a narrow hallway. The walls and floors are all slate gray. Our footsteps echo through the corridor. Briggs following behind me, with the gunmen bringing up the rear.

"You're injured, Major," Richards says without looking back. I wonder if he noticed the bandage earlier or if he can just tell from the uneven sound of Briggs's footsteps. "We'll wake the medical staff."

"Where are we?" I ask.

"You're at a secret underground bunker. That's all I'm at liberty to tell you right now."

He turns. Another hallway. How much time have I spent navigating underground labyrinths in the last few days? This "Liberty Base" is beginning to remind me of the sublevel of Ashwood, and it's not exactly a comforting feeling.

"I was told the president sent for me. When will I be meeting with him? There's a lot to discuss about the Mogadorians and who in the government—"

"It's almost four in the morning. Everyone's taking a two-hour break before regrouping. When you're needed, someone will collect you."

He stops in front of a door and swings it open. Inside is a small room with a desk and a bed covered in a blanket. A minifridge and cabinet sit between two slim doors. It's slightly nicer than I'd expect a dorm room or cheap motel to be.

"You'll find fresh clothes in the closet and toiletries in the bathroom. There's some food and water as well."

"You brought me all the way here to put me in a room and—," I start.

"You'll have to forgive us for not having a gift basket and suite waiting for you, but we're in a state of emergency, Dr. Goode. I advise you to stay in here until you're called for. Don't roam about the halls. I'll keep a man posted outside your door . . . in case you need anything."

"Wait," I say, suddenly feeling like more of a prisoner than someone here to help the president. "You won't tell me where I am, and I'm not supposed to leave my room? What's going on here?"

Richards gets a slight smirk on his face.

"If you want to leave, Doctor, you can. I'll just have a few of my men escort you to the surface and see to it that you aren't able to find this place ever again."

I glance at Briggs, who nods to me in a way I think is supposed to be reassuring. Then I sigh and walk into the room.

"Someone will send for you later," Richards continues. "Get some sleep. It's going to be a long day."

Then the door is shut and I'm left alone. I half expect him to lock me in before leaving, but he doesn't. At least, not that I hear.

I wash my face in the tiny bathroom once I realize that the combination of grime and several days' worth of stubble have me looking like a vagrant. It's only when the water in the sink turns pink that I realize I've got splotches of blood on my hands. From bandaging Briggs or checking on Lujan. Maybe it's even my own—there's a cut on the side of my head and dried blood in my hair. I take out my phone. Whatever Adam did to it, he's a genius: I'm getting a signal, despite what Richards said. I'm about to walk back into the main room and dial my son when I stop, glancing around. Given how secretive everyone's being, I'm sure I'm not supposed to have contact with the outside world, and this place is probably bugged. I can't lose my phone, so I stay in the bathroom, closing the door and turning on the faucet and shower, trying to hide my voice as much as I can.

I try Sam, but there's no answer. Again. I beat my fist against the sink, causing the mirror in front of me to shake.

I dial another number. This time someone picks up. "Hello?"

"It's Malcolm," I say. "Hope I didn't wake you."

"I don't sleep much," Noto says.

"Glad to hear you made it out of that mess."

"Likewise. We have a few injured men, but they'll live. It'll take more than the small scouting party they sent to wipe us out. But the Mogs will be back."

"Probably," I say. "Though I'm not sure Ashwood is high on their priority list right now."

"Doesn't matter. We're packing up everything we can from the archives and heading to a safe house. Orders from high up. The brass thinks Ashwood is too hot right now. I have to say, I agree." He pauses. When he starts talking again, he's a little quieter. "We haven't heard from Walker, but now that the Mogs know we're here, we can't sit around waiting for another attack. Don't worry. We're, uh, trying to take the guard birds with us. Where are you? Are you safe?"

I glance around at the sterile bathroom walls. Steam from the shower is starting to fill the room. I'm suddenly feeling claustrophobic

"You know," I say quietly, "I have no idea."

CHAPTER
NINE

SOMEONE KNOCKS LOUDLY ON THE DOOR, WAKING me up. I stumble out of bed, where I'd fallen asleep in all my clothes, on top of the blankets. My mind is hazy, and a glance at my watch tells me I've only been in the room for a couple of hours.

Richards is on the other side of the door. He gives me a once-over.

"You've got five minutes to pull yourself together," he says. "You've been summoned to the war room."

"Summoned?" I ask, trying to focus and make sense of this. I look at my rumpled clothes. I'm not sure when the last time I showered was. If anyone's going to take me seriously, I might need to make myself a little more presentable.

"Five minutes," he repeats.

I close the door and find a white button-down shirt in the closet that's a little too big and tuck it into my pants, then brush my teeth, clean my glasses, and try to pat down my hair, which is springing out in every direction. I'm just getting my shoes on when there's another knock at the door. Gamera buzzes in the air beside me, but I shake my head, holding a hand up to him. He's saved my life already, and I don't want to risk him being exposed in front of whoever it is I'm meeting. Eventually someone's sure to notice that I've always got a bug crawling on me.

In the hallway, Richards hands me a Styrofoam cup of coffee.

"It's black," he says.

"That's how I take it."

"Good man."

He turns on his heel and starts down the hall.

"You're sure you can trust the people you've gathered here? MogPro—the aliens' human supporters—ran deep. The vice president, the—"

"The administration went through widespread upheaval yesterday when everything went to hell. A veritable FBI hit squad ordered by your friend Agent Walker took care of most of what you referred to as 'MogPro.' They're in custody now. Those who escaped are in hiding. The men and women here have either been vetted or, in some cases, brought out of retirement to serve. Still, we're keeping a close eye on everyone."

My room is definitely bugged.

"Is that part of why we're so isolated? Do the other people here not know where we are either?"

"Let *us* decide who we can and can't trust," he says as we pass by a series of doors that cause me to wonder how many people, exactly, are down here. "Remember that you've been brought here as a special adviser but that your advice should only be given when solicited. Whatever decisions are made here are final and for the greater good of the country—and above all else, they're classified. Sharing any information you hear with unauthorized persons will be considered an act of treason."

"Sure," I say, wondering if it would've been smarter to have stayed in Ashwood after all.

Richards stops in front of two thick double doors guarded by four armed men in military fatigues.

"The fate of America and quite possibly the world is being decided here. There's a chair for you against the back wall. Stay quiet until you're spoken to."

He pushes open one of the doors and ushers me through.

It's dimly lit inside, most of the light coming from the huge monitors that cover the walls, showing news feeds from around the world. At least two of them are showing the footage from Sarah's video about John and the Garde. Another shows shaky cam footage of a destroyed building in Manhattan.

Is Sam safe?

The room itself is almost entirely filled by a giant rectangular table of lacquered mahogany where a dozen men and women sit. They range from my age to people well into their sixties, maybe even a little older. I recognize a few of them as cabinet members. A handful of younger-looking aides flit around in the background, taking notes, tapping on electronic devices, occasionally whispering into the ear of someone seated at the table.

Voices fill the air, overlapping one another, all vying for attention.

". . . the National Guard in Brooklyn. Troops are being mobilized in Georgia but the fastest we could get them there . . ."

". . . obviously it would be a last resort, but we do have untested prototype weapons that could prove to be effective . . ."

". . . saw what happened in China. The warships are protected by some kind of force field. We might as well be bombing our own civilians if we launch missiles at them. . . ."

". . . suggests a full-scale evacuation of major American cities might save millions of lives, but the cost and logistics would . . ."

". . . march forces across the Brooklyn Bridge while simultaneously dropping units into Central Park . . ."

At the far end of the room, Arnold Jackson, the president of the United States, stands with his back to everyone. He's got a landline phone to his ear. After a few seconds he lowers it. I watch as he takes a deep breath, composing himself, before turning around to the table. He doesn't sit, just leans over with his hands pressed on top of the polished wood. There are bags under his eyes. His close-cropped black hair is peppered with gray, more so than I've noticed on TV. He looks like he's aged ten years in the last twenty-four hours. The rest of the room goes quiet.

"The European Union is officially open to the idea of negotiating with Ra despite strong disapproval from several nations, including Germany and Spain. There are widespread riots in Moscow. There's been visual confirmation of a ship over North Korea, but there's no communications coming out of the country, so we have no idea how they're going to react. No one plans to attack the ships after seeing what happened in Beijing and what resistance in New York led to, but everyone is quietly assembling forces for a counterstrike if necessary. And here we are, hiding underground while warships hover over millions of American citizens. So tell me, what do we do now?"

Everyone starts to talk at once. It lasts for maybe five seconds.

"Enough," Jackson says. He turns to an older man

seated at his left who's dressed in an officer's uniform covered in stars and pins. "General Lawson. What's your assessment of the situation?"

Lawson leans back in his chair.

"New York and Beijing were power plays," he says. He speaks slowly, with a vague Southern accent I can't place. "These aliens are smart. They've been slowly infiltrating us for years. That means they know how we function as individual countries and as a planet. They know how we tick. You don't just destroy a city like New York because of a bad-press event. You do it to show you're the ones with the power. That you can do it again. New York was their A-bomb. Hell, I'd bet that the counterattacks in Beijing were orchestrated by the bastards to show the rest of the world that they can't be touched. They're telling us, in no subtle terms, that this world is theirs if they want it. Seems to me like we've got two courses of action: try to outsmart them, or try to blow 'em out of the sky. Neither way's going to be easy."

"There's another option," the president says. "We listen to the Mogadorians. We play along—at least for now. If they start killing more civilians, what other choice do we have?"

"You're talking surrender?" Lawson asks, narrowing his eyes. I shift on my feet as he continues. "I'd rather see humanity's extinction before we become slaves.

There's the possibility that employing some more extreme measure might—"

"I'm not authorizing a nuclear attack on American soil," the president says. "Even if it did manage to take down one of those ships, the fallout would be catastrophic, and the enemy would likely immediately open fire on the other cities."

"Oh, I agree," Lawson says. "Besides, we'll let some other country with an itchy trigger finger test out nukes first. What I suggest is sending out a few small teams in New York. Quietly take some of their smaller ships and soldiers hostage. See what we can figure out or reverse engineer. We should also start interrogating the Mog-Pro traitors who were arrested. *Aggressively.*"

Jackson nods, then points to one of the monitors playing Sarah's PSA.

"And this 'Garde'? John Smith. Have we found him?"

"They're illegal aliens who might have just started an interplanetary war on American soil," a woman with a severe blond bun says. "Ra was talking about peace before they attacked him."

I squint, trying to place the woman, trying to imagine how the Garde might be blamed for this. But then, these people don't know the Loric like I do.

"That was before he turned into a monster on live television," someone else says. Then everyone's talking again.

"They're *aliens*. What do you expect them to look like?"

"Why don't you tell the people of Manhattan that they came in peace?"

"We've got troops looking for him in New York right now." Lawson stands and begins to walk around the table. "Frankly, sir, despite what your FBI informants say, I wouldn't put much faith in *any* of these extraterrestrials. We know nothing about them other than what this anonymous video says. The enemy of our enemy is not *always* a friend. Who's to say this John Smith isn't worse than Ra?"

"He's not," I say, stepping forward. Everyone turns to look at me. "He's—*they* are our only hope of defeating the Mogadorians."

Richards puts a hand on my shoulder and pulls me back, but the president beckons me forward.

"Malcolm Goode, isn't it?" the general asks, drawing out each syllable. "Welcome. You know, I did some research into you when I heard the president sent for you. Seems that many of your theories and ideas were discredited by your colleagues back when you were a professor. In fact, they cost you your job, didn't they? Before you were abducted by aliens." He pauses. I know why. Even when proof of extraterrestrial life is falling out of the sky around us, saying you were abducted still *sounds* crazy to most people. He goes on. "How are we supposed to be sure that you're not just a nut job who's going to tell us next that Bigfoot runs the illuminati?"

"With all due respect, General," I say, feeling the heat rise in my cheeks—a mixture of anger and embarrassment, "I know more about what's happening around the world right now than anyone else in this room."

"If the Mogadorians did have you all those years, couldn't you be a spy?"

Richards speaks up from behind me. "Major Briggs reports that the hostiles *did* try very hard to kill him."

"Not hard enough, I see," Lawson says with a hint of a smile.

"All right, General, that's enough," Jackson says. "Dr. Goode, I understand that it wasn't easy for you to get here. Thank you for coming. I've been briefed on your work regarding intergalactic communication and found it quite interesting. Brilliant even, though I admit some of it was difficult to wrap my head around. What can you tell us about what's going on?"

I take a deep breath.

"Well . . . this has all been in motion for over a decade. Longer, actually. And that's just taking Earth's role into account."

I tell them everything—or at least the highlights—as quickly as I can. My imprisonment. Paradise. Chicago. The Mog encampment in West Virginia. There's no use in hiding anything now. A few of the people at the table snicker or roll their eyes when I tell them about the piken or the powers that the Garde have. Even though they've seen John in action on TV, trying to describe Six's ability to create storms seems like a stretch. But they fall silent when I start talking about how we discovered that the Mogs and the government were working together. Through it all, the president and Lawson both stare at me, not betraying a single emotion.

"And now I'm here," I say finally.

The room is deathly silent for a few seconds. I almost regret not bringing Gamera with me. It'd make a hell of an ending to toss him onto the table and watch everyone's mouths drop open in shock as he morphed. Of course, it's likely this might be interpreted as an attack on the president, which would probably end with both me and Gamera dead.

"We'll need to retake the base in Dulce," Jackson finally says. "I want to know what the hell happened there and *why* we didn't know about it. See if we can track down this FBI squad that was combing the archives in Ashwood too. Offer them whatever they need to protect the information they gathered from the Mog base and find out if they have any leads on how to take down those warship shields. Maybe there's something in those archives. And someone figure out where the hell this place in West Virginia is."

"Mr. President," Lawson says. "This story is all well

and good, but we're talking about a handful of teenagers up against their entire army. Do you really want to trust a sixteen-year-old boy with the fate of the country?"

One of the aides whispers into the ear of the woman with the severe bun.

"It seems like this John Smith is polling well with the nation. They *love* him. At least based on this PSA."

"These kids sound like ticking time bombs at best," a man at the table sneers. "I for one don't want to sit in a room with a pubescent kid who could pull my head off with one thought."

Lawson grins. "I bet our enemies feel the same way."

"Like it or not," I say, "the Garde are your best chance at defeating the Mogadorians without launching a full-scale war."

"If they want to fight, they should be fighting under our command."

"No offense, General, but the government doesn't have a great track record when it comes to the Loric."

"We're talking about less than a dozen Garde and their allies, right?" Jackson asks. He turns to an aide. "Prepare a video conference with our people in the Brooklyn evacuation zone. I want those Garde found. I want to talk to John Smith. *Then* we'll figure out where to go from there."

One of Jackson's aides gasps and runs to his side,

sliding a tablet in front of him and whispering something I can't hear. His eyes go wide.

"Mr. President . . . ," I start.

He raises his hand. "I've got military operations to coordinate and a terrified nation to run. I'll be in touch when we have further questions."

And just like that, Richards is pulling me into the hallway.

"But, sir . . . ," I say, but everyone in the room has already turned their attention to one of the monitors on the wall, where the aide is bringing up some sort of video.

The last thing I see before the war room doors close behind me is Setrákus Ra's black eyes on the screen.

CHAPTER
TEN

NEITHER RICHARDS NOR I TALK ON THE WAY back to my room. That's fine by me. I'm too busy wondering what Ra's demands are and going over all the ways I should have reframed my arguments in the war room, how I could have helped Sam and the Loric more.

When we get back, Briggs is standing outside my door, leaning on a crutch.

"Major Briggs here has been assigned to guard you," Richards says.

"You mean *watch* me," I say.

Briggs doesn't meet my eye.

"It's standard procedure," Richards says. "Guests are always assigned an escort. It's for your own safety."

"You know, I can be of use to you," I continue. "Get me data to go through. A computer. Hell, I'm just staring at the walls in there. It's a cell. Even prisoners have access to libraries."

"This is temporary," Richards say. He frowns. "Look, we're all just trying to follow protocol as best we can. The sheer amount of decisions to be made here . . ." He shakes his head. "I'll be back later. I'm sure the president will want to speak with you after everyone's had time to digest what you explained at the briefing."

"Can you at least tell me if they find the Garde?"

"You'll be informed of any declassified information deemed relevant to your situation. Now if you'll—"

I go into my room and slam the door behind me. Immediately I feel stupid, like a child stomping off to his bedroom because his parents made him angry. But I *am* angry. That I haven't heard from Sam. That I'm being treated like a prisoner. That despite everything we've done to try to protect Earth, the Garde are still being thought of as possible enemies.

I lie on the bed and seethe, trying to calm down. I start to count backwards from one hundred, something I used to do when the Mogs had me conscious— anything to take my mind off the horrible things that were likely to come. Somewhere in the fifties I pass out again, my body desperately trying to make up for all the lost sleep of the last few days.

After a few hours of dreamless napping, my phone rings. I am immediately fully awake, bolting into the bathroom and turning the taps on again.

I don't recognize the number.

"Hello?" I answer, holding my breath as I wait to hear who's on the other end of the line.

"Hey, Dad," Sam says. "I was afraid you wouldn't answer."

Despite everything that's happening, the moment I hear his voice everything is right in the world. Relief washes over me, and for a fleeting moment I think I might break down. I lean my back against the wall and sink to the ground.

"I'm here, son. Where are you? What's going on? Are you safe?"

I manage to close my mouth before another thousand questions come out.

"I'm safe, yeah," he says. "John and I are in Brooklyn. Once the attack started, we tried to save as many people as we could. Then we were looking for Nine, but Walker's team found us in the subway and brought us to a temporary camp. I can't tell if they're about to give us medals, try to get us to enlist or arrest us."

There's plenty I could say about this, but I can tell there's something else on his mind in the way his voice lilts as he speaks. Something he's not telling me. Figuring out what that is seems much more important than catching him up on what I've been through.

"And?" I ask. "What's wrong?"

"Nothing's *wrong*," he says slowly. "At least, I don't think so. But, Dad . . . are you sitting down?"

"Yeah."

"Um, I don't really know how to say this, but . . . I've got Legacies now. Or telekinesis at least. There was a piken coming at us, and I just . . . I *did* it. I pushed him with my thoughts like I was John or Six or Luke Skywalker or something. I'm like a *Jedi*. I've been using it all day."

Noises come out of my mouth that are nothing more than odd syllables and half-formed vowels. I can't process what he's talking about.

My son has powers now? How? Why?

What does this mean?

"Yeah," Sam says in response to my lack of coherence. "That's kind of how I felt at first too."

"But how is that possible?" I finally manage. "Did John transfer his powers to you or . . . ?"

"I don't think so. He's as confused by all of it as I am. Oh, and we met someone else in the city. This random girl who had never even heard of the Loric or Mogs until today. She's got powers too. Dad . . . what if there are others out there? Like, what if humans across the planet started getting Legacies?"

The implications are extraordinary—especially in terms of protecting Earth. What force has the ability to grant abilities like this? Maybe something the others found in the Sanctuary? Are Adam and the others okay?

"Dad? You there?"

"Yes, just . . . trying to make sense of this," I say, my mind still reeling. A smile creeps across my face as I realize that if Sam has this power, he'll be better able to protect himself now. "Let's take this one step at a time. What's your next move?"

"Um, I'm not sure. John's talking to Walker. Nine and Five are somewhere around here fighting. I'll keep you updated. What about you?"

I give him a rundown on what happened after he left. Mostly he responds with "What?!" and variations of "Oh crap!" I tell him that this morning I spoke to the president.

"Whoa. It sounds like they've given you rock star status."

I glance around the bathroom, the living space I've been told not to leave.

"Something like that," I say.

"At least you guys aren't stuck at Ashwood. Eventually you would have run out of waffles."

It takes me a second to realize he must think Walker's agents are with me, but I don't have a chance to correct him. There are new voices on his end of the line I can't quite make out.

"Crap, Dad, I need to go. I'll talk to you soon, okay? Stay safe."

"You too, son. You too."

He hangs up. I sit on the floor, trying to understand what all this could possibly mean.

I'm off the phone for maybe a few minutes when there's another knock on my door. I open it, expecting to see Richards there ready to drag me off to another meeting or something, but it's Briggs.

"Hey," he says. He's still using a crutch and is holding a cardboard box that someone's written "roast beef" on with Magic Marker. "Lunch."

"Thanks." I take the meal. "How's your leg?"

"Much better, thanks. They've got a top-of-the-line infirmary down here. I've never seen some of the machines before."

"Having fun in the hallway?"

He shrugs. "I'm supposed to report in if you go anywhere, but not stop you. You're not a prisoner or anything."

He sounds a little embarrassed by his admission.

"Oh," he says, pulling a book from under his arm and holding it out to me. *The Once and Future King* by T. H. White. "Here. There were a couple of books in the break room, but I think the others were all field guides and operation manuals."

"Thanks," I say. He's still not meeting my eyes. He seems meeker than yesterday—why?

"Anyway, I thought I heard a phone ring earlier. But

that's impossible, since there's no way you could get a signal down here."

I don't say anything. He motions behind me, and I open the door wider so he can step through.

"Your phone works down here?" he whispers when the door is closed behind us. I can barely hear him and respond in the same hushed tones.

"Apparently. Like I said earlier, it's a long story."

"We're not supposed to have any communication with the outside world. I should confiscate that."

Crap. I can't let him take my only connection to my son. Is this why he seems so hesitant?

"Look, the only people who have this number are people we can trust. It's important that I keep in touch with them. They know more about what's going on out there than we do."

Briggs stares at me, not blinking, for what feels like a long time. Finally he speaks again.

"Could I . . ." He hesitates, eyes hitting the cement floor. "Would it be okay if I made a quick call?"

I breathe a sigh of relief and motion for him to follow me into the bathroom, where I turn on the water.

"Here," I say. I switch the ringer to vibrate before handing it over, feeling stupid for not having done so before.

He looks at it as if I've just handed him a live

grenade—something tells me this might be the first time he's disobeyed an order. Or maybe it's just the fear of what he'll find on the other end of the line. His hand shakes slightly when he dials and raises the phone to his ear. As it rings, his breathing gets faster and faster, and his jaw clenches. I can hear the ringing go on, five, then six times.

Finally someone picks up.

Briggs's entire posture changes. He goes slack. For a second I think he's going to collapse onto the floor.

"Mom," he says.

I slip out of the bathroom to give him a moment of privacy, sitting on the bed, putting my head in my hands. My mind is still racing, trying to make sense of what Sam told me.

My son. With Legacies.

I guess I always knew he was special.

It's only then that I think back to the meeting earlier, how the Garde are considered allies but also possible threats to the country.

And my heart drops as I realize that applies to Sam now as well.

CHAPTER ELEVEN

IT'S EARLY EVENING AND I'M A FOURTH OF THE way through *The Once and Future King* when there's another knock on the door, this time rapid, almost nervous. I shove my phone underneath my pillow.

I actually drop the book to the floor when I see the president standing in the hallway, flanked by two Secret Service agents. He's sweating, his eyes wide and pink at the corners.

"Something's happened to my daughter," he says. "Please, will you talk to her?"

"Of course," I stammer, thrown for a loop by his appearance. "I'll do anything I can, but . . . I'm not a medical doctor."

That doesn't seem to matter; he's already heading back down the hallway. Briggs shrugs at me, looking as confused as I am. All I can do is follow.

"She was fine," Jackson says over his shoulder. "The

aide said she was just watching a movie when suddenly she convulsed and something strange happened to her eyes. They were shining. Then she lost consciousness for a few seconds. It doesn't make any sense."

"Was anyone else there?" I ask.

"No. My wife . . . She was in California when all this started. She's in a safe house there."

His voice sounds different from that of the man leading the table of high-ranking officials this morning. We have more in common than I might have guessed. He's a man separated from his family as well, tasked with protecting not only the people of his country, but his loved ones. Trying to figure out how to keep both safe at the same time.

"Does you daughter have a history of seizures?" I ask.

"None. The doctors here said they can't find anything wrong with her. She says she's fine but . . . she's scared. I've never seen her act this way. She *saw* something when she was unconscious. A meeting room where there were a bunch of teenagers who she calls 'the good guys' and one really bad man."

He stops in front of a guarded door and turns to me.

"She saw Setrákus Ra. I don't know *how*—as soon as the ships showed up, we were shuttled away, so she hasn't seen any of the footage. But she described him, just like he looked after he transformed at the UN and in the video he sent this morning."

"My God . . . ," I say. "Wait, this video—"

"Later," he says. "How is she seeing the leader of the Mogadorians? Is this some kind of attack?"

I shake my head, unsure. But then I remember Ella and some of the other Garde having visions in the past.

"It's not unheard of," I say. "Setrákus Ra has invaded dreams before, but as far as I know he's only ever targeted the Loric."

"She said there were hundreds of people who all seemed to be sharing this . . . *vision*. I showed her a picture of John Smith after hearing her describe a boy who spoke to them. It was him."

Jackson's face is full of confusion, eyes boring into me as he tries to understand what's happening to his daughter. When I can give him no answer, he pushes through the door.

The presidential suite in the bunker is, naturally, much better furnished than mine. Apart from the lack of windows, it looks like a normal small apartment. The girl is sitting on a tufted white couch. Her dark hair is pulled into a ponytail sprouting from the back of her head. She's fifteen, maybe sixteen. A woman sits beside her, trying to get her to put a damp washcloth on her head.

"I said I'm *fine*," the girl says, pushing the woman away.

"Thank you, Vera," Jackson says, dismissing the woman. "Can you step outside for a minute? Get some fresh air?"

There is no fresh air down here, but Vera takes the hint and leaves me and the president alone in the room with his daughter. She stops by the door, looking back and forth between the three of us.

"Do you want me to send someone else in?" she asks, no doubt wondering if Jackson wouldn't feel more comfortable with a Secret Service agent in the room.

"No thank you, Vera."

I know I'm not a threat, but it's good to know Jackson doesn't think of me as one either. Or, more likely, this just shows how desperate he is.

The president turns to his daughter. "Melanie, this is Dr. Goode."

"You can call me Malcolm," I say, holding out a hand.

Melanie looks up at me, then back down at her nails, which are pointed and painted a pale matte pink. She seems nervous, and from the way Jackson watches her, I can guess that being on edge isn't the norm for her.

"I don't know anything but what I told you, Dad," she mutters. "It all happened so fast. It was confusing."

"Right," Jackson continues. "I told him the main points. Malcolm knows the Garde. He—"

She looks at me with wide eyes, finally interested.

"You know John Smith?" she asks.

"I do."

Her mouth opens as if she's going to say something and then she closes it again. She seems hesitant to say anything else, so I keep talking.

"Sam, my son, is with him now in New York. Fighting the Mogs. John's his best friend."

Is Sam safe? The question is in the back of my mind, as always.

"Did you see it too, then?" she asks.

I shake my head. She frowns and looks away.

"Why me?" she asks. "Why'd I get sucked into their weirdo dream world?"

"Can you tell me anything else?" I ask. "Did they say where they were? Did they mention . . ." I rack my brain. "Maybe a place called the Sanctuary?"

She shakes her head, squinting her eyes, trying to remember.

"I don't think so," she says. "There were these people from all over the world. They had . . ." She catches herself, pausing. "They told us we could travel using a 'low-light' stone or something like that. A bunch of them popped up on a map that this creepy little girl showed us."

"Loralite . . . ," I murmur. That doesn't make any sense. From what I understand, the Garde needed Eight's teleportation power in order to use the stones.

When did that change? Is this somehow related to the new Legacies?

"What else did John say?" I ask.

"He wanted to get us to join him. He says we can save the world if we rise up against the bad guys."

"And your father said Setrákus Ra was there. Did he . . . say anything?"

"He said he was going to hunt me down. *All* of us." Tears fall on her cheeks. "He said he was going to kill each one of us who was there watching. He . . . Dad, he was horrible."

Jackson gets on one knee and pulls her in close, looking up at me with gritted teeth. My mind reels, trying to figure out what could possibly be going on. It sounds like John was trying to *recruit* people, but none of the Garde have ever shown the power to create some kind of widespread illusion before. Unless it's a new Legacy or . . .

New.

I think of Sam. And of the girl he mentioned. Of the fact that there might be new Garde popping up all over the world.

"Melanie," I say softly. "When did you start moving things with your mind?"

I'm taking a chance, but it's obvious I've hit a nerve. She stops crying—stops *breathing*, actually. Slowly, she pulls away from her father until her bleary eyes are locked on mine.

"How did you . . . ?"

"The same thing is happening to my son," I say, working things out as I speak. "To a lot of people in the world, I think. Probably all those other kids you saw in your dream."

"Then it's not just me? I thought . . . I was afraid I was the only one. I thought maybe I was going crazy and that this whole dream thing was just proof I needed to get locked up in an insane asylum."

"Melanie, what's going on?" Jackson asks, looking back and forth between us. His voice is measured, but it's impossible to not hear the urgency and pain behind it.

Melanie looks at him, her features contorted in a strange mixture of hope and fear, a deep groove appearing in the space between her eyebrows.

"This morning I was staring at a picture of Mom I brought with me. You were already gone. I wanted to talk to her, for her to be here. And then it just floated over to me. Like, flew off the nightstand and smacked me in the face. I . . . I thought it was something the aliens did to me. Like I was going to die. But then I *kept* doing it to things."

"What?" Jackson's question is hardly more than breath.

"Can you show us?" I ask, glancing around the room. There's a bottle of water on the coffee table in front of us. "There. Can you bring it to yourself?"

She concentrates. Slowly, the bottle begins to wobble, until it's rising off the table. It floats through the air, splashing water over its rim. Jackson is on his feet in a flash.

"Baby . . . you're doing this?" he asks.

"Don't talk to me," she says, her eyebrows furrowing more. "This is hard."

"But . . . *how*. How are you—"

"*Dad*, I said—"

The bottle suddenly crunches, sending a jet of water up in the air between the three of us. Then it drops to the floor.

"I'm not very good at it," Melanie says quietly. "My room is . . . kind of a mess."

"Why didn't you tell me?" Jackson asks. He keeps shaking his head, trying to make all the puzzle pieces in his head fit together.

"I was *scared*."

Jackson smiles, but then something must dawn on him, because his face quickly contorts into a grim frown.

"Mutation," he murmurs. "Unnatural abilities . . ."

"This is nothing to be afraid of," I say, even though I'm not sure of that at all. "Though . . . Melanie, you may get *more* strange abilities. All the Garde have more than one. I think telekinesis is usually the first to surface."

She looks up at me with huge brown eyes, mouth

agape. Then she turns to her father.

"We have to help them," she says.

"Who, baby?" Jackson asks.

"The Garde!" Her voice is louder, more serious. "We can't let that monster beat them and then take the rest of us. He's already invaded Earth and blown up New York. And the way he stared at me when he was yelling, telling me he was going to kill me—all of us . . ."

She takes a deep breath and swallows hard, wiping her eyes with the backs of her hands, smearing them with mascara and eyeliner. She notices this and suddenly looks embarrassed.

Jackson hugs her again, and questions start to spill out of her mouth. Why her? What other things can the Garde do? Is this contagious? I do my best to reassure her, but I don't have many answers myself. Finally, exhausted, she turns to her father.

"Can you just leave me alone for a little bit?" she asks.

"Melanie . . . ," Jackson starts.

"Like *ten minutes*, Dad," she says. "I just found out I have superpowers, and I kind of want to freak out for a little bit. Alone."

Jackson nods and stands, ushering me to the door. As soon as it clicks behind him, he pulls me out of earshot of the Secret Service agents and speaks in hushed tones.

"What's *wrong* with her?" His breath is shaky, like he's trying not to completely lose it. Which, given what he just saw, is pretty warranted. "How did this happen?"

"I don't know exactly what's going on, but I can assure you nothing is *wrong* with her." This comes out a little harsher than I expected, probably because I'm thinking about Sam again. I take a deep breath. "I think this is happening to lots of people. I don't know how many, or how they're chosen, but from what I can deduce the same powers the Garde have are being given to humans—kids—around the world. Telekinesis. Maybe other things, I . . . I don't know."

"Did the Garde do this?"

"I don't think so. When I . . ." I remember that I'm not supposed to be in contact with the outside world. "This is happening to my son, Sam, like I said. When I talked to him about it, it sounded like the Garde were as surprised as he was when he got this ability. And the Mogs certainly wouldn't want to empower the people they're trying to conquer. I don't know what force is at work here."

Jackson keeps shaking his head, moving his jaw back and forth as I speak. He processes things for a moment, wiping a sheen of sweat off his brow.

"We received a video this morning," he eventually says. "Ra knows about this. He said it's the Garde's 'mutations' that are giving people powers. He insists we turn anyone showing unnatural abilities over to him for 'treatment.'" His eyes meet mine. "He wants my daughter."

"And my son," I say, my pulse doubling. It's always been dangerous for him to face the Mogs, but now that he's got powers they'll be targeting him specifically. "We can't let the Mogs have them."

"Of course not," he says quickly. Then he composes himself. "I don't know if he has a way of tracking people with new powers, but if he can . . . He's given us forty-eight hours to hand over the Garde and anyone who's been mutated. After that, he's declaring war."

"No . . . ," I say. A useless protest. "You can't just hand innocent people over to him. And the Garde are our only chance, like I said earlier. They're on our side. You have to trust me. You have to believe in them. Hell, I've dedicated years trying to help them. I've trusted them with my son's life. Think of what that means, from one father to another. You can't turn them over."

Jackson bangs a fist against the wall beside us, clenching his jaw.

"Dammit," he spits, all the frustration and fear boiling over. Then his voice gets quieter. "Why her? She's a teenager. A *child*."

"People her age are the reason this planet hasn't completely fallen already. I've watched sixteen-year-olds obliterate entire squadrons of Mogadorians. These kids can walk on walls, conjure storms—some of them can heal wounds that should be death sentences. Even the unpowered among them are fighting with every ounce of strength, doing what they can.

"And we have no idea how many of these kids who just got superpowers are in the US, right? Jesus, we're talking about American citizens. We can't hand them over to invaders."

I think back to what his daughter said, trying to make sense of everything that's happening. The shared dream. Ra's threats. The Loralite stones.

"If there are teleportation areas popping up around the world, you may also be dealing with an influx of these newly powered individuals traveling to the US. It sounds like John Smith is rallying them behind him. And *he's* in New York."

"A whole army of superhuman teenagers," Lawson says from behind me. "Interesting."

Jackson shoots him a pointed look. I don't know how long he's been standing just around the corner, but he's obviously heard plenty.

"These kids you're talking about could make for good soldiers if we provide them with strong leadership," he says. "Not *Melanie*, of course. She'll stay hidden away for security reasons. But if there's an army of brand-new superheroes out there, we'll want them fighting on *our* side. The faster you can get a leash on them, the better things will be in the long run."

"They aren't *dogs*, General," I say, turning to him. If he tries to put a leash on my son, I'll remind him that I don't have to have superpowers to fight.

"Of course not. Sounds like they're weapons. Isn't that what you're getting at?"

"They're *kids*," I say. "Probably scared out of their minds."

"Welcome to war, Mr. Goode." Lawson sneers.

"*Doctor*," I say, a petty correction I haven't made in over a decade. I can feel my pulse throbbing in my temples.

Lawson's nostrils flare a little. "Everyone's terrified, *Doctor*. That's something we can use."

I turn my back to him. "Mr. President, I know this is all a lot to process, both as a father and as a leader. But just remember: whatever's happening, your daughter is wrapped up in this now. She may not be Loric, but she may as well be one of the Garde. Remember that as you make your decisions. You can't give them up. The Garde are *not* our enemy. The Mogadorians are."

Jackson holds my gaze, nodding slightly, before turning to Lawson.

"If these . . . *human Garde* are going to start appearing

in America wanting to fight, our job will be to make sure they don't do anything foolish, but not to subdue them. We can't fight a war on two fronts. General, call everyone back to the war room in thirty minutes. I want to firm up our plan of action. Our primary threat right now is the race of aliens that has warships parked over our cities. We've still got over forty hours of 'peace' to come up with a plan." His lips purse a little bit. "And I want to talk to John Smith myself."

"Yes, sir," General Lawson says, disappearing around a corner.

"And Dr. Goode, I want you there as well. Now, if you'll excuse me, I'm going to check on my daughter."

He goes into the suite, leaving me alone in the hall-way.

Back at my own room, Briggs is shifting his weight on his crutch outside my door.

"There was, ah . . . ," he says. "It sounded like there was maybe something buzzing in there earlier."

I don't respond. All I know is that I have to get to the phone. Sure enough, I have a string of missed calls from the number Sam reached me from earlier. I press all the wrong buttons trying frantically to redial, not even bothering to hide from any bugs or recording devices. Finally, it connects.

"Dad?" Sam's voice is frantic, shaking. I don't real-ize I've been holding my breath until I hear him speak, and the air rushes from my lungs in relief.

"Sam, thank God, what is it?" I ask. "Are you okay? Where are you?"

"Oh, shit," he says. "I thought something had happened to you too. I . . ."

Too?

"I'm fine, Dad, but . . ." In the background I can hear shouting, pained and animal. "Something terrible's happened. Could you . . . Dad, we need you back."

I don't hesitate to answer. I know that elsewhere in this bunker the leaders of the nation are gathering again. There's a seat for me at their table now.

But my son needs me. And it's not like I can't advise the president from afar.

"Of course, Sam," I say, motioning for Gamera to follow me. "Just tell me where to go. I'm already on my way."

"I . . ." He pauses. When he talks again, it sounds like he's holding the phone away from his ear. "John, wait, where are you . . . ?" Hushed voices I can't understand, and then "Dad, let me call you back in five, okay?"

He's hung up before I can ask any of the dozens of questions I need answered, chiefly *What the hell happened*?

Still, I've got five minutes to figure out how to escape from a secret bunker. I think back to Richards telling me that I could leave whenever I wanted but that he'd have men escort me out, making sure I couldn't lead anyone else back to the bunker. At the time it had seemed like a thinly veiled threat, but I don't *think* the president would actually let Richards kill me—especially not now. Still, it would definitely be faster and easier for me to get out of here unnoticed.

The trouble is, I'm not even sure where I am. Maybe sixty miles outside of DC if the train ride was an hour? Farther? And what do I even do for transportation?

In the hallway Briggs must be able to tell something's wrong—and that I'm bolting.

"No," he says, shaking his head.

"I thought I wasn't a prisoner," I say.

He doesn't have an immediate answer for me.

"It's my son," I say. "I have to go."

"My orders are to report—"

"Please, Samuel," I say. "This is my family. If your mom was in trouble you'd go, right? Especially if she was wrapped up in everything that's happening like my boy is. My son needs me, and I'm leaving. If you try to keep me here, you're just ensuring that I won't help."

I can see the conflict in Briggs's eyes. He glances around the halls.

"Follow me," he says. "Quickly."

He doesn't wait for me to answer before walking in the direction opposite the war room and the president's suite. We go through a series of gray corridors. He nods

to the people we pass, who probably assume he's leading me to or from some appointment. Finally, we reach
the big cement room where we first entered the bunker.
Our train car still sits in the center of it.

The man in the lab coat has his face buried in an
electronic tablet. He glances up when we enter.

"I'm here to relieve you, Joe," Briggs says. "Clearance
Juliett Delta Kilo."

Joe—I guess—squints at us. "I'm not due for a break
for another hour."

Briggs snorts. "You want to keep working, that's fine
with me."

The man's nose twitches as he turns his attention to
me, raising an eyebrow.

"Our guest's a science guy." Briggs shrugs. "He's
interested in the software we're using. Plus, it's boring as shit down here, and he's keeping me entertained
with stories about ETs."

"Fine, whatever," Joe says. He gets up and leaves,
muttering something about how bad the food is here.
Briggs glares at him as he exits.

"We go way back," he mutters. "That guy's such a
prick."

"Come with me," I say. "You're going to be in trouble
when they find out you helped me."

He shakes his head. "I'd be in more trouble if I
deserted. Besides, technically you're *not* a prisoner.

I'll just tell them you manipulated me into helping you and I fell for it. Which . . . probably isn't far from the truth. Unless you want to hit me over the head with my gun or something, but I think I'd *rather* them think you outsmarted me than overpowered me. No offense."

"Briggs, I . . ." But I don't know what else to say. "Thank you."

He taps on the controls. I scrawl a number down on a notepad I find lying nearby.

"This is my number. See if you can get it to Richards. Tell him this is how Jackson can reach me. Tell them . . . it's a family matter. Believe it or not, I think the president might understand."

On the wall opposite us, a metal panel slides away, revealing a small elevator.

"That'll take you topside," Briggs says, pocketing the note. "Eventually someone will come looking for you. Better not be in the area when they do. They might insist you come back."

"I think I've run more in the last few days than in my entire life," I say as I jog to the elevator. Gamera buzzes after me.

It's only when the door starts sliding shut that I realize I don't know what's waiting for me above. "Wait, where are we?"

"Didn't Richards tell you? Liberty Base." He gets

a little grin before he disappears behind the closing metal door.

I'm shot up what feels like several stories before I finally come to a stop. The door opens, and for a moment the sunshine is blinding. I step out onto a bed of grass and pine needles as my eyes adjust.

I turn in time to see the wall behind me slide shut, until it looks like nothing but another section of the giant white stone wall in front of me—a dam of sorts. I take a few steps away, trying to figure out where I am. That's when I see a faded brochure and map on the ground, half buried. "Liberty Reservoir," it reads. I dust it off. According to the map on the back, I'm north of DC, not that far from Baltimore.

"All right," I say, glancing at the dragonfly on my shoulder. "Let's find a road."

I start to jog. Gamera zips forward, morphing in midair, until he's turned into a horse. He rears back and then stands in front of me, shaking his mane.

I think I've found a faster way to get away from the bunker.

My phone rings as I hoist myself onto Gamera's back. Sam's on the other end of the line when I answer.

"Hi, Dad," he says.

"Son," I say as Gamera starts to gallop. "Where am I going?"

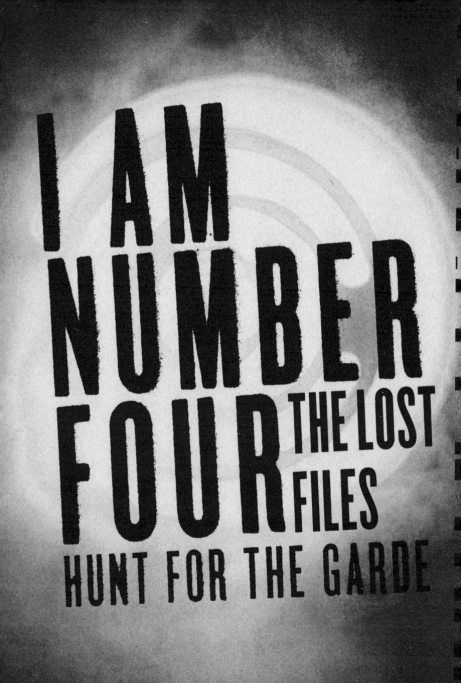

I AM
NUMBER
FOUR THE LOST
FILES
HUNT FOR THE GARDE

PART ONE
PHIRI DUN-RA

CHAPTER ONE

THE LORIC MAY CALL IT THEIR "SANCTUARY," but today it's a war zone.

Their people will die here.

Killing the last of the Garde has always been on the forefront of Mogadorian minds. I know *I've* thought much about it, at least. Not for my own vanity or sense of accomplishment, but because I know that it is the greatest way I can serve Beloved Leader. To please him.

That's all I want, all I need out of life.

There was a time when I thought I was close to receiving Setrákus Ra's favor. I'd worked my way through the ranks, showing my superiors how mercilessly I could deal with any who opposed us. How swiftly I could turn the vatborn into well-trained killing squads. Eventually I was given command of an entire platoon in our West Virginia base, where I could show Beloved Leader once and for all that I was his most faithful, most capable commander.

But then I failed him. A few of the Garde scum under my watch escaped. I was disgraced, and given the choice to be put to death for my failures or re-stationed in Mexico, tasked with finding a way into an impenetrable Loric site. The decision seemed like an easy one. I chose the latter, hoping that I would be able to make up for my mistakes. Instead, I failed him again.

But that's all going to change. Beloved Leader is here now, and I will show him that I am worthy of being his disciple. He will witness me on the battlefield and see that I am the embodiment of what he preaches in the Great Book. I will show no mercy, spare no enemy.

"Protect Beloved Leader!" I shout as I run from my cover in the jungle, leading a small group of vatborn and trueborn soldiers I've rescued from Garde impris-onment. As we cross the battlefield, I see Number Six. One of my eyes is swollen shut thanks to the Loric bitch punching me while I was tied up earlier. She should have taken my trigger fingers—*killed* me if she was smart. I fire at her back. She goes down. I bare my teeth. I will make sure her death is slow and agonizing.

I will make Beloved Leader proud.

We charge forward. Ahead of us, our savior stands in a crater, holding the Garde called Marina in the air with his extraordinary powers. He bashes her into the ground below over and over again until her body goes limp. The Loric and their allies may have destroyed the pipeline Setrákus Ra created to harvest the Loralite, but they're being beaten down, reminded of our superiority.

This is war. This is glory. This is Mogadorian Progress.

⊐

We continue our surge forward amid blaster fire from every direction. I reach Beloved Leader too late. One of the Loric allies—a human male with the audacity to use our own weapons against us—manages a lucky shot that scorches our infallible commander's ear. Had I been just a little faster on my feet, I could have thrown myself in front of the blast, happily dying to protect Beloved Leader from even the slightest pain. By the time I get to his side, he's already thrown Marina's broken body at the boy, sending them both rolling out of sight.

Up close, I can see blood dripping from a few wounds on our commander's body. He leans on a sword.

"Beloved Leader," one of my fellow Mogadorians says, stepping forward and placing a hand on the commander's arm as if to help him stand.

Setrákus Ra responds by placing a palm on his underling's head. There's a half second when the soldier looks like he's in ecstasy, like he's been blessed. Then the hand on his head clenches into a fist, the trooper's skull caving in like a piece of rotten fruit before turning to dust.

Our Beloved Leader needs no help. These injuries are nothing to him.

"Back to the ship," he growls. "We'll make them feel our power."

"You heard our glorious leader," I shout. "Hold nothing back!"

Weapon fire continues to fill the air, coming from all sides, even from the *Anubis* itself. There are painful wounds on my hands from getting too close to the force field around the Sanctuary, but I don't let this slow me down. I shoot constantly. I know Beloved Leader doesn't need my help, but I show him my loyalty by being front and center as we march out of the crater, taking any harm meant for him. The other troops fall in line too, forming a ring around him as we move.

We will serve him until we are nothing but dust.

"I will destroy every speck of life for miles," Beloved Leader growls as we start up the ship's ramp. "Everything beneath us will burn, and once we've wiped out the Loric and their allies, I'll dig the remnants of the Sanctuary from the ground myself."

"Not even their bones will remain," I say.

We're near the top of the ramp when something in the air changes.

Wind hits us, a hurricane gale that must be the work of the Garde. Debris—rocks, metal, biting sand—slams into us, causing me to cover my face with my arms as I take a few steps backwards, trying to brace myself.

Beloved Leader stands strong, though. He turns to face the wind and holds a hand out, palm open. The wind fighting against us dies down, but I can feel some other force in the air as he grins. He is so powerful, his might driving our enemies back. The battlefield of the Sanctuary explodes with shrapnel and chunks of stones.

This is what our victory looks like.

Beside me, Beloved Leader laughs.

I see the projectile too late—I am *always* too late. It's hardly a glint of metal in the air before it hits him; a piece of the broken pipeline is buried in Beloved Leader's chest.

The sound of his laughter turns into a gasp as he doubles over, stumbling back.

"No!" I scream, rushing back to his side.

In that moment, despite the blasters continuing to sound around us, there is only me and Setrákus Ra, huddled together in the entryway of the *Anubis*, my body blocking him from further attacks. The rest of the world—the universe—ceases to exist.

He looks down at the shrapnel in his chest and then up at me.

"Inside," he grunts, dark blood dripping over his lips.

I move as quickly as I can, shouting to the others to help me. We pull him into his ship. We're barely clear when I slam a hand down on the controls that close the loading door, shielding us.

Chaos breaks out in the loading area as all the troops start shouting at once. One of the low-ranking trueborn steps forward.

"We should pull the pipe out, right?" he asks, a little uncertain.

"You won't touch him," I say.

"If *I* were him, I'd want—"

"But you are *not* him." I fire one shot directly into the soldier's head. His augmentations begin to disintegrate before he hits the ground. The others back away. I am a trueborn commander, and even if my military record has been tarnished as of late, I'm likely the highest-ranking person in the docking bay.

Other than Beloved Leader, long may he reign.

The front of his armor is slick with inky blood leaking from the wound. There's something strange in his eyes, so unexpected from him that it takes me a moment to recognize the emotion as shock.

He struggles to get up, batting away the troops who try to offer him assistance. His eyes meet mine, and he whispers two words.

"Crush them."

Then he collapses onto the floor.

CHAPTER
TWO

WE SOMEHOW MANAGE TO GET OUR HIGH COM-
mander into the nearby elevator. His body is heavy,
almost too much for us to carry. His ragged, gurgling
breaths fill my ears. If it were anybody else, I would
assume that he was near death, but I know this is no normal Mogadorian in front of me. He is forever, immortal.
This is a momentary setback. Not even that—it must be
part of his plan, something he has foreseen.

As we rise through the *Anubis*, the other troops in
the elevator with me are silent except for occasional
outbursts.

"Hail our Beloved Leader!"

"Long may he reign!"

"Praise his name!"

When the doors open, a few medical staff are waiting for us. It's fortunate we're on the *Anubis*, as doctors
are hard to come by on Mogadorian vessels, even on the

warships. It's usually not worth the trouble of trying to heal or treat the vatborn when more can so easily be created. As for the trueborn, it's sometimes better—or more honorable—to die on the battlefield than return a disappointment.

At first the doctors are afraid to even touch Beloved Leader, but I bark at them, and he's hoisted onto a gurney. He grunts, and then he's rushed to the medical bay.

I start to follow, but then something occurs to me: we're still parked at the Sanctuary. Our enemies are somewhere just outside, and our commander is currently unconscious.

Who will lead us?

What would Beloved Leader have us do?

His last words fill my mind.

Crush them.

Then it becomes clear. He has given me a command. Purpose. A divine order. He's leaving it up to *me* to take control and see that his will is done.

If I can do this, I will have proven myself many times over to him, surely.

So instead of following the doctors, I make for the bridge. My long, black braids have come loose in the battle, and they whip the air as I sprint through the hallways, the sounds of my footsteps echoing behind me.

I burst onto the bridge. The officers are running around, shouting at each other. The medical teams have apparently already reported in to them. It seems that several crew members left to be by Beloved Leader's side, while others nervously hover around their terminals, waiting for commands.

"Where are the Loric bastards?" I shout as I make my way to the viewing window at the front of the bridge.

"They've just taken off," one of the officers says. Based on his terminal's readouts, I'm guessing he's our navigator. "They have a Loric ship somehow. We're waiting for—"

"Follow them," I say.

"But Beloved Leader is the only person who—"

I raise my blaster to the officer's head.

"I am Phiri Dun-Ra, trueborn daughter of the honorable Magoth Dun-Ra," I say, slowly and clearly. "And at this moment I am the voice of Beloved Leader. He has given me orders to crush the Garde. If you don't put us in the air in the next five seconds, I'll do it myself."

He hesitates only a beat before the *Anubis* takes off.

"Fire as soon as you get them in sight," I say.

I open a comm line to the medical bay, but there's nothing to report. Setrákus Ra is still unconscious. The doctors are trying to figure out how best to proceed with the extraction of the pipe. They've contacted some kind of specialist, whatever that means.

Which leaves me to command the ship. To execute Beloved Leader's order.

To ensure Mogadorian Progress.

I pace around the bridge, watching the Loric ship on our radar screen. We're gaining on it, but not quickly enough.

"Call for reinforcements," I shout. The officers follow my orders. They know who I am—some of them even recognize me from when I was leading troops at the main base. "Map their trajectory and alert the other warships on this continent that a Loric vessel is in the air. We don't let this ship escape. And someone send more troops to the Sanctuary. Many of the Loric were wounded. Perhaps mortally. Capture anyone left behind."

"Incoming transmission from the West Virginia base," an officer says.

"Pull it up." I gesture to one of the many electronic panels around the bridge.

"I'm sorry," he says, his voice a bit shaky, like he's unsure of how to proceed. "But I've been instructed that this is a private message for whoever is in command of the ship." His brow knits together. "Is Beloved Leader able to—"

"I am his voice *and* his ears right now," I say. "Take me to a place where I can receive this call."

The officer leads me out of the bridge. I'm taken to a meeting room. The officer leaves me there alone as I tap on a control panel. A trueborn appears on the screen on the opposite wall. There's a jagged but thin scar running across the dome of his tattooed head—one I know he got from the traitor Adamus's attack on Ashwood Estates.

"Ah, Phiri Dun-Ra," he says with a slight smirk. "When the chief doctor contacted me, he mentioned the *Anubis* was in the air. I should have known it was you who'd taken control."

"Dr. Zakos," I mutter. "I have a ship to destroy. If you have a message for me, speak now."

Zakos and I have not always seen eye to eye. He was often a guest of Beloved Leader at the base in West Virginia when I was still stationed there. He oversaw all sorts of experiments and augmentation programs dreamed up by our leader. Once a superpowered piken of his design got loose in the tunnels surrounding the facility and ate half my men when we were sent to retrieve it. The doctor shrugged off these casualties as necessary losses. Meanwhile, I had to train a new squad.

When the Loric Garde escaped a few days later, it was that team of new soldiers who lost them in the tunnels.

"It's admirable that you've so quickly stepped into Beloved Leader's boots," Zakos says, "but chasing this ship is out of the question unless it's headed to the West Virginia base."

"Of course it's not," I say.

"Then I'm afraid you're going to have to abandon your pursuit." His face gets serious. The self-satisfied smirk disappears. "Beloved Leader needs my attention. *Now.* His wound is serious, and every second that passes, it grows worse. The *Anubis* is not equipped to handle his injuries."

"Beloved Leader will not be killed by a pathetic Garde," I say, my voice getting louder. "He will rise again to conquer this world."

"Of course he will," Zakos says. "But he'll rise much faster if I can get him into the healing vats. The longer you chase the Loric ship, the longer Setrákus Ra will be out of commission. He'll have to spend more hours in the vats while you are free to . . . do what, exactly? Command the *Anubis*? That sounds an awful lot like treason, Phiri. *However,* a disgraced trueborn such as yourself would likely find favor with Beloved Leader if he awoke and heard that you had sped up his recovery by rushing him into my hands."

I grit my teeth, unable to respond at first.

"He told me to crush them," I say.

"If he holds that against you, I'll take responsibility for it myself," Zakos says. "Time is of the essence, Phiri Dun-Ra. I've alerted General Krah that Beloved Leader is . . . unable to be reached right now. He agrees that this is a matter that no one outside of the *Anubis* needs to know about. Understood?"

I nod.

"Good. I'll be awaiting your arrival personally."

The feed cuts out.

I don't move for a few moments, trying to figure out what to do. If we let these Loric slip through our fingers, who knows when we'll have the chance to kill them again? This will be yet another failure on my part. And dammit if I don't want to watch each and every one of those bastards beg for mercy as I torture them.

But Zakos is right. Beloved Leader comes first, always. Though he told me to crush the Loric, I can't be responsible for prolonging his recovery. And besides, the best way to ensure their demise is to have Setrákus Ra giving orders. He saved our people. He crushed Lorien. Earth is his whenever he decides that he wants it.

If I should be put to death for letting the Loric escape, so be it. So long as Beloved Leader walks among his subjects at full power once more.

I go back to the bridge.

"Update me," I say.

"We'll be crossing the United States border in ten minutes," the navigator says. "We've gained on them slightly, but they've got a hell of a pilot. We're having trouble closing the gap, and they're outside of our weapons' range."

I nod.

"Send as many skimmers as we can spare after that ship, but the *Anubis* is disengaging," I say. "Plot us a course for the West Virginia base."

"Would Beloved Leader . . . ," the navigator says, unsure of how to finish the sentence.

"Now," I shout.

And then I'm forced to watch as the Loric ship disappears from our radar screen.

CHAPTER
THREE

I GO BACK TO THE MEDICAL BAY AS WE SHOOT towards West Virginia. The doctors there have removed most of the pipe in Beloved Leader's chest using some sort of laser. Now it sticks out just an inch above his body.

"He's alive, but *barely*," the trueborn in charge whispers to me when I pull him aside.

"He is *fine*," I say, narrowing my eyes. "To say otherwise would be heresy. Remember that."

"Of course," he says quickly. "I'll make sure my staff remembers that as well."

It's early morning when we land, still dark. Before we move his gurney out, I instruct the doctors to put a sheet over him, just in case there are stray troops roaming around somewhere. They shouldn't see him like this. No one should.

Dr. Zakos is waiting for us outside, along with half a dozen other trueborn scientists who serve as his staff.

"Straight to the vats," he says to two of his men, who sprint inside with Beloved Leader's body. Then he motions to the others. "The rest of you retrieve any Loric energy the *Anubis* managed to siphon out of the ground at the Sanctuary. You know what to do."

The men grunt and make haste. Zakos then turns to me. "You did well, Phiri Dun-Ra. Beloved Leader will surely commend you."

"How long do you think he'll be out?" I ask.

"Hard to tell based on the reports the doctors sent. But he should regain some consciousness soon after he's put into the vats. Unless his injuries are worse than anticipated." Zakos casts a wary eye on the ship behind me. "I'm impressed you made it here so quickly."

"The crew of the *Anubis* are our best," I say. "They know how to push the ship to its limits."

"Yes." He rubs his chin. "Quite the crew indeed. Given everything they've witnessed, I wonder if they should stay on the ship and make sure everything's in working order." He gestures to scorch marks on one side of the hull. "Plenty of repairs and diagnostics to be run, I imagine."

I see what he's getting at. Our leader will be okay—he'll awaken stronger than ever, no doubt—but there's no reason for the rest of our fleet to know that our commander is healing in the vats. The fewer people who know about what happened at the Sanctuary, the better. When Beloved Leader is at the helm again, none of this will matter, anyway.

"I'll take care of it," I say.

"Good." Zakos nods. "Most of our higher-ranking officers are on warships at this point, but those who are still here are aware of your homecoming. I believe your old quarters inside are vacant, if you'd like to use them."

I nod.

"And I'd recommend a cryo pack for the eye. It looks like shit."

"I've been in battle," I say. "Not holed up in safety experimenting on piken."

"As Beloved Leader's most trusted disciple, the one in charge of overseeing his plans for Mogadorian Progress, it's in the fleet's best interest to keep me safe, isn't it?" He turns to the base, talking over his shoulder. "I'll need some time alone with him. Come see me in a few hours. We've much to talk about. I think you'll find what I'm working on very interesting."

I wonder what this might mean. With Zakos, it's never easy to tell. I turn back to the *Anubis*. A few of the ship's crew are loitering at the end of the loading ramp.

"Back to your posts," I shout at them.

I follow them aboard and patch myself into the PA system.

"This is Phiri Dun-Ra, voice of Beloved Leader," I say. "All crew members and troops stationed aboard the *Anubis* are to stay on the ship until further notice. In addition, we are now on a communications lockdown. Any off-ship transmissions must be cleared with Beloved Leader first."

Then I head off the ship.

It's been so long since I've been inside the base that I'm unprepared for the acrid smell of it. It looks the same, except that the rivers of green liquid that flowed through the main chamber have been replaced by a viscous black ooze, not unlike what Setrákus Ra uses to augment and better our forces—probably due to whatever experiments and further augmentations Beloved Leader began testing since I left. Still, my mind floods with memories of this place, of training troops and demanding the best of every vatborn Mogadorian sent to me, breaking whips and stun rods over their backs when they weren't up to snuff. I pass the piken and kraul pens and the cell blocks where I watched humans, Loric allies, and even the occasional Cêpan or Garde cower in fear. I can't see them, but I know the interrogation chambers are past the cells, stocked with all sorts of instruments and tools designed to extract information.

I didn't realize how much I'd missed this place.

I ignore my quarters and head instead to the central command room, the heart of Mogadorian Progress. I want to know what's happening with the rest of our operations. Unlike the rock walls of the main chamber, it's sleek, every surface a dull-gray metal. Computers and monitors cover the walls. A table in the center of the room displays a digital map of our warships across the globe. Most of the trueborn inside appear to be young officers-in-training.

"Phiri Dun-Ra," a gravelly bass voice says.

I turn to find General Krah. In the grand scheme of things, it's rare that a Mogadorian dies of old age. So much of our lives are spent fighting that we tend not to expire from "natural causes." Krah may prove to be an exception, though, and not because he's shied away from battle. The trueborn's face is a web of scar tissue and unnatural grooves.

"General Krah," I say, nodding to him in deference.

He crosses the room in a few heavy steps. When he speaks again, his voice is quieter so that only I can hear it. I brace myself. When I was kicked out of the mountain base, Krah was one of the officers responsible for choosing where I would be relocated.

"Dr. Zakos informed me of the situation you found

yourself in." He narrows his one good eye at me, study-ing my face. The other is a milky white, rendered useless by some injury long ago.

"I acted as I thought Beloved Leader would want," I say. "But I regretfully let the Loric scum escape. Our skimmers lost their ship somewhere over Texas." My eyes fall to the floor. "I understand this failure is unfor-givable. If it warrants an end to my life, I will offer my neck to your blade willingly."

Krah grunts.

"You've always been a good soldier, Dun-Ra. Even when you fail, your loyalty never wavers. You were right to bring Beloved Leader here, long may he reign. If you die because of your actions, it will be by his hands, not by mine."

I nod, a small wave of relief rushing over me.

"Sir." One of the officers-in-training stands, remov-ing his headphones. "Several of our warships are still asking about the Loric ship the *Anubis* was chasing. I believe many of the captains would like to engage it if possible."

"Of course they would," Krah says. He glances at me. "I know you were hoping to head the bastards off, but you've made our entire North American fleet rest-less."

"How should we respond?" the young trueborn asks.

"That they're to remain put," Krah says. "That Beloved Leader will tell them when they have new orders." He raises his chin a little. "And that our invasion of Earth is going just as he designed."

CHAPTER
FOUR

KRAH FILLS ME IN ON THE STATE OF OUR CAM-
paign. For now we're in a holding pattern. The *Anubis*'s
unexpected flight to the Sanctuary changed our time-
line. Once Beloved Leader awakens, his plans will
resume, but for now the warships wait in silence. The
only anomaly has been the humans who've suddenly
begun to display Garde-like powers. But according to
Krah, they're more of a curiosity than a threat at the
moment. The affected humans appear to all be little
more than children, untrained and incapable of using
their newfound abilities in any way that might harm
our cause. In fact, it's believed they may prove to be
useful in other ways.

I get more of a sense of this when I visit Zakos in the
afternoon.

There are five metal slabs that serve as beds lining
the walls of his laboratory. Three are empty. One is

covered in blood and what looks like chunks of human flesh. One has an unconscious human girl with short, red hair strapped down to it. Zakos is bent over her, prodding her with some sort of baton wired to an electronic tablet in his hands.

"Doctor," I say.

"Ah, Phiri." He drops the tablet on the girl's stomach. She doesn't react. "I was just about to send for you."

"Who is this child?" I ask. "I thought we'd learned everything to know about human anatomy."

His eyes light up a bit at this. "So had I. And yet this girl has exhibited signs of Loric power. Telekinesis, to be specific. We have reports that other Legacies have been displayed by these newly powered humans as well."

"Which is why you have her drugged, I'm guessing."

"That's right," he says.

"And that one?" I point to the slab where blood is congealing.

"An unfortunate blunder on my part. It won't happen again. I tried to use the same techniques as my predecessor, Dr. Anu, to isolate Legacies. Unfortunately, *his* methods apparently only worked on Loric physiology. I've made some adjustments to his methods. As you can see, *this* specimen is still alive. And if she does die, well, several of our warships have teams devoted to collecting new samples for me. I don't think I'll have any problem finding more subjects."

I step closer to the sleeping girl and take a better look at her. Slender metal probes stick out of her chest and arms. Her eyes move back and forth beneath thin lids.

"How did they get these powers?" I ask.

Zakos dismisses the question with a wave of his hand as he moves to a computer terminal.

"I'm not concerned about the how so much as what we can do with them. The how we'll figure out later. The how I might be able to reverse engineer. Or, more likely, Beloved Leader will be able to explain."

"How is he?" I ask.

"See for yourself."

I follow him through a door in the back of his lab and out into a huge open area. The place smells like sulfur, and there are big black rectangles spotting the metal floor, pits full of the dark sludge that gets pumped into augmented soldiers, and that incubates the vatborn.

These are the healing vats.

"He rests below us," Zakos says. "Already he has begun to recover. It won't be long before he walks among us again."

"So quickly?" I ask.

"Yes," he says, sounding a little annoyed. "He designed this system when he brought us the vatborn and the Great Book of Mogadorian Progress. You must trust in his knowledge, Phiri."

I grit my teeth at the implication that I don't and manage to keep myself from clawing at the doctor's face. Meanwhile, he's taken an interest in my bandaged palms.

"May I?" he asks.

I begrudgingly offer him my hands. He takes off one of the bandages.

"Burns," he says. "Energy based, but not blaster fire. You should have told me about them sooner."

"They're from some sort of force field I encountered at the Loric Sanctuary," I say. "I don't need them healed. They're a good reminder of what happens when I am less than Beloved Leader would like me to be."

"He would like you at your full potential." Zakos drops my hands and points to one of the dark rectangles in the floor. "I'll get you some clean bandages. If you'll spread a little bit of the vat liquid on your palms, they'll be healed in no time."

I walk over to the vat and stare down into the slick darkness. A few seconds pass before I stick two fingers into the black sludge. It's viscous and warm, but when I spread it over my wounds, it starts to tingle, turning cold.

I let out a sharp breath.

"Yes," Zakos says, coming up from behind me. "It can be quite jarring."

He takes my hands again, cleaning off the excess ooze with a towel before starting to rewrap them in clean, white bandages. He's finishing up my first hand when he speaks again.

"You are a strong soldier, Phiri Dun-Ra."

I don't respond.

"I *need* strong soldiers."

"For what?" I ask. "To retrieve more subjects for you? I'm not a delivery service."

"Of course not," he says with a slight smirk. He starts on my other hand. "I misspoke. He needs you. I'm working on something for Beloved Leader—a project he is *most* interested in. A new way to arm our troops."

"He's developed new augmentations?" I ask.

"Something like that. But only the strongest among us will be able to wield his new weapons. Not just true-born, but those with physical and mental strength. Endurance. And loyalty."

He looks me in the eyes.

"That's you, Phiri," he says. "Before he flew to the Sanctuary, Beloved Leader left me with very specific plans and goals concerning the future of Mogadorian Progress, and I know that nothing would make him happier than to emerge from the vats with a new force to command. Will you serve our glorious commander and ascend to the level he requires of you?"

I stare back at him, trying to process what he's saying. But in the end, I know there is only one answer to this question.

"I will do whatever Beloved Leader asks of me."

"I was hoping you'd say that," he says as he finishes bandaging my other hand. "I'll begin the preparations at once. I'll send for you when I'm ready. Go get some rest." He grins. "Evolution can be a painful process."

CHAPTER FIVE

AFTER MEETING WITH ZAKOS, I HEAD TO MY OLD quarters at the mountain base. It holds none of my personal belongings other than a few old uniforms and a dog-eared copy of the Great Book. And yet it feels good to be back there after so many nights camped out in Mexico, wondering how the hell I was going to break through the Sanctuary's force field. On the small bed in the room I sleep the deep, dreamless sleep of one who has been running on nothing but adrenaline for days.

I've barely woken the next morning when Dr. Zakos sends for me. It's well past sunrise. I know my body needed the rest, but I still feel lazy, like I should have been awake at dawn and doing something, anything, to help the invasion move forward.

I catch myself in the mirror before heading to the lab. My eye isn't as swollen as it was but has begun to bruise, turning one side of my face into a mixture of purples, yellows and deep blacks. My mind flashes with thoughts of being tied up in Mexico, beaten by Adamus and Six.

I promise myself that if I ever see them again, I will bleed them slowly, making them watch helplessly as their friends die in front of them before I even begin to consider gifting the two of them the release of death. Not for the disgrace they caused me by taking me as their prisoner, but for the injuries they inflicted on Beloved Leader. They will pay dearly.

Someone has cleaned up the blood in Dr. Zakos's lab, but he's not around. I loiter there for a few minutes, letting my eyes run over the various notes and documents littering his workstation: designs for new monsters, potential weapon upgrades, scrawlings about the humans who've developed Loric powers.

I'm interrupted by a ragged gasp behind me.

I turn on my toes and draw my blaster in one fluid motion. From the end of my weapon I see the red-haired girl on the metal slab. She looks different than she did yesterday. She's paler, and her cheeks are sunken in. Her lips move, but no words come out, and unlike before, her eyes are open—big and green and bloodshot, staring off into space.

I step over to her side. There are all sorts of new contraptions around her bed, big pieces of machinery and computational equipment with needles, tubes and electrodes hanging from them. I crouch beside her.

"Lucky little human," I say. "You have no idea what an honor it is to be in your position. Whatever Beloved Leader and Dr. Zakos have planned for you will surely make our armies stronger, speeding up Mogadorian Process and the invasion of your planet. Any pain you endure in this laboratory is for the greater good of my people. You should consider yourself fortunate: unlike most humans, your death will have meaning."

When I finish, her eyes suddenly jerk towards me, wide and full of terror. I smile, knowing she's heard me. That she understands.

She takes another gasping breath, and then her eyelids flutter and she falls unconscious again. That's when I hear a voice filtering into the room from the vats. I go through the door and am immediately hit by the same sulfuric smell as yesterday, even stronger now.

"Dr. Zakos," I say, and then I register what's happening in front of me.

Zakos stands in his white lab coat over one of the dark pools. He's got an electronic tablet in his hands. In the vat below him is Beloved Leader, submerged up to his shoulders in black ooze. His face is covered with a slick coat of the dense liquid.

"Beloved Leader," I say, dropping to my knees with such force that for a second I think I may have cracked my kneecaps. "Forgive me; I didn't mean to intrude."

"Rise, Phiri Dun-Ra," he says, his voice a deep bellow filling the room.

"Ah, there you are," Zakos says. He raises the tablet in his hands. "I was just updating our illustrious commander as to the state of his fleet and everything that's happened in the last few hours. Including your flight from Mexico."

"You took control of the *Anubis* when I was . . ." My leader pauses. "When I was indisposed."

"I did . . ." I hesitate. "I acted as your voice. There was chaos where there should have been order, and I tried to rectify that and act in your interests. I know that I had no right to do this and offer my life as—"

"You have done well, Phiri," he says, cutting me off. "In fact, I have plans for you. Call it a reward. By my design, Dr. Zakos has developed a new form of augmentation. I want you to be his first test subject."

"Me?"

"Who better than one who has shown she will stop at nothing to prove her loyalty? The process will be painful. It may push you to the brink of death. I need someone with the will to survive, to endure—to serve as my voice while I mend myself here. My voice, and my *fist*. We're going to make you stronger, unbeatable, and in doing so you will become the face of this world's end. You'll emerge from this process renewed, my most powerful weapon."

My heart pumps in my chest. Something rushes through me, a feeling of contentment and joy unlike anything I've ever felt.

"All you have to do is make it through the process alive," he says.

I try to speak without my voice shaking. For a moment, I remember the blood and flesh on the lab table yesterday. That could be me, the first to test this new augmentation.

But it is his will.

"It is my purpose to serve you, Beloved Leader. Thank you for honoring me in this way, despite my failure to capture the Loric fleeing the Sanctuary."

He lets out a few short laughs.

"Don't concern yourself with the Loric right now, Phiri Dun-Ra. Their fate is sealed. I've foreseen the end of the Garde and their allies. Their downfall will come from within." His lips curl up into a smile, dripping black ooze over his sharp, gray teeth. "I haven't just been healing down here in the dark. I've been dreaming."

Before I can get any sort of explanation of what that means, he begins to sink back into the vat.

"A few more hours, I think," he says to Zakos before the ooze rises above his lips. "Then I want to see how our new soldier has turned out."

"Of course, Beloved Leader."

And then he's completely covered.

Once he's disappeared, I can hardly contain myself. I realize that I've been holding my breath, and letting it out causes my vision to momentarily go hazy as a rush of adrenaline jolts through me.

I am the voice of Beloved Leader. I am the fist that will smash the Loric, and then the humans. I am fulfilling my purpose.

When I finally look up, Zakos is standing over me. He's stowed the tablet in one of his big lab coat pockets and now holds what looks like a bone saw in one hand. He points to the door of his lab with it.

"Well then," he says. "You heard Beloved Leader. He's pleased with you and looks forward to seeing how I might be able to improve upon your abilities. So . . ." He grins. "Shall we begin?"

PART TWO
VINTARO ÜSHABA

CHAPTER SIX

HUMANS ARE WEAK PIECES OF KRAUL SHIT.

At least the Loric put up a fight.

I was new to war when we invaded Lorien. Practically fresh out of the vats. Raised and trained to annihilate an entire civilization. There was a blaster in my hand as soon as my fingers could curl around the trigger. I was part of the youngest batch to fight in the invasion. We had one directive: to live the words of the Great Book. *Conquer. Consume. Cauterize.* To make Beloved Leader proud.

Hail our Beloved Leader!

We were told that the Loric were a people who upheld peace above all else. But they didn't accept their fates without resistance. The so-called Garde—the Loric with powers—fought hard. I lost half my squad to a girl shooting lasers out of her hands and a man who could control flames—and those weren't even the strangest things I saw that day. But the Garde didn't live up to their purpose. They failed to protect their planet and their people. Of *course* they did. They had no chance against us. Against me. But they died honorably, fighting until their last breaths.

Most of them, that is. I destroyed buildings where Loric cowards were holed up, hiding and praying to their useless leaders. Hoping someone would save them, or that we'd just keep on moving and forget about them.

I'm not sure how long it took for the planet to fall. Everything happened in a blur of bombs, blaster fire and blood. And then it was over. What I do know is that the fight was finished too soon. When we left Lorien, I felt feral, like I could have spent the rest of my years torching that planet's fields, destroying its cities—or better yet, pulling the last of the survivors from their hiding places and slitting their throats in Beloved Leader's name.

Instead, our ships finished off the planet, destroying any hint of life that managed to survive our assault. And Setrákus Ra was pleased.

Forever may he reign!

Afterwards I was sent to Earth. In many ways, it's a combination of Mogadore and Lorien, inhabited by a people who somehow worship peace and war in equal measure. At first, I had high hopes. I thought I was *lucky* to be stationed here. That the humans would make worthy prey.

They don't, for the most part. They submit. They're easy to control. I've found no sport in dominating them, no thrill in the victory of beating them.

Here on this blue-and-green planet I've been working in the shadows for years, long before we made our presence known. I was one of the many sent to seek out the last of the Garde, who proved to be much better at hiding than they were at fighting. Because of this, I've learned all about the humans. I had to, in order to disguise myself and blend into the population when needed. I've faced them head-to-head as I've hunted the remaining Loric, intimidated people of power into joining us and silenced those who saw too much. In all these years, I hardly ever broke much of a sweat. Even when torturing people for intel—like those who unknowingly harbored Garde or tried to alert the humans to our presence—they gave up information so easily. I never *really* got to work them over. Or if I did, it was just for fun, after they'd told me everything I wanted to know already.

I'd thought everything would change when our warships descended over their cities. I guess it did in some places where the humans and the Garde actively fought against us. Not in Chicago where I'm stationed, though: where I led a squad of soldiers in a raid on a Garde safe house not long ago, collecting one of Beloved Leader's most valued targets. Here we allow them to evacuate because Beloved Leader—*Praise his name!*—has plans for this planet, maybe even its people. It is not Lorien. We are not here only to destroy. I do not question his reasoning. I know it to be infallible.

And so I've been on patrol, stamping out small pockets of resistance ever since we showed the humans the true face of their masters. A handful of police officers here, a mob of angry students there. A couple of people desperately trying to get out of the city—who happened to be in the wrong place at the wrong time—just to keep my blood pumping.

What I wouldn't give to be in one of the cities where there's a real fight going on. I can feel it in my muscles and bones. The need to fire my blaster and swing my blades. To hold my enemies up by the throat and look into their eyes before finishing them off. I actually miss the old days, before we made ourselves known. I miss the thrill of the hunt. I miss the sweat of battle and the feeling of someone's pulse when their neck is in my hands. I crave carnage and bloodshed. Anything but the boredom of dealing with humans.

Which is why, when I receive word that my captain wants to see me in the council room of our warship a few days after we stopped over Chicago, I can't help but run my tongue over my teeth and hope that he's giving me a chance to do some real damage. To get back in the fight and end all this waiting around. Not to mention the fact that to be in the presence of the ship's captain is an honor in itself. I'm a vatborn squad leader—someone who has proven his worth in battle—but my orders still come from lower-level trueborn officers.

I take a skimmer up to the warship and wait in the council room with two other vatborn veterans. They've got scars on their faces, and one of them is missing several teeth. They've seen action. They're good soldiers.

We stand shoulder to shoulder as we wait. None of us speculates as to why we've been summoned. At least not out loud. We'll know soon enough, and then we'll carry out our orders. Swiftly. Mercilessly. We'll make our comrades proud.

The captain enters and sizes us up, nodding to himself as if to approve of the selection before him. He says our names. We step forward when called. I am last.

"Vintaro Üshaba." The captain pauses for a second. "Why have you chosen this name for yourself?"

He means my first name. Like all vatborn, my last name is taken from the place I was created.

"'Vintaro' in the old tongue means 'to raze.' That is what drives me."

The captain smirks a little. He seems to like this.

"I've called you here for a special mission," he says, beginning to pace back and forth in front of us. "Ever since it came to the attention of Beloved Leader that some humans have begun to exhibit Garde-like powers, your squads have been on the lookout for such specimens on the ground. He—in his infinite wisdom—would like to examine a few of these tainted humans himself. From now on, we're taking a more proactive approach to collecting such prisoners. I'm told you three are some of the best of my vatborn on this ship."

I grunt, nodding my head in agreement but keeping my eyes on the floor.

"Your jobs are simple. You'll each lead infiltration squads and find these Loric-powered humans. Our recon officer will supply you with leads. You have whatever resources you need available to you. Though, remember: we're to uphold the 'peace' we promised to the cities who don't resist us." He shows off a row of gray teeth. "Keep your mayhem in the dark."

"Sir!" we all say in unison.

He makes for the door, telling us that more information will be given to us soon and that our squads have already been chosen. They are awaiting our orders. He's about to step into the hallway when he stops.

"One more thing," he says, turning back to us. "It's crucial that the subjects are alive when you bring them back." He pauses for a moment, shrugging. "Anyone who stands in your way is expendable. Now, you're dismissed. Get back down to the barracks and begin your preparations. I want you deployed as soon as the recon officer shares her intel with you."

When the door closes behind him, I grin. I can't help it.

Humans with Loric powers. I don't really know how that's possible, and I don't care. I don't *have* to understand. All I know is that I have a mission. I'm back in the fight, and no prey will escape me.

It's time to go hunting.

CHAPTER
SEVEN

A FEW HOURS AFTER THE CAPTAIN IS DONE WITH us, the recon officer sends a list of names and locations to each squad leader's tablet. We divide the targets based on location. I assemble my men. They talk quietly to each other. I don't join in or bother to figure out who is who. It doesn't matter what they call themselves—I'll learn their names when they're telling stories of our victories in the future. When they've proven themselves. All these troopers have to do is follow my orders. And they will. It's what we were born to do, what will win *his* favor.

Hail our Beloved Leader! Forever may he reign!

Our first target is a teenager in a wealthy suburb north of Chicago who has been talking on some form of internet media about how he just made his computer float across the room. There are a few photos pulled from his web profile that I can use to identify him.

We load up a skimmer with weapons, restraints, and syringes full of a sedation compound, just in case these humans are able to use their newfound powers with any sort of skill. Then we head to the boy's home, where the messages originated, according to the IP address. It's far enough away from the city proper that they must think they're safe. That we might overlook them.

Stupid humans. As if our reach didn't span this entire galaxy.

The street is tucked away and quiet, full of big houses on big plots of land. The mansion we're going to is at the end of a cul-de-sac. Secluded. Still, we take out a few power lines before landing, killing the street-lights. Combined with our stealth shielding, it makes for a fairly quiet approach.

We tread silently, the four troops following my lead. There are dim lights moving in the windows of the house. The orange glow of candles and the intense white of flashlights and battery-operated electronic devices. The people inside are likely confused, scared.

Just how we want them.

The front door is large and thick hardwood. It's a narrow entryway for my squad, so I motion to my left, and they follow me around the side of the house, where floor-to-ceiling sliding glass doors look in on a large room. There's a woman standing inside. She's lighting tall candles in some sort of centerpiece on a side table.

Her eyebrows are knit together, forming deep grooves as she moves from one wick to the next.

She sees us a moment before one of my troops throws a huge cement planter through the glass door, shattering it. The woman barely gets a chance to scream before our blasters open fire. She falls quickly, knocking the long candles over as she goes down. They ignite a piece of cloth laid across the table, lighting up the room with warm flames.

A small smile spreads across my lips.

"Find him," I grunt, and my men move.

The house is too big, with too many places to hide. Fortunately, most of the people inside come rushing to us, trying to figure out what broke the glass. Why the woman screamed. There are more humans than I'd anticipated. Maybe friends or family of the owners hiding out in the big house—evacuees from the city who figured they could lay low for a while farther away from the warships. They go down just as easily as the first woman did, most too shocked to react to the sight of our faces. Our weapons. I wonder if their brains even process what's happening before they fall silent.

The humans are like the Loric in some ways. Anatomically, for instance. Their bodies don't disintegrate and disappear, becoming one with the universe. With Beloved Leader. Instead, they lie there. Dead. Bleeding. A reminder to everyone who sees them that they were unable to survive. They rot if left in the open, at a far slower pace than our trueborn—the best parts of our leaders disappear just like the vatborn do. A human's end is disgraceful. There's no honor in a death like that.

The acrid scent of blaster fire fills the air, mixing with the smoke rising from the flames, which continue to spread across the table. I inhale deeply. For the first time in a long while, I feel satisfied. I feel like I'm doing what I was born to do.

The boy we're after makes a brief appearance before turning tail and fleeing. Running up a set of stairs. Coward. We chase after him, leaping over bodies. Our boots stomping on cold, shiny tile floors in the home's entryway. Before we get to the first steps, a shot rings out. A human holding a double-barreled shotgun starts to reload. One of my men is down. It's his own fault— it was his *duty* to be watching our left flank. He's not dead, but injured. His left arm is gone, along with his blaster. Fortunately, he still has a dagger. He draws it from his belt and leaps. His shouts are pure rage as he lands on the human, taking him down. The man's head hits the tile floor with a *crack*. That alone probably killed him. But just in case it didn't, there's the blade. Blood pools on the floor. I leave my trooper to his work and head upstairs with the other three squad members.

We find our target in a bedroom, hiding under a desk. I drag him out and lift him in the air with one hand, holding up the electronic tablet next to his head with the other. It's him.

"Stop, please," he says, beginning to beg. "I'll do anything. We've got money. Is that what you want? If you let me go to my parents' room, there's a—"

I jab a syringe into his arm. He goes limp. I let his body hit the floor and motion to one of my men, who picks up the boy and throws him over his shoulder.

"Move out," I say.

Downstairs, my one-armed soldier stands over a mangled mess that was once a body. He appears to have used the hot barrel of his blaster to cauterize the stump where his arm used to be. Human blood drips from his uniform.

"Piece of shit," he says, kicking the lifeless corpse. "That was my good hand."

We leave the way we came, stepping over the fallen. The flames from the overturned candles have spread to the carpet but are threatening to die out. I spot a large cabinet full of bottles nearby. Alcohol. I pull the whole thing down. Glass shatters. The alcohol spreads across the floor. As we step through the space where the sliding door had been, the liquid ignites behind us with a satisfying *whoosh*.

Technically, the fire will make it harder for anyone to determine what really happened here. But honestly, that wasn't what I had in mind when I pulled down the cabinet. I just wanted to watch the place burn from the sky once we made it back to the skimmer. To see the night lit up in flames.

And just as I expected, the sight of it as we shoot into the sky is glorious.

CHAPTER
EIGHT

WE DROP OFF THE SEDATED CAPTIVE AT THE warship. Our injured man is replaced with a new soldier. He curses under his breath, insisting he can still fight, but I need everyone on my team operating at one hundred percent. Then we head for our next targets. Two more teenagers, this time in Wisconsin, where we don't have any warships located.

Our first stop is outside of Milwaukee. A house, much smaller than the one we'd found in Chicago. It wouldn't take but a few minutes for this one to burn to the ground. It's the middle of the night when we arrive, setting the skimmer down in the street once again. The neighborhood is quiet. The front door is unlocked. We find one adult inside. He's asleep. Never hears us coming. The subject does, though. He cowers in the corner of his bedroom, tears streaming down his face as he shouts that it was all a joke. He was "pranking" his friends. And he thought it would be "cool" if aliens showed up so he could meet them.

At least he gets his wish.

The only time he shows any sort of bravery is when I reach out to grab him. He swings a lamp at me, breaking it against my chest. I am unfazed. He tries to bolt past me but only gets a few steps away before the butt of my blaster slams into the back of his head, causing him to crumple like a puppet whose strings have been snipped. I motion to one of my subordinates, and the target is sedated and loaded up.

The whole encounter takes five minutes tops. We are precise and merciless in our movements.

It's a short flight to our final target of the night. This one in Madison. I fly the skimmer myself, enjoying the feeling of the controls in my hands. My men are silent in their seats behind me for the most part. Eventually, the new squad member speaks up.

"What happened to Görde?"

He must mean the soldier who lost his arm.

"Shotgun," one of the others says. "Human took us by surprise. He lost his arm. Made the guy pay for it, though. Mauled him like a starved piken who'd just spotted a juicy kraul."

"Beloved Leader would be proud."

"Maybe," I say. "Or perhaps he'd condemn the bastard for letting the human injure him in the first place.

Görde should have been paying attention. Watching his flank. *Our* flank."

After that, my troops are quiet.

Our last target has been traced to an apartment complex in what looks like a rundown part of town. She's different from the others we've picked up if only because it wasn't her own stupidity that put her on our radar screen: someone somewhere tipped off an agency our computer experts are monitoring. We land in a small park across the street. What little grass there is crumbles under our feet as we march through the night.

"Eyes open," I mutter as we make our way to the complex. "Lots of people crammed in tight living conditions. We can expect resistance."

The troops grunt behind me. There are a few humans loitering around the parking lot. When they see us, they freeze. It takes them a few seconds to understand who we are. What we are. Then they run. I move my finger to the trigger of my blaster, expecting them to reappear with weapons or more people. To try and keep us from moving in closer to their homes. But they don't return.

Typical. Humans hide themselves away instead of facing their threats head-on.

The apartment building is made up of outdoor hallways, the front door to each unit opening to the open air. We find the one we're looking for on the first floor. The door goes down with one kick. My men flood in.

Out of the corner of my eye I see blinds part in the window next door, but when I turn my head to investigate, they snap closed again.

No one comes out.

There are no adults inside, only the girl we're after. She springs from the couch, long, black hair falling over her face. Dark eyes wide with fear.

"What do you want?" she screams. "Who . . ." But she doesn't finish. She must understand at that point.

I glance at the photo and stats on my tablet. Perfect match. This was easy enough.

"Take her," I say.

My men step forward.

That's when things start to move.

First it's just the shit strewn about the apartment. Soda cans, books, a few dirty dishes. They start to float above the stained carpet. The girl throws her arms out to her sides. Then there's a sudden bass sound, followed by a wave of invisible force. I'm still in the doorway, and the wave hits me like a brick wall, sending me flying backwards onto the concrete outside. The front window of the apartment bursts out, glass landing all around me. My men inside take the brunt of the attack. Several appear to have broken noses. The shabby coffee table and the trash and junk that had been floating around are now all piled up against the walls.

I pick myself up off the ground.

Standing alone with nothing else around her, the girl looks more helpless than before. Long, black hair floats around her head like she's been electrified. Slowly, it starts to fall down. Tears fill her eyes. She pushes her hands out again as my men get to their feet.

But this time nothing happens. No wave of telekinesis. Not even a breeze.

She looks frantic. Her eyes even wider now, mouth open in a silent scream.

"Looks like your power's failing you," one of my troops says with a grin.

She clenches her teeth and curls her hands into fists. The girl has fight, I'll give her that. She's worthier of our time than most humans.

"John Smith is going to hunt you down," she screams. "I've seen him in my head. There are a bunch of us. Hundreds. You'll never get away with this, you fucking monsters!"

I recognize the name she clings to. I know his face—the faces of all the Garde who have challenged us now that they too have come out of the shadows. But she places her faith in false hope.

"John Smith can't save you." I step into the apartment and motion to my squad members. "I told you to take her."

She bites and claws at my men. Eventually she goes

slack. An empty syringe breaks as it's tossed aside.

On the way out, I see more eyes in the windows around us. Peeking out through parted curtains and slits in blinds. The other apartment doors stay locked. No one tries to stop us. Maybe it's the thrill of the hunt or the high of the destruction we've wrought tonight, but knowing that all of these people think they're safe behind doors makes my blood burn. There are explosive throwing disks on my belt, and for a moment I think of letting them loose. Toppling the entire complex.

But that's not my mission. Our mayhem must be kept out of sight. At least until Beloved Leader decides that the humans are of no more use to him.

Praise his name!

Neither of our targets stirs on the flight back to the warship. A few of my men inspect flesh wounds they received during the girl's attack.

"Damn human bitch," one of them mutters. The new addition. "We should wake her up now and show her what pain means. Cut her up just enough to say it happened while we were trying to capture her."

"Touch that girl and I'll turn you to dust myself," I say. "Beloved Leader wants these subjects alive. They're his property. Would you mutilate something that belongs to him?"

The soldier is silent.

"Glory to Beloved Leader," another says.

Again, the skimmer is quiet.

The sun is still down when we get back to the warship. I'm sent up to the labs with our targets, carrying both humans over my shoulders. They're light enough. Fragile.

There are several trueborn Mogadorians in the ward, huddled around various human specimens who've been secured tonight. Like our teenage boy from the Chicago suburb. He's awake now. Gagged. Eyes big with fear as he's poked and prodded by our doctors.

One of the trueborn turns to me as I enter. He wears a long, white lab coat. I've never seen him before, but that's not surprising. I rarely mix with my trueborn superiors.

His eyes light up when he sees the humans bound up behind me. "A new delivery of specimens. How wonderful."

He motions to a few empty metal tables. I place the targets on them.

"This girl definitely has telekinesis," I tell him. "She put up a fight when we cornered her. You may want to keep her sedated."

A grin crosses the trueborn's face as he assesses the human.

"Perfect," he says. "What is your name, soldier?"

"Vintaro Üshaba."

He nods. "You've served Beloved Leader well,

Vintaro. Your work will help us usher in a new age of Mogadorian Progress."

Another trueborn steps up beside him.

"The ship is prepped and ready for the flight to West Virginia."

"Wonderful," he says, starting for the door. He points at the girl as he leaves. "And load her onto the ship. It sounds like she may be strong enough to survive Dr. Zakos's procedures."

CHAPTER NINE

I SLEEP SOUNDLY. SATISFIED.

I wake up hungry for more.

The vatborn barracks are in one of the warship's lower levels, a giant room with a wall full of small sleeping units, just big enough for us to sit up in. They're stacked one on top of the other, from the floor to the ceiling. Inside is a thin foam pad and a wadded-up spare uniform for a pillow. It's all we need. I get only a few hours of sleep before an intercom near my head sounds a shrill buzz. Then a voice from the speaker orders me to report to the council room again.

I leap from my sleeping unit, whizzing past the seven below me, landing in a crouch. Then I'm moving through the ship as fast as I can, up the stairs to the higher decks where the trueborn eat, sleep and work.

How many targets will we get today?

My fingers twitch in anticipation.

Thank Beloved Leader for this glorious opportunity.

I'm the first to arrive in the council room, but the other two squad leaders from yesterday follow quickly. They're as excited as I am to be seeing action.

"Did you bring in all your humans last night?" the vet with the missing teeth asks.

I nod.

"We lost one," the other says, his dark lips grimacing. "A human was trying to fight us off and shot at everything that moved. Including our target."

"Idiot weaklings," the squad leader with the gap-filled grin grunts.

"Had to punish a soldier for it. He'd been toying with the human, playing around. Taunting it. I asked him, 'What would Beloved Leader think if he knew that you'd gotten his prey killed?'"

"What did he say?" I ask.

He shrugs. "I think I've still got some of his ash on my uniform. Ask him yourself."

The other leader burst out in laughter at this, slapping us both on the back. I tense up, gritting my teeth. I probably would have punished my own squad too if they'd done something so stupid. But this is no laughing matter. We're here to complete a mission, to follow *his* orders. Not to joke around. His squad's failure makes us all look bad.

But I don't get a chance to comment on that fact. The

doors open, and our captain walks in. Immediately, we're all at attention. This time the reconnaissance officer trails after him. Her head is tattooed in web-like patterns and shaved except for a long, black braid sprouting from the base of her skull.

"Dr. Zakos was thrilled with the work the three of you did last night," the captain says. His hands are clasped behind his back. "You may not be aware, but the doctor answers to Beloved Leader himself. You've brought honor to your names and to this ship. Well done."

The three of us grunt and nod.

"Today we have a . . . more interesting task for you," the recon officer says.

She taps on a tablet in her hand, and a video plays on one of the screens lining the walls. Humans in front of some sort of waterfall. Talking to the camera. Pointing to a blue stone.

"This video was uploaded to the internet just a few minutes ago," the officer continues. "It's a message for the Loric, but broadcast for anyone in the world to see. It's possible we're the first Mogadorians to pick up on it."

"These appear to be four more 'human Garde,'" the captain says. "I'm sending all three of your squads to collect them. Assuming they're still there. Your secondary directive is to investigate the blue stone on the video. Take a laser cutter. Bring back a sample. If this turns out to somehow be Loralite, Beloved Leader will no doubt be pleased. We'll give you some lead time before we share our discovery with the other captains. I want this to be *our* victory."

"This is a big opportunity," the recon officer says. "Securing the humans and taking control of a possible Loralite deposit will bring glory to you and our ship."

"As you may have guessed based on the context of the message, it's possible the Loric or their allies will be there. You're to exercise extreme caution." One side of the captain's lips curls up a little. "And brutality."

This is better news than I could have expected. Still, something doesn't sit well with me.

"Sir," I say, taking a slight step forward. My eyes are on the ground.

"Speak freely, Vintaro," he says.

"If it's possible the true Loric Garde might be there, should we not . . ."

I trail off, unsure of how to continue. It's not my place to question the judgment or commands of my superiors.

"You're wondering why we don't send half the fleet to stop them," the captain finishes my thought.

I don't respond. It doesn't matter—he keeps talking.

"Our orders are to secure Chicago. As soon as you're en route, I'll put in a priority-one request that I be allowed to send a more substantial amount of troops to the location where this video was shot: Niagara Falls. However . . ." He pauses for a few seconds. "High command has been slow to respond to requests for the last twenty-four hours. As you know, Beloved Leader is very busy at this moment."

Hail our Beloved Leader! Forever may he reign!

The captain crosses his arms over his chest. "Now, if you *do* happen to run across the Loric while on this mission and they try to interfere, it would of course be your duty to take them out. And doing so would bring glory that would follow you for the rest of your life."

My vision goes red. I hardly comprehend the rest of what the officers say. All I can think of is facing the Garde. Of taking out their leader, John Smith. How his arrogant face might look as my hands grip his neck.

And before I know it, the captain and reconnaissance officer are gone.

In half an hour, we've assembled and briefed our squads, loaded our skimmers, and are flying towards Niagara Falls. I assign one of my men to pilot the craft while I triple-check our weapons and supplies, going over possible scenarios in my head. Once we've obtained the humans, should we delay our return? Wait around for the Loric to show? How long? And what if we're not the first Mogadorians there. It sounded as though anyone could have picked up on this broadcast. If other squads from other warships show up trying to claim our targets, or take credit for killing the Garde . . .

How far do we go to ensure that victory belongs to our warship?

Or to my squad, for that matter?

"Vintaro," one of my men says. It's the newest member. I stare back at him. His nose is bruised and smashed from last night's run-in. He tentatively adds, "Sir."

"Speak," I say.

"We will make Beloved Leader proud," he says. "We'll bring honor to our warship, and the captain will know that it was Vintaro Üshaba who led us to victory."

He hits his chest with his fist and grunts. I return the gesture. My heart drums under my knuckles. All my life, this is what I've wanted. What any Mogadorian wants. To excel, and speed our progress across planets and stars.

"Four targets," I remind him, and the others. "You've seen their faces. Lock them down, then find the possible Loralite deposit. Put a hole in the head of anyone else who dares stand against us."

"We're just a few minutes away," the pilot calls back. "We should— *Shit*."

"What?" I ask.

"One of the other skimmers just hit their afterburners."

I watch as our allies shoot ahead. Trying to be the

first ones there, I'm sure. To claim the humans.

"Catch them!" I bark, and I can feel our acceleration in my guts.

I open up a comm line, reporting back to the warship.

"This is Vintaro Üshaba. We have no visual on the targets yet, but we're approaching the—"

"Look!" the pilot shouts, bringing up a visual onscreen.

The other skimmer is hovering above the side of a roaring river. Troops jump to the ground. There are humanoid figures in front of them, but we're too far away to make out what's happening clearly. As we get closer, though, it's obvious these humans are fighting back. The other squad members are firing at them.

"Bastards!" I slam my fist against the back of one of the seats in our ship. "They'll kill our targets! Get us—"

There's a flash of some kind of red energy across our ship's windshield.

"What the—," the pilot starts, but the sound of the explosion and our hull ripping apart drowns out the rest of his words.

CHAPTER
TEN

I'M BLOWN BACKWARDS, INTO THE REAR OF THE ship. Everything is rushing air, fire and ash around me.

Our pilot's dead. So is the soldier who was sitting in the copilot's seat. It's difficult to see what happened exactly, with the thick, black smoke filling the cabin, but it's obvious they're gone.

And that we're falling.

I lunge forward and hit a few buttons, enacting some emergency protocols. For what it's worth. The skimmer rotates as it drops, but I manage to get us evened out enough so that when we hit the ground, crashing into a wooded area near the falls, we're right side up.

It's only once we've stopped skidding and the smoke starts to clear that I can assess the damage.

Getting to my feet, I realize my left wrist is broken. A setback, but one I can overcome. I only need one hand to fire a blaster. I could kill without either arm if I needed to.

"Report," I shout, the sound of the nearby waterfalls nearly drowning out my voice.

"Sir," someone says.

From the back of the skimmer, the newbie emerges, coughing. There's a cut on his forehead, but otherwise he looks fine.

"Is it just you?" I ask.

He nods.

I glance at the controls. Our communications systems are shot. Somewhere near us, I can hear blasters firing.

I gesture to the hole in the cockpit, and then we're climbing out.

"What's your name, soldier?" I ask my only remaining squad member.

"Drak Üshaba," he says.

This takes me a bit off guard.

"We come from the same vat," I say.

He nods, his eyes searching the trees around us as we get our bearings. A good soldier.

"But I think I was born quite a few broods after you," he says.

Our skimmer crashed not far from the falls. I spot two piles of ash beside metal railings set up to keep people from tumbling into the water. The two remaining skimmers circle overhead, firing at targets I don't immediately see. A few more of our troops from one of the other skimmers are hunkered down behind large rocks, shooting from cover.

"Drak Üshaba," I say, taking out my blaster with my good hand. "We have a mission to complete. Let's make our vat, our warship—our Beloved Leader—proud."

He grunts in reply. We rush into the fight.

I spot two targets: a blond-haired girl hiding in the trees a hundred yards away from us, and a stout, brown-haired kid trying his best not to fall off the rocks and into the water while waving his hands around. Possibly using Loric powers.

Drak sees them too.

"Take the girl," I say, and he disappears into the trees. "Nonlethal shots. We'll ride back in one of the other skimmers. They'll have room for us."

I hustle to the side of the railing above the brown-haired kid and aim carefully. The humans are putting up a hell of a fight—much more than I'd expected. But this is far from over. We can still capture them. I can still achieve victory.

I fire. My aim is good. I hit the boy twice in his rear. Just enough to take him down without killing him. He falls, crying out. I think. The sound of the water is so loud.

It's probably why I don't realize the person sneaking

up on me until it's too late.

"Oy!" a voice shouts.

I turn. There's a human boy standing ten yards away. His hair is an odd color. Unnatural. Almost white and sticking up on the top of his head.

I turn my blaster on him. He grins and shakes his finger back and forth. Something flies over his head. A streak of red, pulsing energy. The boy clenches his fingers into a fist and swings it down. Must be using telekinesis. Before I can leap out of the way, the red thing hits the ground behind me just on the other side of the railing. Exploding. Sending me flying through the air along with a shower of smoke, rock, debris.

I hit the ground and roll, finally coming to a stop with my back against something hard. My head smacks against whatever it is, blurring my vision. There's a sudden pain in my chest.

"Thanks," the boy calls over his shoulder, but all I can make out is a dark-haired figure, much too small to be a Mogadorian, disappearing into the trees. The boy turns his attention to me. "Man, I've got to work on my aim. I almost got poor Bertrand caught up in all that. Ran's bomb was supposed to actually *hit* you. Still, I bet that bloody hurts, doesn't it?"

I look down. There's a length of metal rod sticking out of the right side of my chest. Part of the railing I'd been standing by. One of my lungs is destroyed, certainly. I must be in shock, though, because I don't feel much of anything other than a cold tingling in my fingers.

I look around. Where is Drak? Where are the other troops?

"Damned humans . . . ," I spit out. "Weaklings . . ."

The boy smiles in a way that sets my blood on fire. "Seems to me like these 'human weaklings' are taking out all your men. You shoulda brought more aliens with you." He lets out an exaggerated sigh. "Guess I shoulda guessed you ugly bastards would pick up on our message. Maybe the Loric aren't far behind." His face lights up. "Wait, is this some kinda test or something? Because I think we're acing it, mate."

My blaster lies on the ground between us. The boy opens his palm, and the blaster flies into his hand. Over his shoulder, I see one of the other skimmers going down. There's something hazy about it. Like it's been covered in some kind of cloud or swarm. It crashes into the water.

I try to stand. That's when I realize the rod has gone completely through me. The back end is embedded in a tree. I twist my body in an attempt to dislodge it. That's when the pain comes.

I yell. The boy holds the blaster up, aiming at my face. Based on the angle, it looks like he'll miss. But if I stay here, he'll hit me eventually.

I won't let this *child* end me. I have only one option. Maybe I'll even survive. Maybe the wounds aren't that bad.

With every ounce of strength in my body, I lunge forward. There's a sickening, wet sound as I slide off the metal. I feel a blast of heat shoot by my ear, searing the air. The kid missed.

But he's not really my concern now.

"Oof," the kid says. "Looks like you're already dead."

I crawl forward on my knees. Dark liquid gushes from the hole in my chest, covering me. Coating the leaves. I look down at my hands. They're turning gray. A bomb of exclamations goes off in my head.

You've failed! Kill them! It hurts! Don't let this human *beat you!*

And then comes the loudest of all as my fingers start to break apart. Disintegrating.

Hail our Beloved Leader! Forever may he . . .

PART THREE
REXICUS SATURNUS

CHAPTER
ELEVEN

STANDING IN THE CENTER OF THE GREAT GLASS window on our warship's bridge, I have an unobstructed view of the invasion of Earth.

It's surprisingly quiet, as if the humans have already accepted their fate, choosing compliance over opposition. This is good for us. It means that when we actually come down out of our warships and take the planet, we won't be met with much resistance.

And yet, despite knowing this, I can't shake an uncomfortable feeling in the back of my mind. Something almost like guilt.

I think I might actually feel sorry for the humans.

They're fighting back in other places like New York and Beijing, of course, where my people are doing what the Great Book says is our purpose in life. In those cities, our ground troops are seeing action, flexing their trigger fingers, bathing in the blood of those who stand against them while our pilots rain fire from above, destroying any who would oppose Mogadorian Progress. Domination through combat. No one can hope to stop us. The Garde—or the humans who've somehow gained powers in the last few days—don't stand a chance against the vastness of our armies. And neither do their allies. Be they human, Loric or something else. Eventually, all of them will be nothing but dust. Forgotten.

Just like the rest of us. Except Setrákus Ra, I guess. He'll rule our people forever if the Great Book is to be believed. Though, he *did* write that himself, so we only have his word to go off of. Fortunately for him we grow up reading his manifesto, so we never even think to ask if it's true.

Most of us.

With all its talk of war and honor, the Great Book left out how much waiting can be involved in an invasion. In Toronto, where I'm stationed, though, things are fairly calm aside from a few of our patrols keeping watch over the streets below. I'm not in the thick of it. I guess I should consider myself lucky for being assigned to such a quiet location, especially after everything I went through in Dulce and Plum Island. I was given a slight promotion after "capturing" the traitor Adamus. No one knew I'd actually helped him escape, obviously, because I'm still alive. When he broke out and that Plum Island facility was closed down, I had some options as to where to go next. I asked to be reassigned to a warship. Something about being on Earth had started to make me feel uncomfortable. Or maybe *too* comfortable. I liked it too much.

I needed to clear my head and try to make sense of everything that had happened.

Fortunately, as a trueborn, I'd done a lot of training on how warships are run, so after a few crash course refreshers, I ended up as a navigator. The recycled air of the warship has taken some getting used to, but all in all, it could be worse. At least I've got a good view. From the windows looking out from the front of the ship's bridge, I see mostly an expansive lake that seems to go on forever, disappearing in the horizon. It's nice. I've even rotated the warship to get a better view. Just slightly, so none of the other trueborn milling around the bridge notice.

It's probably more chaotic in the city itself, where evacuations continue. We allow the people of Earth to run, knowing that eventually—inevitably—they'll bow before us. The fewer casualties we cause among their population, the more humans we'll have working for us once we take over completely. They'll gather resources for us, build shrines in our honor and palaces for our war heroes. Or they'll die. That's the Mogadorian way. Or that's *Beloved Leader's* way, and therefore ours.

I wonder where those who are running are going, where they think they can escape to. I've crossed the country below, hitchhiking and hopping trains. I've spent time among the humans. They're a resilient species, if a bit lacking in technological advances. But they're severely outgunned. They must realize that after the destruction of New York, which, from what I understand, is—*was*—one of their most splendid cities.

I almost want to help them.

I shake my head, trying to get rid of such thoughts. I focus on the water, letting my fingers connect the dots of stars reflected off of the lake below. Trying to think of nothing at all.

Eventually there's a hiss of pressurized air behind me as one of the doors to the bridge slides open.

"I want status updates from every department," a voice barks, snapping me back to reality.

I recognize immediately that it's Captain Jax-Har and turn, posture rigid at attention. Medals decorate both sides of his uniform. A sheen of sweat on his head causes his complicated skull tattoos to shine under the lights. Two other trueborn follow after him: our communications officer, Denbar, and Mirra, one of the few trueborn females in our military. All their faces are blank but look somehow paler than usual. I wonder where they're coming from within the ship and what they've been talking about. Even though I'm a trueborn officer, I still lack top-level security clearance. Plenty of meetings take place without me being present. The fact that I'm kept in the dark is the captain's decision. I understand his hesitation to include me since I've only recently been assigned to his crew. Still, I can't shake the feeling that when Jax-Har looks at me, he knows the truth, somehow, someway. That I helped Adamus. That I killed our own people. That I betrayed Beloved Leader.

I remind myself for the thousandth time that if anyone really *did* think this, I'd be executed without hesitation. But the paranoia remains. Maybe because I myself have trouble understanding my past actions and why I helped Adamus when I could have easily left him locked up on Plum Island. Why I betrayed my people just to help an enemy (even if at moments during our time together, we felt like something else, like friends).

Or maybe it's just that spending so many days with Adamus awakened something in me. A series of questions I consciously try not to ask, a secret I keep locked away in the darkest part of my head that surfaces every night when I'm alone, half asleep, guard down.

Because of Adamus, I have doubts about the Mogadorian cause.

"Officer Saturnus!" The captain steps over to me. I bow slightly in acknowledgment, and then we stand facing one another at the center of the window. I'm bigger and stronger than most Mogadorian troops—even many trueborn—but Jax-Har towers over me.

"How long would it take us to reach Beloved Leader's base of operations?" he asks.

"One moment, sir," I say, walking back to my terminal, where I tap on a keyboard and bring various figures up on the screen. "We could be at the West Virginia base in approximately two hours."

Jax-Har nods but doesn't say anything. He just stands there, looking over my shoulder at nothing. A few seconds pass in silence.

"Shall I . . . plot a course?" I ask.

His eyes snap into focus as he scowls at me.

"Did I give you that order?" he spits.

"No, sir," I mutter.

He turns away, shouting at Denbar, who stands in front of a large computer terminal on the other side of the bridge.

"Get me an open channel broadcasting to the *Anubis* and the base in West Virginia."

Denbar does so. When Jax-Har speaks again, his voice booms, filling the room.

"This is Captain Jax-Har of Warship *Delta*, currently stationed above the Canadian city of Toronto." He pauses momentarily, brow furrowing for a few seconds before continuing. "We are awaiting orders and requesting guidance from Beloved Leader so that we may forge ahead and ensure Mogadorian Progress. Please advise."

Something about this is odd. I listen to his words and try to piece together why he seems so flustered— almost *nervous*. He's been doing stuff like this all day, sometimes asking about the whereabouts of a supposed Loric ship, other times contacting West Virginia just to "check in." Then I realize why this seems so odd: he's actually *asking* for commands. Either he's gotten bored waiting for action and is succumbing to some sort of bloodlust or . . .

Has something happened in the fleet that I don't know about? When was the last time we *did* get an order from Setrákus Ra?

What is Beloved Leader doing now?

The captain motions to Denbar, who cuts off the line.

"Alert me immediately if we receive a response," Jax-Har says. He takes a few steps towards his captain's chair before stopping, looking at me over his shoulder. "And, Officer Saturnus, if I find you away from your terminal during one of your shifts again, I'll have your feet nailed to the floor in front of it. We're not here on a sightseeing mission."

"Sir," I say again.

"Captain!" Denbar rushes to him, holding out an electronic pad. "We've received a message from our people in the American capital. Level-one clearance."

In a few long steps, Jax-Har crosses the bridge, swiping the tablet from his subordinate's hand. His face flashes with concern for only a moment.

"Come with me," he says, motioning to the officer.

Mirra, who's been busying herself reading ship diagnostics, steps forward.

"Captain, shall I—," she starts.

"Stay here," Jax-Har says. "Make sure the rest of the crew is in order."

Denbar winks at her. Jax-Har glances at me again, and then the two men are gone, out the doorway.

Frustration flashes on Mirra's face. There's a ruthlessness and cunning behind her eyes that I've only ever seen from our most feared warriors, which is kind of terrifying since, of everyone on the ship, she's perhaps the only person I'm friendly with. We both grew up in Ashwood Estates. She's several years older than me, though, so I don't have much memory of her. Now, she's Jax-Har's second-in-command. Or she's supposed to be, at least. I get the feeling that Denbar's trying to take that position away from her, which is probably why they always seem to be at each other's throats.

I start over to her, hoping that whatever annoyance she's feeling will make her more willing to tell me what's got the captain so upset. Then I remember Jax-Har's words and pause, standing awkwardly in the middle of the bridge for a moment before taking a few steps back.

Mirra notices, and stomps over to me.

"Is there a problem, Saturnus?" she asks.

"You know, you can call me Rexicus," I say. "Actually, back home and at the Dulce base, most people called me Rex."

"I'm aware."

Perhaps "friendly" isn't the best way to describe my relationship with Mirra. It might be more accurate to say that I sometimes try to strike up conversations with her about growing up on Earth, and so far she hasn't shoved a sword through my stomach.

I try to soften her up.

"Did you see the moon reflecting off the water?" I ask. "It reminds me of that park a couple miles south of Ashwood. Did you ever go there?"

"Is this why it looked like you were about to defy the captain's order and step away from your station just now? To reminisce about an orbiting satellite as seen in a man-made pond? You're not a child, Saturnus."

She knows about the pond.

"So you *have* been to the park."

Mirra turns her back to me and starts to walk away.

"Wait," I say, a little too loudly. I glance around, but the handful of other trueborn officers around are minding their own business. Or at least pretending to.

She faces me again, the brow over one dark eye raised in annoyance.

"Are things . . . okay?" I ask as quietly as I can. "Normal? With the ship and everything that's going on? With the invasion? Things just seem . . . tense."

"What do you mean?" Her face may as well be made of stone. She betrays no hint of emotion. "Everything is going exactly as Beloved Leader expected it would. His word is prophecy and truth."

This is one of the problems with Mogadorians. Or at least with those who have no doubts about Setrákus Ra's plans.

So, like, 99.99 percent of my people.

"Well, it's just that I've never seen a captain ask for orders before. We wait until we're told what to do. That's our job. And I've been on the bridge for most of the last twelve hours. We haven't received any transmissions from the *Anubis* or West Virginia."

"High command is no doubt busy with more important things at this time."

"When *was* the last time we got orders?" I ask.

She opens her mouth to speak, but no words come out. Instead, she just looks at me for a few seconds, searching my face.

"You'd have to ask Denbar," she says flatly.

I try to reframe my question.

"What would *you* do if you were captain?"

"I wouldn't bother Beloved Leader like some pestering—," she says, and then stops. Her eyes narrow.

I grin. I've caught her.

"Officer Saturnus," she says, loud enough for everyone else on the bridge to hear. "Your shift must be over soon if you've been on the bridge for twelve hours. I'm sure you're exhausted. Before you leave, though, I want you to run possible flight patterns to every second-tier city target in North America. Double-check your numbers. Triple-check them. We need to be prepared for when our next orders come in."

She smirks and then turns away and heads back to the main controls.

Great.

I glance around, but no one makes eye contact with me. Most of the people on the bridge were born on Mogadore, or on ships. There's a noticeable brutality to them, an economy in their speech. They say only what they have to, when spoken to. They don't pretend to care about camaraderie. And above all else, they obey, without question.

But I grew up on Earth. So did Mirra. Even if we were in Mogadorian homes, they were designed to look like human communities. We sneaked human entertainment and learned how the species functioned so that we could better understand them—could *conquer* them more easily. Some of that must have rubbed off on us. I wouldn't say that it's been difficult adjusting to life on a ship, surrounded by a bunch of uptight Mogs. But it's different. Especially after spending so much time on Earth. Sometimes I miss just talking. Or having someone to talk to.

Underneath that hard exterior, maybe Mirra feels the same way.

One thing's for certain: it's obvious something's got our captain spooked. Still, I have to be careful. Questions are a dangerous thing up here. Ask the wrong one and you're dead.

Or you're labeled a traitor.

I start looking at the routes Mirra mentioned. There are so many cities left. A whole world out there to conquer. And yet, I can't shake the idea that despite what the Great Book says—that progress can only be made through war, death and bloodshed—there might be another way. After living so much of my life among the humans, I can't help but hope that it doesn't become another Lorien. Or another Mogadore, a place I've never even been.

I wish my people were maybe a little more like the humans. A culture that has war, yes, but also respects peace and tranquillity. Bloodshed is ever present but not the entire focus of their lives for the most part. There's room for the innocent and pacifistic to survive.

Hell, in that sense, I wouldn't mind us being more like the Loric.

I steal one last glance at the quiet, still water outside.

I wonder what Adamus is doing now.

Is he even alive?

CHAPTER
TWELVE

AFTER COMPILING ALL THE DATA MIRRA ASKED for, I completely crash in my room. It's late morning when an alarm sounds. I wake up in a fog, disoriented, trying to figure out why the speakers in the ceiling are blaring an alarm, when someone comes on the intercom telling me to report to the council room. I move as quickly as I can, wondering what's happened—if we're finally going to stop pretending that we're here for anything but total domination. My blood pumps faster, and I can't help but bare my teeth.

Mogadorian programming: One whiff of battle and I'm firing on all cylinders.

But there's another side to the feeling. A worry I can't place. Or, rather, that I *can* place but don't want to think about.

If we're moving into full-blown war, how many innocent lives will we take? How many of those places

I'd passed through and people I'd met on my way from Dulce to Plum Island will be annihilated?

I splash some cold water on my face and try to shake the doubt away. Since I'm a trueborn, I have my own sleeping quarters and bathroom, though it's nothing special. I can touch almost every wall when I stand in the middle of the floor. It's still better than the group barracks the vatborn are stuck with. At least here I get a little privacy, some time alone with my thoughts. It's a blessing and a curse.

I throw on my uniform and hustle down the hallway, the footfalls of my boots echoing off the metal floor. When I get to the council room, most of the other officers are already there, sitting around the big, oval table. I take a seat beside Mirra.

"Good morning," I murmur.

She doesn't look up from the readouts on a tablet in her lap, but nods and makes a *hmmmm* noise. It's not exactly a "Good morning to you too," but it could almost be mistaken for a greeting. I'll take it.

I tap on the table in front of me, and the glossy black surface folds open, revealing a small computer terminal. I log in, bringing up our current position and the ship's diagnostics. We've barely shifted an inch since I went to sleep last night. I guess you don't become the most feared species in the universe without some damned fine engineering.

Eventually almost a dozen officers take seats at the table. When Captain Jax-Har enters, we all stand. He waves a hand, and in unison we sit, a well-oiled machine. He stops at one end of the room, staring at the shiny tabletop, maybe at his own reflection in it. The space around his eyes is always dark, but it looks like he hasn't slept all night.

Something is definitely going on.

Finally, Jax-Har begins to talk.

"Earlier this morning a group of humans who we believe to be among those with newly developed Loric powers posted a video on the internet. It showed these Earth scum arriving at a landmark known as Niagara Falls, just on the other side of the body of Lake Ontario, which we're currently stationed above. The video also shows a blue stone that we believe to be Loralite, a mineral with astounding properties. A mineral that's very *valuable* to Beloved Leader. Somehow, the Loric are using this to transport their new troops across the planet."

Beside him, Denbar nods. He's obviously in the loop on this.

"Digital scouts on the warship stationed over Chicago were the first to pick up on this video." Jax-Har pauses long enough to glare at the officer in charge of our own research and reconnaissance efforts. "In response, they sent three skimmers to investigate."

There's grumbling around the table about how it should have been *our* troops who picked up these targets. Since the first reports of so-called "Human Garde," Beloved Leader has made it known that capturing the anomalies are a high priority.

I'm pretty sure I can hear Mirra grinding her teeth beside me. I bet she would've loved to have captured those targets herself.

The captain continues.

"The skimmers reported in shortly before reaching Niagara Falls and haven't been heard from since. Due to the Chicago captain's *insistence* that the site was their find, we only learned of their operation within the last hour. I sent our own forces to investigate. They found the wreckage from our ships but no one alive—Mogadorian *or* human. There was evidence that the troops sent from Chicago were killed."

From what I understand, these powered humans are largely untrained and not so much threats as nuisances and subjects to be studied. Several specimens have been picked up across the planet with little to no resistance. It seems they're just as confused by what's happened to them as we are.

So who took down these skimmers? The *real* Garde? Their allies? Human resistance forces?

"There have been other recent . . . *setbacks*." Jax-Har starts to walk around the table, letting his heavy boots thud against the floor. "What I'm about to discuss is top-clearance information that doesn't leave this room. As trueborn Mogadorians of honor, I am trusting your silence. Know that betraying this trust will be considered treason, and if I so much as suspect you of breathing a word of this to anyone else, or even to each other, I'll put my own blade through your heart. Understood?"

He looks around the table. We all nod. Even without the warning, I doubt anyone would mention anything from one of these meetings to anyone else.

The captain sighs.

"I'm aware that some of you heard radio chatter about our troops in Mexico calling in reinforcements and losing a Loric ship. You saw the Loric scum soil our Beloved Leader's appearance in New York—something they paid dearly for. And we've recently been informed that one of our enclaves outside of Washington DC has been taken from us."

Mirra goes rigid at this, inhaling a sharp breath. I have to admit, the wind is taken out of me for a moment as well. He has to mean Ashwood. My father was the only family I ever had, and he died years ago, before the first attack on the estates. But Mirra . . . I don't know who she still has there. Based on her reaction, I'm guessing she had no idea this happened.

"Our Beloved Leader is no doubt setting all of his

energies to ensuring Mogadorian Progress. As such, we wait in the sky for his directives. However, just across the water from us is a possible Loralite stone, something of untold strategic value to our enemies."

He stops at the end of the table opposite to where he started, standing at attention himself.

"As such, I've made a decision as captain of this warship to leave our post. We will take this enemy resource for ourselves, and slay any bastard who dares approach it. If the Loric *are* using it as a transportation hub, our cannons will vaporize anyone who appears. I have no doubt in my mind that when Beloved Leader hears of our initiative and boldness, he will reward our quick thinking."

The captain is silent then, letting his eyes drift among his subordinates. He doesn't ask if we agree with him—even if we didn't, there's no room on the ship for any sort of vote. This is not what the humans would call a democracy. We swear our allegiance to the highest-ranked Mogadorian and follow his or her orders without question.

Still, I know what everyone else must be wondering. Is Jax-Har going against the wishes of our Beloved Leader? What does that mean for us? If Beloved Leader *doesn't* agree with what he's doing, does that make all of us traitors?

And if he's making this call on his own, what are the

rest of the captains throughout the planet doing? And where the hell is Setrákus Ra?

It takes a few moments to work through all of these questions in my head—to understand the real breadth of what Jax-Har is suggesting.

"Officer Saturnus," he says, pointing at me. I'm jolted back into focus.

"Sir," I say.

"Set a course for Niagara Falls. I've sent word of my intentions to the command base in West Virginia. If I don't hear back from them in an hour, I'll take their silence as approval." He turns to Denbar. "Prepare to patch me into an open channel. The other captains will be wondering what we're doing, and I don't want to give them reason to believe we've been hijacked or something."

"We'll crush the Loric and anyone who aids them," Denbar says, slamming his fist on the table. The others around me at the table join in, until the room is full of thunder.

"Strength is sacred," Jax-Har says, quoting the Great Book. "Now, get to work."

CHAPTER
THIRTEEN

IT'S A STRAIGHT SHOT ACROSS THE WATER TO Niagara Falls. There's nothing for us to avoid, no military bases to steer clear of or other warships in the way. We just have to move. A child could probably plot a course there. And so once I'm finished I stand around my terminal, pretending to look busy. The captain isn't on the bridge. I wonder how the other Mogadorian leaders have reacted to the fact that we're leaving our post.

Jax-Har is acting on his own, against a direct order from Beloved Leader. For the first time since I was folded back into the Mogadorian army, I feel like others around me might be questioning the chain of command, even if it's in a small way. It's at once thrilling and terrifying. And of course, the bridge is silent. What could the other officers be thinking?

So many frustrating questions float through my

mind that I don't notice Mirra until she's standing beside me.

"Follow me," she says, and is walking away before I have the chance to ask what this is about.

I follow, though. I have to. Not just because she's a senior officer, but because maybe I'll actually get some answers if I talk to her.

As we approach the door to the bridge, Denbar enters. He looks surprised to see us.

"Where are you two going?" he asks.

Mirra ignores him, walking forward. Denbar keeps talking.

"The captain specifically requested that Officer Saturnus plot—"

"You've completed your assignment, correct?" Mirra asks me, turning around, putting Denbar between us.

I nod. "That's right."

She tilts her head back and looks down at Denbar over the tip of her nose. "Scans detected an anomaly in our geo-mapping systems earlier this morning. It's probably nothing, but I'm having Officer Saturnus double-check the hardware to ensure everything is in working order before our mission. If you have a problem with that, I suggest you take it up with the captain. Or I can leave Saturnus here, and if something goes wrong later, you can explain to the captain why our systems failed yourself."

Even I can't tell if this is true or not. I start trying to recall everything I know about geo-mapping, just in case.

Denbar looks taken aback for a few seconds, but that quickly morphs into something else. His eyes narrow, and a glint of teeth show through his lips. He glances at a nearby monitor.

"We'll be heading out soon."

"I'm aware," she says, turning on her heel and leaving.

Denbar's glare then falls on me. I shrug, and he walks off in a huff.

I meet Mirra in the hallway.

"That egotistical little kraul," she mutters under her breath as she continues walking, not looking at me. "Still can't handle that high command appointed *me* as his superior."

She moves so fast that I have to double my normal pace to keep up. Eventually she takes a sharp right, heading into an elevator that leads down to the belly of the ship where many of our vital systems are housed. As a top-ranking officer on the warship, she's one of the few people with access to such a place.

As soon as the doors close, she turns to me.

"Your questions yesterday," she says. "Where did they come from?"

"What do you mean?" I ask.

Her lips purse a bit. "You don't seem to trust the way things are going right now. You were wondering why the captain was asking for orders. Questioning his judgment, perhaps."

This is quite an accusation, but she doesn't seem angry, which makes me think this might be her attempt at a joke.

"It just seemed odd."

"Agreed," Mirra says. She starts to say something a few times before she actually speaks again. "I'm talking to you in confidence, Rexicus. Because I think some big things are about to happen, and if that's true, I'll need someone like you to . . ." She searches for the right words.

"Be a friend," I offer.

She called me Rexicus.

"To navigate the ship," she clarifies.

We'll work our way to "Rex."

The elevator stops, the door opening to a pristine, empty hallway leading to the systems core. But Mirra doesn't get out. Instead, she leans on the entryway, blocking the door from closing. There's something different in her eyes. Excitement, confusion and just a hint of fear.

"Things haven't been going well lately," she says. "You heard what the captain said."

"Ashwood."

She sighs a little, nodding. "My family stuck around after the first attack by the traitor Adamus. I'm not sure how long they stayed. I'm not sure . . ."

She trails off, and I'm stuck thinking how strange it is to hear Adamus's name coming out of her mouth. Sometimes I forget that others don't know him like I do. Or like I did. Even though I'm not sure how *I'm* supposed to think of him. It's a reminder that though Mirra is opening up to me for the first time, this isn't the same as Adamus and me talking as we hopped trains. This is business. In fact, she and Adamus would probably try to kill each other if they were ever in the same room.

"There have been more defeats and setbacks," she continues, shaking off any thoughts of her family. "And rumors. It's said that Beloved Leader himself was at the attack in Mexico. The one where reinforcements had to be called in."

My mouth drops open. If Beloved Leader was on the battlefield, the Loric or humans or *whoever* fought against him shouldn't have stood a chance. At least, not according to The Great Book. He is the personification of invincibility. Any time he's retreated from battle or appeared to be overpowered—like at the United Nations—it's only been a feint, a fake out to draw our enemies into the open.

Or that's supposed to be the case. That's what we're told.

The spark of doubt in the back of my mind flames up again.

"So what does that mean?" I ask, choosing my words carefully. I'm not sure where she's going with this.

"It means that since that attack, we haven't received any direct orders from Beloved Leader. Everyone's supposed to be holding their ground, but our enemies are moving. These human Garde are popping up all over the place. Their forces are growing."

"So you're on board with the captain's plan?"

"Officer . . . ," she says, then shakes her head. "*Rexicus*. Last night we had a meeting with several other warship captains. Everyone's nervous, or angry, or both. No one said anything in the open, but . . . people are starting to imagine the unthinkable. The captain from Moscow actually asked who would be next in line if someone needed to take Beloved Leader's place 'temporarily.' It's madness. And Denbar's always there whispering in Jax-Har's ear, telling him all sorts of lies probably."

My head swims, trying to make sense of everything. To make sense of why she's telling me all this. Could it be that she too is questioning the Mogadorian way?

And if so, is that why she's come to me? Because she's figured out that I'm another doubter? If things are about to shift, perhaps *we* could be that change.

"You . . . ," I start. I check to make sure the hallway

is empty before lowering my voice to the faintest whisper. "You think Beloved Leader might be dead or something?"

Her palm meets my face so quickly that I don't even realize I've been slapped for a few seconds. Then the stinging pain rises in my cheek.

"What the—"

"Don't speak such blasphemy," she says. Her eyes are big and wild now. "Beloved Leader is immortal. You *know* that. He'll lead the Mogadorian Progress long after you and I are gone. I thought you were a believer, Rexicus Saturnus, not a heretic. Not a *traitor.*"

I raise my hands up in front of my chest. I may not be sure of what's going on, but I do know the last thing I want is for Mirra to be pissed at me right now.

"No, no," I say, trying to keep my hands from shaking. "I was just making sure *you* weren't one."

"Don't you see?" Mirra asks. "The Great Book tells us we must follow Beloved Leader's plans without question and without fail. If his last command was that we stay above Toronto, moving this ship anywhere else is an act of treason."

Everything clicks together suddenly. Mirra isn't telling me all this because she thinks Beloved Leader may not be everything he claims. She's telling me this because she truly believes that by moving from Toronto, our captain is betraying the entire army.

"We should be over the city, ready to fire on it at a moment's notice," she says. "Ready to burn it to the ground for the glory of Mogadorian Progress. Don't you see, Rexicus? This is a test! Beloved Leader is trying to find those who are truly worthy of his favor. Like me. Like *you* too if you follow me. Jax-Har has lost sight of the path. He must be stopped. We can't allow him to doom us all. We'll show Beloved Leader that *we're* his strongest warriors—disciples who follow him without hesitation—and then he'll reward us by letting us bathe in the blood of the humans and Loric."

She takes a deep breath. "Are you with me?" she asks.

I don't know what to say. Despite all the doubt I've had about Mogadorian Progress and the way we've invaded Earth, crossed an entire solar system to hunt down a few remaining Loric, I never expected to be in a position like this. On one hand, I see where Jax-Har is coming from. Maybe Beloved Leader is dead, or injured. Captured, even. Maybe he's not fit to give commands. And if so, what does that mean for the Mogadorian fleet?

And then there's Mirra. Is her vision of the future really better than Jax-Har's? Or any other commander's in our army?

I want a third choice. Or I want to know what to do. Or I want to go back to the time before I met Adamus, when I was like Mirra, so unquestioningly devoted to Beloved Leader that I was blind to everything else.

But I can't tell her any of that. I'm not sure she'd let me walk away if I said no.

So I nod.

"What do you propose we do?" I ask. "You're talking about leading a mutiny against Captain Jax-Har."

"We don't have enough time to act before going to Niagara Falls," she says. "But we must be swift. There are other officers on my side. True believers. We aren't alone."

"Who?" I ask. It's hard to fathom the idea that some sort of rebellion has been happening under my nose. More confusing is the very idea that other people on the ship—officers no less—are even entertaining the idea of a coup.

What's becoming of my people?

"I'll make my move during the officers' meeting tonight," she continues. "You shouldn't have to do anything, but if things go bad, be ready to back me up and take down any who oppose us. When it's done, get us back to Toronto as quickly as you can."

She leans in to me. "We're in the right here. We're doing this for Beloved Leader." She actually smiles. "He's going to be so proud of us. He'll give us entire states to cull and reap."

She steps back into the elevator, letting the door finally close.

"Everything will work out according to his plans, Rexicus. You'll see. Remember, strength is sacred."

It's the second time today I've heard the quote, though I can't tell if she's using it to mock Jax-Har or out of complete faith in the Great Book. Probably a mixture of both.

The words repeat in my head. Not in her voice, but in Adamus's. It feels like a long time ago that he said the same thing to me, when I was battered and broken, barely able to stand as we walked away from Dulce and into the desert. At the time, the sentiment had kept me going, reminding me that Beloved Leader expected my best, that it was my duty to fight and grow stronger for my people.

Now as I look at Mirra's manic expression, I'm wondering if the words could have another meaning.

CHAPTER
FOURTEEN

WE GO BACK TO THE BRIDGE IN SILENCE, BUT my head is whirring.

"Everything check out?" Denbar asks when we walk in, though from his tone I don't think he really cares.

"Fine," Mirra says, stealing one last knowing look at me before heading to her station beside the captain's chair.

The sun is high in the sky by the time Jax-Har stomps onto the bridge. His skin is pallid, and the portions of white around his black eyes are bloodshot. Knowing Mirra's stance on what's happening, it's easy to see how she'd view him as a madman, a blasphemer. He looks like someone at his wit's end, even more than he did an hour ago at our meeting. He's fully aware of what he's about to do.

"Is the course set?" he asks.

"Yes, sir," I say.

"Nothing from West Virginia?" he asks Denbar.

"Negative, sir."

Jax-Har is quiet for a few moments. Then he turns his tired eyes back to me.

"Take us to Niagara Falls," he says.

I nod and tap on the terminal in front of me. The warship starts to move, picking up to a casual speed. There's no need to rush or show off. We're so close already.

"ETA fifteen minutes, sir," I say.

Mirra stares at me. She nods a little when I notice and then walks over to one of our science officers and disappears into the hallway with him, saying something about Loralite deposits. I turn back to my terminal and pretend to busy myself going over numbers and data I already know by heart.

It's usually quiet on the bridge, but today the silence feels unnatural, heavy. I guess we all know what this means, that in some ways we *are* disobeying orders, even if we're probably doing what's best for the Mogadorians—or at least what makes sense.

It's strange, when I really think about it, that something so seemingly simple as moving a short flight away from our stationed location could be viewed as an act of betrayal or a lack of faith. Mirra isn't exactly an outlier when it comes to fanatical devotion to Beloved Leader. That's our entire mindset, how we're raised to think from birth. To even be considering the idea that Beloved Leader is fallible is fundamentally anti-Mogadorian. This sort of conflict doesn't exist for us—*can't* exist based on the way our society works.

And yet, here we are, flying over Lake Ontario.

I glance back at the captain, who's doing his best to look composed even though his fingers thump along the sides of his chair. He has no idea what Mirra has in store for him. *I* hardly know. I can barely wrap my head around it. But I can feel something in the air, kinetic. Change.

What does that mean for me? Am I really going to help Mirra take down our captain? Or sit by and watch it happen? Who else does she have on her side? Would the troops listen to her? Probably, if she convinced them that Jax-Har was a traitor.

I *could* tell the captain about her now and stop her little insurrection. I don't know that Mirra would be any better than Jax-Har. Perhaps worse in the long run. She wants to bathe in the blood of our enemies, which happen to be billions of humans on a planet I've come to kind of like as it is.

Who do I side with?

Who would *Adamus* side with?

I'm not sure where this question comes from, but I know the answer immediately. He'd get off this damned warship and find the Loric. He'd help stop whatever we

Mogadorians had in store, knowing that whatever our plans were, they'd no doubt end with blood flowing in rivers across the planet below. The planet we grew up on. The only one we really know as home.

My terminal beeps.

"Approaching target destination," I say.

We break through a cover of clouds, and then, suddenly, it comes into view.

I don't know what I was expecting—fire, death, fighting—but all I see are the waterfalls, a river rushing over a cliff, crashing down and rejoining itself. Raging, continuing, only temporarily disrupted.

As we get closer, I can also make out three downed skimmers, but the falls are so breathtaking that I have to be consciously looking for the wreckages to spot them.

Mirra comes back to the bridge, the science officer beside her. He looks . . . unchanged. I catch Denbar staring daggers into Mirra. It's only when the captain motions to him that he takes his eyes off of her.

"Send the fleets I assembled down to inspect the stone," Jax-Har says. "See if we can get a sample. And launch the first air patrol units. Keep an eye out for any hint of movement. If the Loric show, we won't be taken by surprise. Don't give them time to even realize we're here. Fire at will."

"Yes, sir!" someone replies.

"Officer Saturnus, I want you mapping the movements of the Mogadorian fleet in North America. Not just warships, but skimmers, scouting parties—anything and everything. There were . . . *objections* when I announced our plans earlier."

Of course there were. I wonder if he's afraid that other ships have come after us or just wants to know if they'll follow our lead. Maybe both.

"Won't Beloved Leader be thrilled?" Mirra asks flatly.

Jax-Har looks at her with a blank expression on his face.

"Yes," he says. "Forever may he reign."

The rest of the day passes in a blur. Our patrols don't detect anything unusual. I'm unsure whether or not the science division is able to carve off a rock sample. Jax-Har is basically silent in his captain's chair. Mirra keeps finding excuses to leave the bridge. I can only imagine what she's doing.

Tracking our fleet's movements keeps me busy, and I'm able to bury myself in the work, trying not to think about the future. That all changes when I break for dinner, taking my meal back to my room. I don't touch my food, though, just sit on my thin mattress and try to make sense of everything happening. Something is going down at the officers' meeting tonight. In the end, either Jax-Har or Mirra will be leading our ship.

Mirra said I don't have to do anything. That she'll handle it. Maybe I should just let them kill each other and wait for the smoke to clear before I choose a side. No matter who's commanding, my role won't change. I'll still be standing at my terminal, watching the destruction of Earth from hundreds of feet above the cities. That's surely the endgame for both of them. Complete takeover. In the long run, it doesn't matter who's in control. I'm on a warship. We were *built* to destroy.

My thoughts go back to what Adamus would do. Completely abandon our people. It wouldn't be too hard, as a trueborn officer, to take a skimmer, pull out the tracking systems and head for open sky. I could maybe try to track down Adamus and see what he was doing—though, if the entire Mogadorian fleet can't find him, I'm not sure if I'd have any luck.

Or I could just fly somewhere far away from the warships, could probably keep a hood on and pulled over my face enough that people would think I was just a pale, tattooed human. I could get by on my own somehow. Somewhere.

But even if I do disappear, so what? We've got this world surrounded. We're primed for full invasion. Our peace with the humans is a sham. Eventually we'll be everywhere. I'd only be buying myself a year or two before my fellow Mogadorians found me and tortured me as a traitor. I'd be constantly looking over my shoulder, wondering if they were on to me.

A memory comes. The last time I saw Adamus. We'd already freed the Chimæra, and just needed to get them and Adamus out of there before anyone found him. I was helping. I'd killed several vatborn to ensure his safety. I told myself at the time that it was because I had a debt to Adamus after he'd pulled me out of the rubble at Dulce and saved my life. That this was the only reason I was helping him.

But that wasn't true. I think I realized it even then. I'd already paid my debt. I'd pulled him onto a moving train when he was almost certain to fall and rescued him from being captured when the Mogs came for us outside of Manhattan. Hell, just the act of busting him out at Plum Island and not letting him rot in a cell made up for him giving me water in the desert. No, I was helping him for another reason.

I liked Adamus. *Adam.* I wanted him to survive.

These feelings went against everything I knew, and they don't make any more sense to me now, in the warship. But as I think about what happened on Plum Island, I know without any doubt that I made a huge mistake there. Adamus offered me the chance to go with him, and I refused. I told him war was in my blood and that my place was with the Mogadorians, my purpose to dominate and destroy. I told him that the next time I saw him, we would be enemies.

Only, deep inside, I wasn't sure about any of that. And now I realize I should have joined him.

I lie back down on the mattress and stare at the ceiling. Tomorrow, no matter what happens, I'll still be Mogadorian. Adamus may have found a way out, a new place in the world, but I made my decision that night.

Besides, I'm just one person. One Mog. It's not like I'm really going to make a difference. Not when there are so many other warships hovering over this planet.

I wonder how many more Jax-Hars are out there in the sky right now. How many Mirras.

And maybe more importantly, how many Mogadorians like me. Are they out there, in their bunks and barracks, feeling lost too?

CHAPTER
FIFTEEN

MIRRA IS THE ONLY OTHER PERSON IN THE council room when I arrive for the night's meeting. She's bent over a tablet, examining readouts like she always is. As though it were a perfectly normal night.

I take a seat beside her out of habit, realizing too late that this is no doubt a terrible idea.

"Good evening," I mutter.

"Hello," she says.

She glances at me from the corner of her eye and then does a double take.

"You look troubled," she says.

Her face is the blank, severe stone I'm used to from her. Eyes narrowed slightly, as if she can see my every thought.

"Just worrying about what Beloved Leader must think of our change in position," I say, which isn't technically a lie.

She seems satisfied by this.

"Don't worry. Everything's in order. Just sit back and witness." She pats her blaster. "For Beloved Leader."

The door behind us opens, and others start to file in.

Dread fills me, settling in my stomach, cramping. My eyes dart around between the dozen officers at the table, trying to figure out who the other allies Mirra mentioned to me might be. And who might push back against her. Maybe it's just because I haven't really talked to many of them or gotten to know them, but I can't imagine any of these trueborn as mutineers.

I hope for Mirra's sake that I'm wrong. Then for Jax-Har's sake that I'm not.

And then I find myself asking Beloved Leader for strength and guidance, without even realizing that I'm doing it until I'm murmuring verses from The Great Book under my breath.

My fingers graze the grip of my blaster. Sweat's starting to prickle on my body, and I close my eyes and try to calm down. I think of the quiet, still water of Lake Ontario and the rushing falls just below us. I try to let those thoughts drown out all the mental alarms going off in my brain.

Jax-Har comes in with Denbar. I catch only the last bit of their conversation, but I hear enough to know that several other captains are furious with what he's done. This must weigh heavily on him. I can see it in his bent posture, in his swollen, bruise-colored features. I almost feel bad for the guy.

"Let's begin," he says. His voice is hoarse, like he's been yelling all morning. "Officer Saturnus, update me on the fleet's locations."

"There's been no movement among the warships, sir," I say. "Skimmer patterns appear to be normal as far as I can tell."

"No one headed our way?"

"Negative, sir."

"What did the other captains have to say about your decision to abandon your post?" Mirra hisses.

"Most respect my boldness and agree about the strategic value of the Loralite," the captain says. He doesn't seem concerned about her tone at all.

Before I can even process how odd it is that he didn't snap back at her, putting her in her place, she continues.

"And the others? Those who don't agree?"

"I'd say they likely have no business commanding a ship." He locks eyes with her, staring her down. "I'd say they're so afraid of disobeying Beloved Leader that they don't see opportunity when it presents itself. They have forgotten that the teachings of the Great Book preach the honor not only of loyalty, but of boldness and making use of all possible resources." His upper lip peels back in a snarl for an instance. "I'd say they are a disgrace to the Mogadorian people."

Mirra doesn't respond, but I can feel the heat rising off of her.

"If you have something else to say, my lost little executive officer, now is the time," Jax-Har says with a hint of a smile.

"Bastard!" Mirra shouts as she stands and pulls out her weapon. Another officer a few seats down gets to his feet as well.

That's when the first blaster goes off.

The shot hits its target with perfect precision, burning a hole straight through the middle of Mirra's right bicep. Her weapon clatters onto the table. Then a second shot, disarming the other standing officer.

Mirra's eyes go wide, incredulous. She stares at the officer across the table from her, the one who fired.

"No, Balda, you—," she starts.

"Serve Beloved Leader," the officer says, finishing her sentence for her. "And whomever *he* sees fit to put in command."

She looks around the table. Almost everyone has a weapon drawn on her. Only a few people look confused. The other officer who stood with her glances at the door.

It's obvious from the look on Mirra's face that several of the people pointing weapons at her were those she'd considered to be her allies in this. In her plight to prove her own loyalty, she underestimated that of her peers.

She turns to me. The shock on her face changes to worry, her brow scrunching together. She doesn't say anything, but she doesn't have to. I know she's condemning me, condemning *all* of us.

I don't even have the guts to keep watching; I look away.

"He is a traitor," she screams, pointing at our captain. "He will lead you off the path of Mogadorian Progress. Do not follow him blindly!"

Jax-Har, for the first time in days, laughs.

"Hail our Beloved Leader," Denbar says.

"Forever may he reign," Jax-Har adds.

And then everyone opens fire.

Mirra's body falls back, toppling over her chair. Her ally goes down as well. I keep my eyes on the table in front of me, not wanting to look back and see their bodies, wishing that the trueborn fully disintegrated like the vatborn do, or that I was anywhere else in the galaxy.

I'm a fool for not leaving with Adamus.

Silence fills the room. It takes a few seconds for me to realize that everyone's looking at me.

Denbar's got his blaster aimed at my face.

"Whoa," I say. "I didn't . . . I mean . . ."

I can't seem to construct a sentence. I raise my hands in front of my chest—a completely un-Mogadorian thing to do, offering up surrender.

"We know she tried to recruit you," Jax-Har says. He speaks calmly, like his second-in-command didn't just attempt a failed coup. "The others came to me, one by one. You did not. And yet, you didn't so much as reach for your weapon when she stood. Tell me, commander: Where do your allegiances lie?"

My pulse beats in my head.

"If I questioned your leadership, I wouldn't have brought us to Niagara Falls," I say slowly, enunciating each word. "I trust in Beloved Leader's wisdom. I trust in your command."

Jax-Har stares me down but eventually waves his hand to the side. The others lower their weapons. I'm safe.

For now, at least. My time on this ship suddenly seems very short.

I glance back, against my better judgment, and look at Mirra's disintegrating body. And I realize I have to do something. The doubts that have been growing inside my head are too heavy for me to stay here, following orders that will no doubt end in the slaughter of an entire planet. I have to get off this ship or I'll be murdered. Or I'll go mad. I'm not sure which is worse.

The doors open again, and someone runs in—another trueborn, a little younger than me. The officer-in-training who answers to Denbar and monitors communications overnight and during meetings.

"Captain Jax-Har!" He takes a few steps in before he stops, looking around wide-eyed, trying to digest the situation, the bodies on the floor.

"This is a closed meeting," the captain barks.

"But, sir . . ." The kid looks a little scared now. "Officer Denbar told me to report in if anything of note happened on the comms. The captains are all fighting—"

"They've been doing that all morning."

"Yes, but, sir, now there's someone else on. Phiri Dun-Ra, who was stationed in Mexico. She has news about Beloved—"

"Turn on the comms!" Jax-Har says, twisting to Denbar and pointing a thick finger at him.

Denbar taps on a terminal. Phiri Dun-Ra's shouts fill the room, her voice laced with venom. We hear only a few words. "Garde." "Legacies." They're meaningless without context and difficult to make out over the sound in the background—someone, a human boy I think, is screaming out in pain, his cries so primal and terrified that I have to fight the urge to cover my ears with my hands.

This is what the future holds for everyone. I can't just sit back and resign myself to follow along with whatever my captains and commanders ask of me. There has to be more to the Mogadorians—to *me*—than war and brutality.

It's not too late to change.

And then something breaks me, causes my blood to stop pumping. Someone else starts to speak on the comm line.

I don't even process the words at first. All I can do is focus on the sound of Adamus Sutekh's unmistakable voice, and what it means.

Adam is alive.

And I can't believe what he's saying.

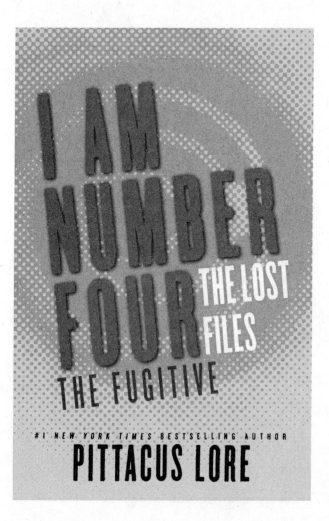

CHAPTER
ONE

This is the thought that screams through my head every one hundred miles or so on the road when I have a moment of self-doubt. Or maybe it's a moment of clarity? I don't really know which. But when I face the facts—that I've stolen an FBI agent's laptop, pissed off some evil aliens and am now driving across the country in order to try to find my missing ex-girlfriend, Sarah, who happens to be dating a *good* alien—I can't help but think it's true. I'm an idiot. Or I'm crazy. Or both.

Whatever I am, it's too late to go back to being who I was before aliens blew up my school and took over my town. Not too long ago I was hot shit at Paradise High, with a bright future ahead of me. Now I'm the dude who's wanted by government agencies and bad ETs from the planet Shark-Face.

I down an energy drink and crush the can in my

fist, tossing it to the passenger seat floorboard, where it finds a home with a bunch of its empty brothers. I've been on the road for about nineteen hours, and I didn't exactly start on a full night's sleep. The only thing keeping me going is a mixture of adrenaline, worrying about Sarah and what are probably enough energy drinks to kill an elephant. One glance in the rearview mirror tells me I'm way overdue for sleep, my eyes all bloodshot and dark looking, but I don't have time to take things easy. Sarah's in Dulce—or at least, that's what the email I read on the stolen FBI laptop said. Before I tried to access a file called "MogPro," and the whole computer shut down. Now, the computer won't even turn on. It's just sitting on my back floorboard, wrapped in my letter jacket.

I try not to think about what the FBI or the Mogs might be doing to Sarah. I can hardly even wrap my head around the fact that the FBI—or at least the agents in Paradise—are working with the aliens. Instead, I focus on the fact that I'm on my way to bust her out . . . somehow. After a few more hours of empty roads on my fifteen-hundred-miles-in-one-day journey from Ohio to New Mexico, I'll be there to try to save her. Me. Alone. Against a bunch of pale-ass aliens and probably the FBI, NSA and the Illuminati or whatever.

My phone dings—a burner, one I bought at a truck stop an hour outside of Paradise. The sound reminds me that I'm not *technically* alone on my mission to save Sarah. There's someone helping me. He's the only person who has this number.

I look at the text.

GUARD: Getting close to the NM border?

I glance up to see a sign on the side of the road telling me that Colorado State Highway 17 will turn into New Mexico State Highway 17 in ten miles. GUARD has been weirdly good at guessing where I'm at since I've been on the road.

I text him back, saying I'm about ten minutes out. Almost as soon as the message goes through, I get another ding.

GUARD: Gas station on the NM side of the border. On the right. Pull off there: I've got some stuff for you.

My brain basically explodes when I read this. I'm actually going to be face-to-face with GUARD: head conspiracy theorist at the They Walk Among Us website, hacker extraordinaire and kind of my only friend now that Sarah's gone. Even though I've never met him. Even though I've never even talked to him on the phone because he's as obsessed with his own privacy as he is with the Mogadorians and Loric.

Okay, so maybe we aren't friends, exactly. I guess we're more like partners in all this alien shit. He's the computer brains, and I'm the good-looking brawn who's going to save the girl and then figure out a way to keep what happened in Paradise from going down anywhere else.

The idea of being face-to-face with GUARD sends my thoughts into overdrive as I start imagining us pulling some badass action-movie moves while we storm the alien base in Dulce. Liberating anyone who's been taken hostage by the Mogs in a montage of explosions. Then the pounding in my chest starts to drum faster, and I remember that this is real life, no matter how strange it all seems. I think of the huge Mog dude I saw while I was acting like a spy at the police station in Paradise. He was a black-eyed giant, built like a professional linebacker. He easily had two hundred pounds on me and was probably packing all kinds of alien weapons. Then I think back to all the gross-as-shit Mogs we faced at the school. I mean, I managed to fight my way out of that whole mess and protected Sarah in the process, but the idea of going up against those guys again makes me want to turn around and head back home.

I crank up the radio and tell myself it'll all work out.

I'll be okay. I'll save Sarah. GUARD and I will do it together. He'll know what to do.

It's two in the morning when I cross the border from Colorado into New Mexico. Sure enough, there's an old-looking gas station at the first exit. This time of night, the place looks deserted.

It's only as I turn into the station that my head throbs and I wonder if I'm in danger for some reason. But that's impossible. I've been supercareful, and God knows GUARD isn't going to screw up on his end when it comes to flying under the radar. I still feel uneasy, though.

I blame the sudden paranoia on my lack of sleep.

I park at one of the pumps because it's the only place that's lit up, loud industrial lights buzzing overhead. Being under the light makes everything else seem that much darker, so I flash my headlights twice, half to get a better look at the area around me and half because I've seen enough movies about gangs and secret meetings to know this is sometimes a sign. No one appears, though, so I jump out and start to gas up since I'm already stopped, keeping my eyes on the lookout for any movement.

I'm five gallons in when a tall figure emerges from the darkness of the side of the station.

"GUARD?" I call out.

The figure doesn't answer, which isn't exactly a good sign.

I suddenly wish I had a weapon other than my

throwing arm—a perfect pass isn't going to protect me if this dude's a Mog. My heart beats so loud I'm guessing the other person can hear it over the buzzing lights. I clutch my fingers around the gas pump. If things go bad for me, maybe I can hose the dude down and throw him off balance long enough to make a break for it.

Fortunately, I luck out. It's obvious from the moment the person steps into the light that she's no Mog. First off, I don't even know if there *are* Mog women. Secondly, she's dark skinned, unlike any Mog I've seen. She doesn't exactly scream FBI either. She's got on a motorcycle helmet that leaves just her face exposed. Between that and the form-fitting leather jacket, I'm guessing she's got a bike stashed on the other side of the gas station. I can't get too relieved, though, because she looks like she's pissed off as she approaches. That's when I notice there's a box under one of her arms. I keep my hand on the gas pump.

I don't realize she's taller than me—by about a head—until she's a few yards away. I don't think I've ever met a girl who's made me feel so short. Actually, she's not really a *girl*. I'm guessing she's in her midthirties, but with the crappy light and her helmet, it's hard to tell exactly.

"Uh . . . ," I murmur. I don't really know what to say. "I'm not sure . . ."

"Jolly Roger?" she asks.

It takes me a second to answer because no one's ever called me that in real life. Hell, I don't think I've ever even said the words out loud. Technically I *am* JOLLY-ROGER182, at least when I'm blogging on They Walk Among Us.

"Yeah?" I ask, as if it's a question.

I'm still trying to wrap my head around what's happening when she pushes the box into my chest.

"Sign here," she says, holding a pen out to me with one hand and pointing to a sheet of paper on top of the box with another.

I do as I'm told, only halfway registering the courier service listed at the top of the page. Sure enough, the package is intended for Jolly Roger. This must be GUARD's way of keeping my real name out of the equation, which is smart, I guess. Still, I can't help but be bummed that he sent a courier instead of coming to the station himself.

I thought I was finally going to meet GUARD. I thought we were going to team up.

The woman keeps her eyes focused on me. Not blinking. Her intensity creeps me out a little bit, keeping me from wallowing too much in the fact that GUARD's not here.

She takes the page back after I've signed for the package but keeps staring at me, like her dark-brown eyes are trying to read my mind. Finally she speaks.

"You should get off the road and get some sleep." Her voice is stern, more of a command than a suggestion. "You look like shit."

And then she walks back off into the darkness.

I fling open my truck door and get in, tearing into the box. I pull out all kinds of stuff I don't recognize: computer equipment, maps, little electronic gadgets. There's a smartphone in the box, along with a stack of cash that's got to be at least a grand. There's even a black, padded messenger bag—I'm guessing to carry all this stuff around in.

What is going on?

Suddenly, the phone's screen comes to life, powering on. After a few seconds, a text message pops up.

GUARD: Thought you could use some supplies. Instructions are on the phone. Careful: they'll self-delete after you've read them. Good luck. -G

GUARD sent me a care package.

There's no return address on the box. I jump out of the truck cab, but it's too late—I can already hear the whine of the courier's bike fading away somewhere down the highway.

The gas pump clicks. I'm about to pack everything back into the box when I notice one last item at the bottom of it. I pick it up: a metal cylinder about half an inch wide and four inches tall that's covered in weird markings I've never seen before. Near the top is what appears to be a button. There's a Post-it note attached that has "do not press me" written on it. I'm suddenly afraid I'm holding some sort of next-gen bomb.

Looking back and forth between the possible weapon and the stack of cash, one big question is louder than all the others going through my head: Who the *fuck* is GUARD?

CHAPTER TWO

I PACK EVERYTHING UP AND GET BACK ON THE highway—I'm only a few hours from Dulce, and now that I have a bunch of weird gadgets and cash, the last place I want to be is parked out in the open under the lights of a gas station. So I drive, fighting the urge to go over all the notes on the smartphone. Once I get close to where the secret Dulce base is supposed to be located, I give in and pull off to the side of the road to get my shit together. I can't exactly charge into a secret government base and demand to talk to Sarah Hart. I start by taking a full inventory of the stuff GUARD sent me, carefully reading the notes on the new phone, which I'm supposed to use to communicate with my unseen partner now.

Most of the stuff in the box seems to be computer related. There's a little netbook that's got a stealthy Wi-Fi hotspot installed inside that will bounce my location to satellites around the world, making anything I do impossible to track. That way I'll be able to communicate with people and upload stuff to They Walk Among Us without worrying about a bunch of black helicopters swooping in on me. There's also a USB drive that's supposed to help get the FBI computer I swiped up and running again—GUARD thinks that the files I saw disappearing before the screen went black may still be hidden somewhere on the hard drive. The trigger-looking thing covered in weird symbols *is* some kind of cutting-edge grenade. GUARD says it should only be used in a life-or-death situation. All I have to do is press the button on top and throw. There's no explanation as to what it actually *does* or what the symbols mean. They don't look like any alphabet I've ever seen, and I can't help but wonder if GUARD somehow managed to snag an alien weapon.

I kind of wish he'd also sent along a laser pistol or something.

The cash is self-explanatory. Well, not really. The fact that GUARD would just up and send fifteen hundred dollars—I counted—to someone he *sorta* knows makes me wonder if he's actually some kind of hacker billionaire operating out of a secret lair that looks like something out of *The Matrix*.

I shove everything into the messenger bag, including my old burner phone. As cool as all the gadgets are, the most helpful thing in the box for me right now is the stack of satellite images and blueprints of the Dulce base. All the maps I found online showed nothing but desert where it should have been, but the stuff GUARD sent is comprehensive, laying out the big-ass complex and giving me a good idea of the size of the thing and where I might be able to sneak in. There are even blueprints of what the underground levels of the place might look like.

It's intimidating as hell.

Flipping through the maps, I don't know how I'm going to be able to find Sarah in this mess. She could be anywhere. She might not even *be* there anymore. My body feels like it's sinking in on itself as I consider how impossible this mission is. How stupid I am for thinking I can just waltz in and rescue her.

I crack open another energy drink, guzzling it.

Man up, Mark.

I put my truck into gear and get back on the road. I'll have a better idea of what my plan should be once I get there. Surely.

After about fifteen minutes of driving, I take an unmarked side road that's circled on the maps GUARD sent. The base shouldn't be that far now. I turn off my lights and drive slowly. There's just enough moonlight for me to sort of be able to see. For a few minutes, I see nothing but hilly desert in front of me, but then I finally spot a tall chain-link fence in the distance that's topped in razor wire.

That's got to be it.

There doesn't appear to be any gate or path leading to the base perimeter, so I say a quick prayer, blow a kiss to the dashboard of my truck and off-road through the desert, trying my best to avoid any big shrubs or rocks and pretending not to worry about the fact that, for all I know, there could be mines and stuff all around out here.

But there aren't any. Or at least I don't hit any of them. Instead, I get within a few yards of the fence and park. Just in case there are hidden cameras around, I fish a baseball cap out of the back of my truck and pull it down low, trying to hide my face as much as I can.

The fence is at least three times as tall as I am, and I can't see most of the base because of a mesa or hill or whatever that hides it. There aren't any lights on—or at least not outside. I wish I'd thought to buy night-vision goggles or that GUARD had sent some along. I squint, trying to make out what all the dark shapes are in the moonlight. It looks like there are burned-out Humvees and other kinds of military vehicles littering the desert around the base. From what I can tell, something crazy definitely went down here recently. Something *epic*.

It reminds me of Paradise and the way my school looked after John, Henri, Six—after we'd *all* fought and escaped from the Mogs. This is the kind of shit that happens when good aliens and bad aliens collide. Were the Garde here? Was John Smith here? Maybe Sarah doesn't even need saving anymore.

But she would have contacted me if she were free, right? And what if dumbass John and his other ET friends *did* try to save Sarah but got captured?

What if I'm the only person left to bail *them* out?

I have to get in there. Now.

"Okay, Mark," I say. "Time to save the day."

I walk beside the fence for a few minutes, trying to see more of the base while at the same time wondering if I've got anything in my truck that might be able to snip a hole in the chain length. But I luck out, because I get to a section of the fence that's been knocked down— maybe even blown apart, judging by the mangled little pieces of metal littering the ground.

That's my entrance.

I think about going back to the truck to grab the grenade thing GUARD sent with me, but I'm kind of scared that it'd go off in my pocket accidentally since its trigger is apparently just a *button*. Probably the lamest possible outcome of the night would be me trying to be a hero and blowing myself up instead, leaving Sarah all alone in a cell.

So instead, I take a deep breath and step through the hole in the fence.

Once I'm inside the perimeter of the base, I jog towards some of the wreckage dotting the desert hills and look for a way to access the main facility, which, according to GUARD's maps, is mostly located underground. I try to stay low and out of sight, hiding behind half-crumbled walls and wishing I'd thought to buy darker clothes since my white T-shirt probably makes me stand out in the darkness. But I keep moving, eventually crouching behind what looks like a collapsed watchtower.

What the hell happened here?

Some of the buildings and vehicles around the main facility look like they've exploded—all scorched and burned-out—while others appear to have been blown apart by some other force. Maybe telekinesis? Maybe John or the other Garde really were here? The place looks completely vacant. Decommissioned. Half of my brain says I should just forget about trying to find a way inside and go back to my truck since it looks like there's no way a major FBI or Mog operation could still be working out of this broken-down base. But I can't do that. I've come too far. And if there's any chance that Sarah is still inside . . .

I think I see a shadow move out of the corner of my eye. I hold my breath and stand frozen for what feels like a long time, trying to figure out if there's anyone around—squinting in the moonlight. But there's nothing. The wind whistles, and I exhale.

I run to one of the charred Humvees, staying close to the ground, and roll behind it. In movies, spies and badass cops are always rolling behind cover, but all this does is get sand all over me and in my eyes. I try not to cough as I blink for half a minute, telling myself not to be a douche bag and try to pull any fancy moves anymore. I just have to get in, find Sarah and get out.

I spot my entry point. There's a bunch of debris lying around a pit about twenty yards away from me where it looks like the ground has collapsed into some kind of sinkhole. I can just make out a few walls and stuff below—the hole must lead straight down into the facility. All I have to do is jump down and I'm in, no locks to try to get past or anything.

Whatever battle took place here has given me a perfect way into the facility.

I start for the hole, keeping my eyes peeled for any movement. I'm halfway between it and the Humvee when a blinding light appears from somewhere to my right.

Shit.

My eyes burn, and I can barely see as I try to run back to the Humvee to take cover. But then there's another light that looks like it's coming from on top of the wreckage. And then there are lights everywhere, stunning me, making it impossible for me to even know which direction I'm facing anymore. I'm not sure if this is some kind of defense system or if I'm about to be beamed up to a Mog ship or something. My head spins, and I start to hyperventilate, completely regretting not bringing the grenade with me.

A figure emerges from the light, silhouetted. I can't make out a face or anything. Can't tell if it's even a human or a Mog. I plant my feet and clench my fists.

If this is my last stand, I have to make it count for something. I shout the first thing that comes to my mind.

"I've come for Sa—"

But before I can finish the sentence, someone attacks me from behind, and there's fabric over my head. Everything goes dark. I swing around, flailing wildly, but I'm struggling against a bunch of people, and before I know it, my hands are cuffed in front of me.

I've made a big mistake.

I'm dragged through the sand until I'm inside some kind of building, my feet kicking against a hard floor. I struggle and shout the whole time, but no one says anything to me. It's like they can't even hear me. Not until they start pushing me down some stairs and one of them threatens to Tase me if I don't shut up. So I do.

The bag over my head is scratchy against my face, and the air inside is thick with my rapid breathing. The more I think about what's happening, the faster and deeper my breath gets, until I'm sucking a bunch of fabric into my mouth every time I inhale.

I'm afraid I'm going to die here. I'm going to be Mog food. Or I'm going to end up a human lab rat. My parents will never know what happened to me. I'm going to become an unsolved case, just some good-looking dude with an all-American past as Ohio's greatest quarterback that ends up on a bunch of MISSING posters for a while.

You're an idiot, Mark.

Someone forces me into a chair and rips the bag off my head. The lights are way too bright, and I wince. I try to cover my eyes with my cuffed hands when I realize they've been chained to the center of a metal desk in front of me. I pull against them with all my strength, but there's no way I'm breaking free.

I am in way over my head.

I look around frantically. The room is small and looks empty except for the high-powered lamp shining right in my face. There's nothing in here but me, the desk and the light.

And a voice.

"Mark James," a woman says.

It's a voice I sort of recognize but can't really place. I hear a few footsteps from somewhere behind the light and squint as the woman comes into view.

And then I realize why I know her. She has red hair

pulled back in a severe ponytail. One of her arms is in a sling, peeking out from underneath her black jacket. She couldn't look more pissed off.

"Agent Walker?" I ask.

She sighs and raises her good arm to her face. She closes her eyes and rubs one temple.

"You're a real pain in the ass, kid," she says, shaking her head.

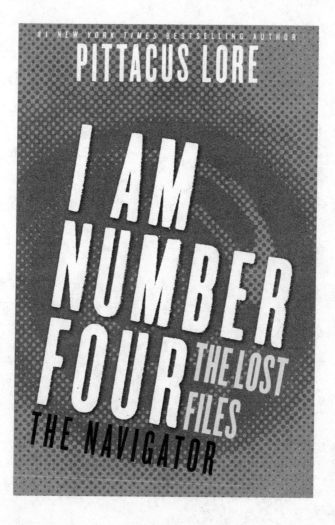

CHAPTER ONE

I'M WOKEN UP BY TWO POUNDING BANGS THAT reverberate through my basement apartment. There's shouting somewhere outside on the street. A single thought shoots through my brain: *They're here.*

My survival instincts take over. I jump out of bed and start shoving anything particularly damning out of sight, hiding data pads and electronic storage devices filled with stolen files in secret drawers and compartments I've built into my furniture. My heart pounds, but I move calmly, methodically, zoning in on my task. I've always worked best under pressure. It's a skill that comes in handy when you do what I do.

I'm leaning over my main computer when a few notes from a guitar or synthesizer filter in from outside, followed by the sound of a cheering crowd. It's only then that my brain starts to logically assess what's going on. I pause to take stock of the situation, my fingers hovering over a keyboard, ready to wipe a hard drive full of incriminating data logs. There hasn't been any more banging or knocking. There's no official from the Lorien Defense Council bursting through my door. Just some music and the sounds of people . . . laughing?

It's only then I remember it's the day of the Quarter-moon celebration.

The music riff stops. I pause and listen for a few seconds before closing my fingers into a fist and creeping over to one of the small windows located near the ceiling of my apartment. I step up on a chair and peel back a blackout curtain just a hair so I can peer outside. Across the street, Eilon Park is packed with people, its location on the outskirts of the city making it the perfect place for those living in more rural areas to congregate in celebration. A kaleidoscope of lights blinks over the dancing crowds, painting them in neon colors. Somewhere a stage must be set up. There are two more powerful bangs that once again rattle my apartment—a bass drum, I realize this time—before a band breaks into some synth-heavy song to the obvious delight of everyone in the park.

Part of me feels stupid for being scared by a drum, but mostly I'm angry. Not because my sleep was cut short—it's dark out, which means it was time for me to wake up, anyway—but because this sort of government-sanctioned celebration is just one of the many ways that the Elders keep the Loric masses placated. They put on all-night parties and erect flashy monuments and light displays they call Heralds, and we are supposed to thank them—to recognize these events as signs that all is well on Lorien. All is *perfect*.

But it's not.

My feet step back onto the cold stone floor. My heart is still pumping in my chest, and I try to slow it down by breathing deeply and stretching my limbs. The tips of my fingers drag across the ceiling as I stretch. On the streets of Capital City—on the rare occasions that I'm out in public during the day—I tower over most of the population, especially other women. Despite my height I rarely feel claustrophobic in my apartment, which is just one big room. If I ever did feel cramped, I could just clean up a bit, since most surfaces are piled high with books and electronics in various states of repair or modification.

I slip on black pants and a T-shirt before returning to my main computer. My adrenaline is still pumping. Best to put this energy to use.

"Talk to me," I say, logging in to my terminal. "What have you got for Lexa today?"

I open up a few of the data-collecting programs I've designed and find a treasure trove of intercepted messages, alerts and intel. The most useful type of currency: information.

A few weeks ago the Grid, which controls and monitors basically all communications and municipal functions in Capital City, had started to malfunction in various locations throughout my neighborhood. Usually the Grid is impossible to hack—even for someone as skilled as I am—but when my own scanners had alerted me to the issue, I saw an opportunity. A chance for me to gather confidential communications—to show the people of Lorien that there are pockets of corruption in our government and secrets that the Elders and high-ranking officials keep from us. I was able to get to one of the Grid workstations before the Munis lackeys got around to fixing it. I did their job for them—adding a bit of my own hardware to the system. Since then, the "impenetrable" Grid has been mine for the perusing.

And I've been stockpiling all kinds of data.

This is supposed to be one big, happy utopia. At least that's what the Elders—and therefore everyone who buys in to them being all-powerful and all-knowing—want us to think. In order for Lorien to be "perfect," all of us have to abide by certain rules. We fall into categories, which make us easier to classify and control. Garde and Cêpan. If you have Legacies, you're a soldier. If you don't, you're a Mentor or Munis or bureaucrat. You're told to follow certain tracks, and if you don't—if something happens that sends your life careening off your destined path—or if you question the system too vocally, then the rest of the Loric don't know what to do with you. If you aren't working in an expected role, you are flawed. You are different, which isn't a good thing. You might as well be actively working *against* the rest of the planet.

Granted, that's exactly what I'm doing. Not for the sake of anarchy but for freedom. What most people don't know—or choose not to believe—is that there are some of us who don't agree with the way things are run. We've realized that, while this may look like a model society, the cost is our free will.

Some of us have lost too much to Lorien. *I've* lost too much. And I want to see it changed. We need reform. We need *revolution*.

The sounds from the celebration across the street are so loud that my apartment has become an echo chamber of cheers and electronic music. I try to focus as I sort through the various communiqués my programs have intercepted throughout the day. Mostly they're harmless—orders for Munis workers, notes from schools about absent students, traffic statistics. What I'm interested in are the encrypted files. Those are the ones that get personal. You can tell a lot about people based on the words they don't want you to read. I've come across a lot of interesting tidbits—cheating spouses, conned business partners, less-than-scrupulous teachers at the Lorien Defense Academy. There are many people who would pay me well for the information. Or to keep it from going public. I know because, in desperate times, information has kept me fed and paid my rent. What I'm really looking for now, though, is something that will expose corruption in the Lorien Defense Council or the Elders—something that will force the people of Lorien to take a hard look at the way our government is run.

I know it has to be there. I just haven't found any-thing heinous enough yet. But I will. I have to have faith in that. It's the goal that keeps me going, that gets me out of bed. Besides, I'm not just doing this for myself. I'm also doing it in his memory.

I'm doing this for my brother.

My apartment shakes. A little stream of dust filters down from the ceiling. There are some heavy fireworks being shot off elsewhere in the city.

They're really going all-out with the celebrations this year.

An alert pops up that my decryption software is having trouble decoding a message that's just been intercepted from a communications channel I didn't know existed. I'm surprised my monitoring programs even picked it up. Either I'm getting much better at keeping tabs on Capital City or the higher-ups are get-ting really sloppy.

Whatever the case, an encrypted message broadcast

on a hidden channel like this is bound to contain something important.

I run a secondary decryption program, and an unintelligible mess of symbols and letters slowly begins to form words. While it runs, I try to figure out who sent the message and to whom. The former is a bust, leading me back to a computer terminal and address I don't recognize, though I log it so I can track it down later. I have better luck with the receivers. It appears to have been transmitted to only nine ID bands—all belonging to people whose names I don't know. Not a problem. I run a cross-check against the LDC's database of every registered citizen—a database that could really use better firewalls—and sure enough, the names have one big thing in common: they're all Mentor Cêpans.

Curious. Why would nine Mentor Cêpans be contacted via an encrypted message during the Quartermoon celebration, a night when most people like to pretend they don't have a care in the world? I wonder if it's a matter concerning them, or their Garde—what unnecessary risks they're asking those gifted with Legacies to take now.

I switch back to the decryption program. It's still working, but I can pick out a few words. "Airstrip." "Garde." "Loridas."

My entire body freezes.

Loridas.

This has something to do with the Elders. I've been trying to track down more information about their current locations ever since I intercepted a Grid message a few days ago mentioning they were all off-world. Why? What are they up to?

I grin as I lean back, putting my hands behind my head and rubbing them over my buzz cut. Regardless of the message's content, something like this—something straight from the Elders—will definitely be valuable. People get obsessed over the details of the Elders' lives. I could have just intercepted Pittacus Lore's grocery list, and I bet I could sell it for enough credits to pay my rent for a month.

There's a sound from across the room. My modified identity band—which looks more like a silver cuff now that I've integrated a communications system into it—vibrates on the table. Zophie's name flashes on the surface. I don't answer but slip the cuff onto my wrist, wondering why she's contacting me. Possibly for another museum gig, I suppose. Zophie's from what others would call "a good family," which really just means that they're wealthy and spend a lot of that money at charity galas and stuff like that. We were at the Lorien Defense Academy at the same time, friendly but not exactly friends. She was always with a pack of other students, but I preferred solitude, even then, back before everything changed and I went off the Grid. Later—years after the incident—we met again at a Kabarak in the Outer Territories, where I was reconfiguring a computer network. By that point she was heading the Department of Otherworld Studies at the Loric Museum of Exploration. She's the one who brought me back to Capital City to work on a restoration project at the museum, refurbishing the onboard systems of an old fossil-fuel spacecraft. It was good money—enough to upgrade most of my computer equipment, which inevitably led to where I am now. But we haven't spoken at all since my last day at the museum, and that was a few years ago.

Maybe it was a mistake. Maybe she just had too many ampules and wanted to wish everyone in her contacts a Happy Quartermoon.

The sounds of the crowds crescendo across the street. I continue trying to ignore them as I crack open a can of liquid stimulants and take a seat in front of the computer again. More of the message has been decoded, but it still doesn't make a lot of sense. Something about a prophecy coming true and the end of Lorien and . . .

"Evacuation?" I mumble to myself.

My ID band buzzes. It's Zophie again. I sigh and am about to answer when I realize that the music from the celebration has stopped. The crowds are still noisy, but their shouts are morphing. They're no longer sounds of jubilation or celebration but of fear and alarm.

What the hell is going on out there?

I rush over to the window and pull back the curtain. I can just see a bit of the sky.

It's red.

There's a surge in the panicked screams from the park, but since the small window is at ground level, the people sprinting past on the sidewalk mostly block my line of sight. My apartment shakes again, more violently this time. I see the light a few seconds before I realize what it is. Fire. Fire coming towards me in a huge wave, engulfing everyone in its path: men, women, children. I manage to take a few steps away from the window before the glass breaks and half the ceiling falls down around me.

CHAPTER
TWO

I COME TO, CHOKING ON SMOKE AND DUST. MY ears ring. I can hear the sound of people yelling, but their voices are far away and fuzzy. At first I can't even tell where I am—it seems like a small, unlit room thick with haze—until I recognize the arm of a sofa that's in flames a few feet away from me. I'm still in my apartment. Only, the ceiling has mostly caved in and there are smoldering planks of wood where my computer equipment used to be, and I'm half buried in debris. My first instinct is to try to collect some of my personal belongings, but I can't stop coughing and my head is pounding, and I know that what I need to do is get up, out into some fresh air. It's too dangerous to stay here. And so I use the flaming couch as a point of reference and start towards the place where my window should be. I climb on all fours up a pile of rubble until I'm finally breathing in cleaner air and collapse on the lawn. My lungs are on fire. My dark skin is covered in ash and dust.

It's only then that I realize most of my building has been blown away, the apartments above mine completely obliterated. Razed, along with the rest of the structures on my block. I'm probably only alive at all because I was in a basement. Still coughing, I roll onto my stomach and look towards the park where the crowds had gathered for the celebration.

Only, there isn't really a park anymore. The trees are gone. Small fires dot the charred grass, smoke spiraling up towards a crimson sky. There are scores of blackened clumps throughout the park too. I tell myself they're tree stumps or the remains of the stage I never saw—anything to keep my mind away from the idea that these mounds were recently dancing around with their hands stretched up to the sky while drums and synthesizers blared.

My stomach lurches. My mind races, trying to make sense of the world I've climbed up into, which seems so different from the one I was just living in. What's happened? What caused this? I wonder if there's been some kind of gross miscalculation of celebratory pyrotechnics. Or if a Garde's new power has overwhelmed him, turning an unsuspecting kid into an untamable inferno and wiping out an entire block.

The streets fill with people, all shouting, adding

to my confusion. They're singed and bloodied. Some huddle over unmoving bodies on the ground. Others stumble unevenly before collapsing.

I realize that my identity band is vibrating—for all I know it's been going off constantly since I woke up. It's Zophie again. Not knowing what else to do, I accept her call.

"Lexa!" Her voice pours out of a hidden speaker on the side of the cuff. "Hello? Are you there?"

"Zophie," I murmur. My ears are ringing.

"You're okay! I thought you . . . Everything is so messed up."

"What's going on?" I ask, getting to my feet. It's the first of a million questions that are threatening to pour out through my lips. "My neighborhood . . . Eilon Park. Something's happened here."

"No. It's everywhere. We're being attacked. And not just the city. The planet. They're hitting us hard, Lexa. Their targets are strategic. . . . I think Lorien is falling. Everything we'd been warned about—it's all coming true."

The prophecy. My mind races back to the message I was decoding before everything turned to fire and ash. For generations, the Elders have been warning us that one day Lorien would face destruction and death. Some kind of global calamity. It's the entire reasoning behind our society's setup—with our super-powered children trained to be soldiers against some unknown enemy. I'd always thought it was a scare tactic. But as I stumble forward, stepping past the remains of a man dressed in the colorful robes of the Quartermoon celebration, I realize I might have been wrong.

"Lexa," Zophie continues before I can ask anything else. "You have to come to the museum. Right now. It's the only way you'll be safe. I need you. I have a plan."

"What?" I ask. My brain isn't functioning on all cylinders. I'm not sure if it's shock, or the cave-in, or both. "What are you talking about?"

"Just meet me there. I'm on my way now. As fast as you can, Lex. Run. Don't let anything stop you."

There's some kind of interference on her end of the line, and then the connection drops out. I look down at my cuff, thinking about who I should contact if the world really is going to shit. Who I should check in on. That's when I realize I have no one else to call. For the past few years I've been alone, refusing to get too close to anybody. Secluding myself. Making sure I had no strings, no one tying me down.

No one to worry or care about.

I look to the sky. The smoke from my neighborhood has created a layer of smog far above me, all but obstructing the Quartermoon and whatever else is out there causing this.

Who is attacking Lorien? Why? How could—

Beside me, the scarce remains of my building collapse farther, filling my basement apartment with fire and debris. I stumble away, coughing through the miasma of dust and ash that's kicked up.

This stirs something in me. A switch is flipped, and before I know it I'm running. On instinct. It's not until I'm at a full sprint that I realize my body is following Zophie's orders and that I'm headed towards the museum. My home is destroyed. My planet, flawed as it may be, is under attack. I don't know what else I'm supposed to do. I just have to focus and keep moving, heading towards the next goal.

The chaos is everywhere, widespread. Most people I pass are preoccupied with their own survival or with trying to find or help out their loved ones. They yell, asking no one in particular what is happening. I hear a short screech somewhere to my right—blocks away? Closer?—followed by an explosion and a rumbling beneath my feet that almost knocks me to the ground. Capital City is still under attack. And even after everything we did to prepare, we weren't ready. We were caught off guard.

The museum. It's not that far away now. Ten blocks or so. I just have to keep my legs moving and concentrate on the sound of my feet hitting the ground and . . .

Out of the smoke in front of me charge half a dozen figures unlike anything I've ever seen. They're pale, dressed in black and carrying blasters and swords that seem to glow with a light of their own. Dark circles ring their black eyes. Their gaping mouths are full of sharp, jagged teeth. The one in the front is huge, taller than me and three times as wide. He has a long black ponytail, but the sides of his head are shaved. Tattoos wind around his skull.

These monsters are definitely not Loric.

I stop too fast, and in doing so trip over a smoking tree branch, hitting the pavement hard. I'm trying to catch the breath that's been knocked out of me when one of the men—no, *creatures*—raises a blaster and fires at a woman crying over a lifeless body on the other side of the street. She falls forward.

My heart goes into overdrive as I fight the urge to vomit.

I stifle a cry and half-crawl to a nearby bush to try and get out of sight. The creatures continue forward. I look around to find something to protect myself with, but there's nothing. I'm alone—I don't even have a utility knife or anything with me, just the clothes on my back. I've always imagined there was no situation I couldn't handle by myself; I'm going to be proven wrong about this by being murdered on the streets of Capital City.

I clench my fists. I won't go down without a fight, at least.

Suddenly a blinding light flashes through the square. I squint and reel back. The burst appears to completely disorient the creatures in black, who take the brunt of its force. And then the strange men are flying through the air, battering against each other and slamming repeatedly into the ground.

Telekinesis. That means Garde are here somewhere.

The one who appears to be the leader is thrown far—well out of my range of sight. Another one of the sword-carrying bastards is impaled on a broken Grid pole. He roars, and then his body starts to disintegrate, turning to dust. A girl who looks far too young to be facing such creatures darts past the pile of ash, one hand in front of her as she uses her powers to crush another of the attackers. Her metallic red pants reflect the flames of a nearby club called the Pit, which smolders, threatening to live up to its name. Two other Garde flank her, their arms outstretched as the bodies of their enemies crash against each other, eventually turning to dust as well.

"This way," the girl yells to them, flipping back her unnaturally white hair. "I see survivors in the distance."

She points forward, and there's another flash of light. Then they're gone. Whoever those Garde were, I think they may have just saved my life.

DISCOVER THE UNTOLD STORY OF A POWERFUL
NEW ALLY WITH A SECRET WEAPON!

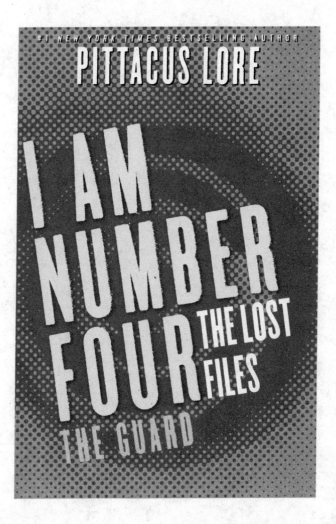

#1 NEW YORK TIMES BESTSELLING AUTHOR
PITTACUS LORE
I AM NUMBER FOUR
THE LOST FILES
THE GUARD

CHAPTER
ONE

ON LORIEN I LIVED IN MY GRANDFATHER'S house on the outskirts of the city, the dormitory of the defense academy, a basement apartment across from Eilon Park—even a Kabarak in the Outer Territories for a few years after my brother died, when I was happy to be lost and disconnected from Capital City and everything it stood for. None of those places exists now that the Mogadorians have destroyed my planet. Now I have only Earth, a world where I am not just a stranger, but one of the last of my people.

I've been on this planet almost two years, but I'm not sure it will ever feel like home. It almost did in a rented cabin in upstate New York for a brief period of time a few months ago. Thanks to the Mogs, that home no longer exists either.

It seems like all of my homes are eventually destroyed. Death tends to follow me wherever I go, taking those I care about most. And so I've made it a priority to stay alone, away from others.

That's how I end up buying a secluded piece of land I've never set foot on in Alabama.

It's dusk when I first see the property with my own eyes, parking in front of the huge wrought iron gate that opens up to a tree-lined drive. The name Yellowhammer Ranch is spelled out in rusty letters arching over the top. The gate looks imposing, but it's mostly ornamental. As a security measure, it's laughable. There's not even a lock on it. The fencing on either side is just as bad, consisting of a few strands of barbed wire: a barrier that will keep out nothing but stray animals. I wonder if the former owners actually felt safer because of these crude strings of metal. Possibly, I suppose. But then, they probably never imagined that their enemies would come from the sky instead of the winding dirt road that leads to the ranch.

I know better.

Still, the gate and fence aren't completely useless. They'll both come in handy when I install perimeter security cameras. Maybe a few remote-operated weapons too, just in case any Mogadorians manage to find me here.

With a little push, the wrought-iron gate moves, squeaking on old hinges. I get back inside my SUV and drive over the cattle guard. The actual house is located a short drive past the gate and is mostly obscured by rolling hills and trees. It's all thick beams of wood on the outside. I ignore the carport off to the side and drive onto the grass, straight up to the porch. The lawn is yellowed and rises just above the ankles of my black boots when I step into it. I circle the house once, taking in the area, keeping my eyes peeled for anything that seems out of the ordinary or that might pose especially glaring security problems. There's nothing around for as far as I can see in any direction other than more barbed wire and empty fields and an old barn out back. I'm alone here. No one to disturb my work. No attachments other than to my mission.

At least if this place goes up in flames too, no one will be hurt but me.

I step over a broken stair at the bottom of the front porch and walk to the wooden door, where there's a big envelope hung up by a thick strip of clear tape. I pull it down and slide out a small stack of paperwork that proves I'm now the owner of Yellowhammer. None of the documents actually has my name on it—I haven't given anyone my real name, Lexa, since I discovered that Mogadorians were on Earth hunting down the Loric. Not that it would mean anything to a Mog if he heard it, anyway—I'm not Pittacus or one of the other Elders. But I *am* careful. Yellowhammer Ranch is technically now owned by a shell corporation I set up, a subsidiary of another organization of my inventing, all of the paperwork looping together in a way that could never be traced back to me.

Lately I've started to collect identities. I've been dozens of people in the past weeks, sometimes in real life and sometimes in the virtual world. I was Julie when I bought the big black SUV in Pennsylvania. I borrowed a man named Phil's IP address when I attempted to hack into the CIA's intranet. I think it was Lindsey who purchased all the firearms in Kentucky and Patti who bought all the computer equipment in Tennessee. I take the names from waitresses, magazine covers and overheard conversations, changing aliases daily, sometimes hourly. Organizing information and data has always been a strong suit of mine, and I bounce between these identities without faltering, storing Julie and Lindsey and Patti away in the back of my head when I'm done with them in case I ever need to use them again.

The people I buy things from at pawnshops and computer stores never suspect I'm not who I say I am. Or if they do, they don't say anything. It's amazing how few questions get asked when you're willing to overpay in cash. And, thanks to the fairly primitive internet firewalls and security systems used by banks on this planet, money is easy to come by if you're someone who's good with ones and zeros and moving them around like I am. In the past few weeks I've skimmed minuscule amounts of currency from millions of bank accounts across the world. Money is one of the few things I have a lot of. Money and questions and anger.

I tip the envelope farther, and a set of keys falls into my open palm.

The ranch was trickier to come by. I knew I wanted somewhere far away from crowded areas, or even the nearest town if possible. Remote places like that were easy to locate, but it took me awhile before I found someone willing to part with their property in a hurry, and without ever even meeting me face-to-face. All I needed was to wire some money and forge a few signatures, and suddenly I owned a piece of this planet.

I take another look around the porch, and I can't help but think of how much Zophie would have liked this place. She spent many nights at the old cabin in New York out on the veranda with a cup of tea, staring at nothing in particular. Probably thinking of her brother, Janus. Back when there was still hope that he was alive.

A shallow ache rises in my chest. It's a feeling I'm familiar with, the hurt that comes when thoughts of Zophie or Janus or my brother, Zane, settle in my mind. No matter how hard I try to numb myself and keep memories of them buried, they always manage to find me again. I remind myself that it's not sadness I should be feeling, but anger. That, at least, I can use. It's what fueled me on Lorien when I wanted nothing more than to take down the Elders and uproot our society. Now, rage against the Mogadorians is what keeps me going half the time. A burning desire for vengeance in the name of everyone I've lost.

But to make the Mogs suffer, I have to get to work. And so I swallow hard, shake my head a few times and unlock the front door.

Inside, the house is dusty, all the furniture covered with white drop cloths. The skull of a big, horned animal hangs over the fireplace mantel. Why the people of Earth choose to decorate their dwellings with the corpses of animals, I have no idea. Killing for sport was an unthinkable crime on Lorien, but based on a few appalling stories I've overheard at hunting-supply stores in my travels here, I gather it's not exactly uncommon on Earth. I can only imagine what Crayton's reaction would be if he were with me, knowing his fondness for Chimærae. There's a pang in my chest as I wonder where he is now. Are he and Ella safe? How big has she grown in all this time since I last saw her?

Again I push these thoughts out of my head and keep going.

I pull one of the white cloths off a table and toss it over the skull, obscuring it. Then I explore the other rooms. The refrigerator in the kitchen has a huge freezer, meaning my grocery trips to the towns half an hour away can be infrequent. The hall closet can serve as my miniature armory, where I can stash a few of the weapons I've picked up lately. I leave the furniture in the spare bedrooms covered and scope out the office located at the end of the one hallway running through the house. This will be where I spend most of my time—the sanctuary in my new base of operations.

I start to unload my SUV.

Until recently I traveled light, mostly because Mogs had destroyed almost everything I had on this planet while I was out chasing a lead on the Garde. For a few weeks I traveled aimlessly, making my way across the United States, an outsider in a world not my own. I thought about searching for the rest of my people: the Garde and Cêpans from the other ship. According to Janus, they'd scattered. That's what he'd said shortly before the Mogadorians executed him on camera and sent me the video. The evidence I've discovered online seems to back this up. I've found hints of them here and there: pictures of an older man and young boy with a Loric chest trying to find passage to another continent, reports of tattooed men chasing a kid in Canada. I'm not sure why they've split up, but for the most part they're covering their tracks well, staying off the grid. I guess their Cêpans are competent, for the most part.

Being impossible to find bodes well for their survival, but not for me finding them.

There's some bigger game at play here, but I can't figure it out. Why are the Mogs after these kids? What's so special about them? Why spend resources trying to destroy the last of the Loric?

These are the questions I've been trying to answer, all while doing my best to help the Garde stay out of sight. If I see something on the internet that sounds like it could be related to them, I try to wipe it away or bury it in broken code. But staying on the move has made this difficult to do. That's why I'm here now, at Yellowhammer. It's a base of operations for a coming war. Because, if the Mogs are here on Earth, it's probably only a matter of time before they do to this planet what they did to my home.

Most of the boxes I have are full of computer equipment I've purchased on my trek across this country. Once everything is piled up in the back office, I begin to piece things together, breaking down machines and wiring them in more efficient ways, building a system that will incorporate the highly upgraded laptop I created in Egypt using Loric data pads. The custom laptop is fine, but the machine I'm building will allot me more processing power and storage space. The work is tedious, but I remain focused. Night falls and then the sun rises. I pause only a few times for water and to stretch my legs.

When my head starts to pound from concentrating for so long, I take a break and walk around outside, taking note of all the places where I can add some cameras and heighten security once the computer is up and running—something a little more substantial than barbed wire. This place will take a lot of work, but by the time I'm through it will be a fortress of knowledge and power. I plan to collect every scrap of information I can about the Mogs. Those bastards who destroyed my planet, who *murdered* my friend, will pay. I'll figure out what they're up to and help the other Loric bring them down. Somehow. Someway.

I pull open the half-rusted doors of the big barn out back. They squeal as if they haven't been moved in a long time. Light filters through a missing section of roof, illuminating a few bales of hay and a scattering of tools hanging on one wall. The place isn't much—in fact, it looks as though one good shove could send it clattering to the ground—but it'll do.

With any luck, soon I'll have a ship in here. The one that brought the chosen Garde and their Cêpans to this planet—maybe the last Loric ship in the universe for all I know.

Because whatever it is that the Garde are here to do,

they'll need all the help they can get. They're being hunted. *We're* being hunted. And when they're masters of their Legacies and decide it's time to strike against the Mogadorians, they'll need the ship.

Hell, I'll fly them to the Mogs myself.

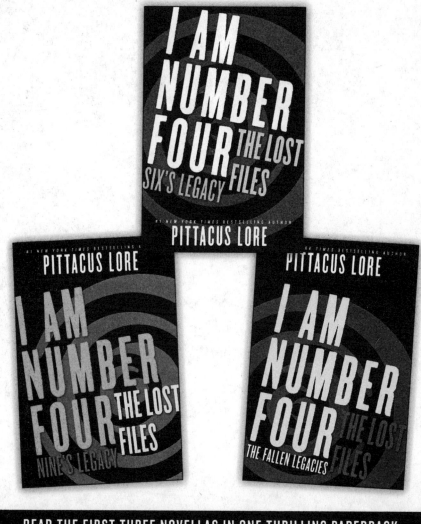

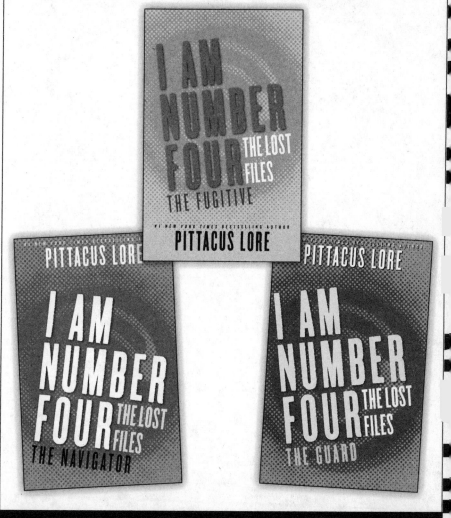